Charity Cases

A Kassel of Philadelphia Novel

Jane Shoup

Also by Jane Shoup

Down in the Valley
Spirit of the Valley
Will of the Valley
Knightfall
The Restoration
Zan, Birth of a Legend
A Choice of Captors
The Key
Ammey McKeaf, Book 1 ~ The Chronicles of Azulland
Heirs to the Throne, Book 2 ~ The Chronicles of Azulland
Into Shadow, Book 3 ~ The Chronicles of Azulland
An American Baroness ~ Sons of Barons Book 1
Nearly a Marquess ~ Sons of Barons Book 2
London's Adonis ~ Sons of Barons Book 3
Santa 2020 the Final Ride
The Time Tunnel of August Kaplan

Acclaim for *Down in the Valley*

'My heart is still in my throat from the tension of reading this page turner. The heart-stoppingly endearing, shy hero, Tommy, who evokes memories of a young John Wayne, is unforgettable. *Down in the Valley* is a keeper.' -Catherine Lanigan, Author of Romancing the Stone

'...a touching, emotional read. Readers will not be immune to Shoup's storytelling talent or her gift of creating three-dimensional characters.' – *RT Book Reviews*

'Shoup moves assuredly through trauma, family discord, and romantic misunderstandings to capture lovely bits of Americana and a bygone way of life.' – *Publishers Weekly*

'. . . wonderfully written. Well-paced and easy to read…but be careful, it'll suck you in and you won't want to leave it until you're finished.' -*eCataRomance Reviews*

Acclaim for *Zan, Birth of a Legend*

'Brilliant, thought-provoking and addictive reading.' -*Affaire de Coeur Magazine*

'Excellent historic context … characters whose bond is irrefutable. An interesting spin on the legend of Tarzan, with a spark of creativity that is all its own.' -*A Romance Review*

Acclaim for *Ammey McKeaf*

'...full of passion, adventure and romance, and every element will stir your inner man to sit up and take notice. Top notch; highly recommended.' -*MidWest Book Review*

'I did not want to stop reading. Anytime life interrupted me, I would growl and hurry with whatever needed my attention so I could return to Ammey's tale. Very highly recommended.' – *Huntress Reviews*

' . . an exciting, creative story that is just the beginning of an adventure. 5 hearts' –*The Romance Studio*

'I could not stop reading this book. I actually was sad when I reached the end. This book is a must read for any fans of fantasy that highlights strong women of character. -*Fallen Angel Reviews*

Acclaim for ***The Restoration***

'There are authors who touch the heart, but this one grabs hold of your soul. When you settle in to read the book, grab a box of tissues. You'll definitely be needing them. -*Romance At Heart*

'If you do not believe in ghosts, you will change your mind after reading this book.' -*Coffee Time Romance*

. . . a tender book that many can relate to, especially those that have shared a loss. Jane Shoup …writes from her heart allowing the reader to be instantaneously drawn into the story.' -*The Romance Studio*

Prologue

Green Valley, Virginia
February 4, 1884

With hunched shoulders and his head bent against a freezing wind, Gregory Howerton made his way to the house, his boots crunching on the ice-coated snow. He had been at a ranch east of Clifton Forge when the weather had taken a turn for the worst. It had made for a miserable ride.

He hurried up the steps to the porch and kicked the snow from his boots before stepping inside where the quiet and warmth enveloped him. He sighed.

"How was your trip, sir?" Janice, his housekeeper, asked as she came toward him with a brisk step.

"Cold." He peeled off his gloves and shoved them into his pockets before unbuttoning and shrugging off his coat. "How's my wife?" he asked as he handed it to her.

"Better today. She received a package from a friend that cheered her."

He hung his hat on the rack. "What friend?"

"She didn't say, but it came from Philadelphia."

He grunted. It was likely from her brother or one of her close friends. Charity hailed from Philadelphia.

"Would you care for some supper?" the housekeeper inquired.

"Yes, but I'll have a bath first," he said as he started off. *And a whiskey.* Rubbing his hands together, he went into his office and poured a shot. He inhaled the fumes appreciatively before downing it. The warmth in his throat and stomach was satisfying

He poured more and then went to warm himself at the fire blazing in the hearth, thinking about his wife. Charity had miscarried their first child nearly a month ago and she'd taken it hard. They both had, although he wouldn't allow her to see how much it had affected him.

She was a remarkable woman, strong enough to become a doctor – a male dominated profession in a male dominated world. But since the miscarriage, she hadn't regained her vitality. It was as if she felt whipped.

He went to their room, knocking lightly before opening the door. Charity sat on the settee in front of the fire with a blanket over her lap. In the firelight, with her hair loose, she stole his breath. That she hadn't struck him as beautiful when he first met her baffled him. She'd intrigued him from the moment he saw her, a lady doctor deeply invested in a near hopeless case, but he'd merely thought her striking. Now he never failed to see her beauty. It didn't matter if she was covered in blood after dealing with a badly injured patient or covered in mud after being tossed from a horse or weary at night or barely awake in the morning. She was the most beautiful thing he'd ever seen. The most beautiful thing in his life.

She smiled to see him. "I thought you'd stay over when it began sleeting."

"Not when I can be here." He walked around and leaned down to kiss her.

She gripped the sides of his face with warm hands. "You're cold."

"I'll be in a hot bath soon." He sat next to her, laying a hand in her lap.

"How was the trip?"

He shrugged. "They're asking too much for the colt, but I'll get him in the end."

"I'm sure you will."

"Janice said a package arrived."

She nodded. "From Tally and Vi. They both sent letters and …a tonic and herbs for a tea. It's a regimen."

"For the melancholy?" he asked gently.

"Not exactly. No. Why don't you take your bath first and then I'll tell you all about it."

He was puzzled by her reluctance. "Tell me now."

"It's a new therapy. An aid for conception."

"We didn't have difficulty conceiving."

"And to carry a child to full term." She paused before adding, "It's my age. I may be too old."

"Nonsense," he stated.

"It's not," she said brokenly.

He pulled her into his arms. "You know these things happen," he soothed. "It doesn't mean it will happen again."

"I feared it. I still do." She pulled away and looked at him beseechingly. "I want to try this." She paused. "I've already started."

He nodded. "All right. I would like to understand it, though."

She reached for the letter and handed it over. "Read it. It's from Tally and it explains."

A corner of his lips quirked. "There's no girly secrets in the letter?"

She grinned. "None you can't know about. You don't mind girly secrets, do you?"

"Not if they're yours. I like those." He leaned in and kissed her lips. "I'll need better light to read it." He got to his feet. "You want anything?"

She shook her head. "I'm glad you're home."

"So am I. Oh, I almost forgot." He reached into his pocket and handed an object to her.

It was a flattish brown rock in the shape of a cross, perhaps an inch and a half in diameter.

She studied it. "What is it?"

"It's a staurolite. It's like a good luck charm."

"Stauro," she murmured. "Meaning cross."

He nodded. "My grandmother used to call them fairy stones."

"Fascinating. It looks carved."

"I know, but it forms naturally that way. Takes a few million years, of course."

"Why is it called a fairy stone?"

"I have no idea. Maybe the fairies made it in the first place. All I know is that I found it on the bank of a creek looking for you." He cherished the amused smile that crossed her face. It had been too long since he'd seen it. "I explained I was coming this way and that it would be my pleasure to get it here."

"Well, I thank the fairies. And you."

"You are welcome on behalf of all of us." He left with the letter in hand, returned to his office and poured another drink. The bathroom had running water capable of getting warm, but it was necessary to add kettles of boiling water to get it to the temperature he liked, so it would be a little while before his bath was ready.

Vi and Tally were dear friends of Charity's from medical college. He'd first met them when they'd gone to her hometown of Philadelphia to get married. It had been important to Charity that her brother, Jack, give her away and that her oldest friends be present.

Thelma 'Tally' Covington was tall, perhaps six feet tall, and attractive. Her medium reddish-brown hair and hazel eyes might have been unremarkable, but one remembered the directness of her gaze. If so inclined, she could stare down most anyone. No flinching, no blinking.

Growing up, her family barely had the means to get by, but the spunky and intelligent girl had become a favorite of the elderly family doctor. He was the one who set her up to attend the Women's Medical College of Pennsylvania. It was made possible by a scholarship program whereby deserving students had their board and tuition paid in exchange for working post-graduation at The Women's Hospital of Philadelphia run by the same patrons as the college.

Viola Ripley, unlike Tally, came from a family that had the means to pay her way through school, but they refused to do it because they disapproved of ladies pursuing a medical

4

education. Only Vi's paternal grandmother had appreciated her drive and passion. It was she that paid Viola's tuition and expenses until a stroke left her without control of her speech, motion or her own finances, at which time Viola's father withdrew the financial support. It had caused a breech in the Ripley family that had never been overcome. Rather than withdraw from the college, Vi had become another recipient of the scholarship.

Physically, Tally and Vi were as different as could be. Vi was petite with dark hair and eyes. She was thoughtful and studious. Tally was of stronger spirit with a sharper tongue and a shorter temper. Vi had been raised to be a lady. Tally had been raised to fight for everything she got. They were still the best of friends and they still worked at The Women's Hospital and lived in a boarding house eight blocks from the hospital. They made just enough to get by, but were grateful to be members of a profession that generally failed to hold them in high regard, much less as equals. It never failed to astonish him.

He sat at his desk, turned up the lamp and began reading.

My dear friend,

I understand the unrelenting sorrow and fatigue you feel. It is emotional and physical – the inevitable toll of miscarriage. But you are <u>wrong</u> to believe future pregnancies will follow the same course. You are strong and healthy. So is Gregory. You are not too old to conceive and carry a child to full term. There is no reason your next pregnancy will not go smoothly from conception through delivery. That said, I have interesting news to share.

Vi discovered a study being conducted by Dr. Clarence Kellerman on this very issue. His theory is that certain women's reproductive organs need a period of dormancy and a building up of hormonal levels before attempting pregnancy again. The study

*has already achieved impressive results. Eighteen out
of twenty–six women have <u>delivered</u> healthy babies.*

*I spoke with Dr. Kellerman about your situation.
Given that you are a practicing physician, you've been
granted permission to receive his ministrations should
you wish. You will need to send a weekly update as to
your health. He needs to know when your monthly
cycle begins and ends. It's possible that you may not
menstruate while you are undergoing the regimen. You
will not be able to conceive during the six months the
regimen takes—*

"Six months," Gregory complained under his breath.

*— but you should not refrain from normal relations
with your husband. In fact, it is important to normalize
your life as quickly as possible. <u>Get back to living</u>.
Doctor's orders.*

*The instructions for the medication are simple. Take
a quarter cup of tonic each morning after breakfast. In
the afternoon, infuse the herbal concoction (he calls it
powder, but it's not a powder consistency) in a cup of
water or tea until it is dissolved, usually the length of
time it takes for tea to steep well. You may add sugar
without the medicine losing efficacy.*

*The tonic may cause a slight dizziness, but it is
purportedly not an unpleasant sensation. Concurrently,
you may feel drowsy with the first few doses of the
herbal powder, but the effect goes away within two or
three days. No nausea has been reported. If you do
experience any adverse sensation, stop taking it at
once and let him know. If you wish to take part in the
study, which I fully expect you will, write to Doctor
Kellerman care of me at the hospital. He sees patients
there on a frequent basis and I will pass your
correspondence on to him.*

You'll have to accept not being able to conceive for the next few months, but after that, you will. Last week a woman of forty-three delivered a child. Her seventh. (She was my patient, not Dr. Kellerman's. Frankly, I know of a different trial I would like to suggest for her.)

The letter continued, becoming more personal and regarding people he didn't know. He set it aside and took a drink. Charity usually wanted specifics of everything medically related and yet she'd accepted this trial on relative blind faith. Of course, it had come from Tally, whom she trusted wholeheartedly.

"Sir," Janice said from the open door. "Your bath is ready."

"Thank you."

"Would you be wanting supper in the dining room or—"

"I'll take a tray in my room. See if my wife will have anything."

"Yes, sir," Janice said and went to do it.

Janice rapped on the door and waited for Mrs. Howerton's invitation before opening it. "Mr. Howerton wants his supper in here and wanted me to ask what we can bring you."

Charity shifted in her seat. "I think I will have a plate with him. I wasn't hungry earlier."

Janice nodded and started to shut the door.

"Janice?"

Janice reopened the door. "Ma'am?"

"Mr. Howerton found this," she said, holding up the stone. "His grandmother called it a fairy stone. Have you ever heard of them?"

"Yes." The housekeeper ventured closer to see it. "May I?"

"Please," Charity said.

"Isn't that something," Janice murmured as she took it in hand and studied it. "It's a healing stone." She handed it back with a smile. "It's a good omen."

"A healing stone," Charity repeated as she stroked the rough surface. "*Hmm.*"

<u>Chapter One</u>

Four years later ...
Green Valley, VA
Friday, June 29, 1888

Charity Howerton kept an office in town and attended it three days a week from ten a.m. to three in the afternoon with the exception of Friday when she stayed an hour later. Medicine was her profession and a passion.

"And again," she said to the man on the examining table as she listened to his heartbeat through her stethoscope. "Breathe in. And exhale."

The man, Sam Blake, was a friend and the foreman at their ranch. He could have walked a matter of a few yards to see her at home, where she also had an office, but he preferred the privacy of town. This was his third visit, this time made at her suggestion.

He was forty-six, strong and healthy. He stood 6'3 and 195 pounds. He had a strong jaw, close cropped brown hair beginning to gray at the temples and hazel-brown eyes with a level gaze. He was honest and often wise. He had a good mind and heart and was fiercely loyal to her husband and family. Unfortunately, he was convinced he was dying of the same heart ailment that had ended his father's life at 46 years of age. Sam knew because of the tightness and occasional pain in his chest. He knew because he knew.

Charity straightened and looked him in the eye. "When was the last occurrence?"

"Yesterday. It's happening more often now. Figure I'm on borrowed time. I need to tell Mr. H soon."

"We have one thing to try first. It's what I wanted to talk to you about."

"Oh? What's that?"

"There's a new study being conducted in Philadelphia. I have family and friends there, as you know."

"Yes, ma'am."

"It's a medical experiment on strengthening the heart."

"Is that so?" he said with a perk of interest.

"Yes, and it's having amazing results. So far, I believe there are fifty participants in the study and they'd all had actual attacks of the heart before entering the study. More than eighty percent have seen their symptoms, which are identical to yours, completely disappear. The other twenty percent have seen improvement. And they were all in worse shape than you, by far."

"How long's this experiment been going on?"

"Just under a year. I know that's not long, but the results are remarkable. Plus, it's simple." She walked over and picked up a bottle. "It's a tonic you take twice a day," she said as she came back. "You can sip right from the bottle. You're supposed to take one ounce, but that's an average swig. If you're willing, I'd like you to try it now."

"Well, yeah. I'm willing. You bet I'm willing."

"Good. Do you have any pain now?"

He frowned thoughtfully. "It's not … pain exactly. It's more like a weight pressing on my chest."

"Where?"

He tapped the center of his chest.

She nodded and took his wrist in hand to get his pulse rate. Watching the second hand on her wall clock, she counted the beats for 15 seconds. There were thirty. Times four, it was a resting pulse of 120. Too high.

"Not good?" he asked.

"I'd rather it be slower," she said calmly. She handed him the bottle. "Try the tonic."

He unstopped it and took a swig. "Not terrible," he commented, putting the stopper back in. "Tastes a little like licorice."

"I know. I tasted it. We'll give a few minutes to get into your system and then I'll take your pulse again. You can lie down if you want" She went to her desk, sat and picked up her pen. She scribbled a few lines in her logbook documenting his pertinent information. Out of the corner of her eye, she saw Sam lie back on the table. His hands were folded on his stomach as he stared at the ceiling. "You may feel a little dizziness."

"It's kind of nice," he murmured.

"I agree. I felt a little dizzy and then relaxed, but then I was fine after a few moments."

"Should you have tried it?" he asked worriedly.

"It was just the once and I won't do it again. I studied the ingredients and knew they wouldn't harm me or the baby," she said, placing a hand on her swollen middle. "The train ride to Philadelphia will be harder on me than tasting the tonic."

He grunted. "You lookin' forward to it?"

"Not the heat or the travel, and not leaving the boys, but I'm excited to see my family and friends. I'm sure my niece's wedding will be lovely." Thinking about it, she pulled out a sheet of parchment to begin a letter. She needed to give the tonic a few minutes to work anyway.

> *Hello, you two! At the moment, a patient who is a dear friend is lying on my table, and I am trying your approach of mind over matter. I've even repeated your recipe, carbonated water with distilled chamomile, licorice root and St. John's wort. I pray it has the same success. The power of the mind is a miraculous thing.*

She glanced up at Sam. "Feeling all right?"

"*Mm-hmm,*" he murmured. "Fine."

11

"Good. We'll give it a few more minutes." She went back to writing.

I cannot wait to see you both when we return home for Alexandra's wedding. I have had quite a challenge finding something attractive to wear. I'm <u>bulging</u>. Our plan is to stay a little over a week, so keep some time open from the twenty-first on. We'll leave on the twenty ninth, the day after the wedding.

She set her pen aside and got up to take Sam's pulse again. Watching the second hand, she counted.

"What is it?" he asked when she smiled.

"It's better." She'd counted twenty, meaning a pulse rate of eighty, which is what it should have been. "It's normal."

He sat up, watching her. "Yeah?"

"Yes. So let's try this. Take the tonic both morning and evening every day for a week and then let me know how you're feeling. If, at any point in time, you feel strange or weak, stop taking it. That shouldn't be the case but let me know."

"Yes, ma'am."

"Most subjects stay on the regimen about three months. That strengthens the heart enough that they've been able to stop. But we'll take it one step at a time."

"Sounds good." He got off the table. "What do I owe you?"

"We already discussed this. There is no cost to you ever."

"I need to pay for the medicine."

"There is no cost. Being part of a medical study is of no cost because it's for research. A hospital is footing the bill. I'm not even sure which hospital."

He looked unconvinced.

"I swear to you, Sam. This is not costing any subject any money," she said solemnly.

"Well, I appreciate it. I have to say, I wasn't expecting this. I thought I was on borrowed time and … about out of it."

"You're not. I feel very strongly that you're not."

He went and retrieved his hat from the rack before giving her a final nod goodbye. "Thank you again."

She smiled and nodded. In the silence that followed his departure, she considered the ethics of what she was doing. In effect, she'd just given him a sugar pill, but as long as the outcome was what they hoped for, it did not seem unethical. She herself had been on the opposite end of the same subterfuge four years ago when her friends had been so concerned that her state of mind would prevent her from conceiving, they'd made up a medical trial and convinced her of its promise.

It was in the fifth month of the trial when she became nauseated that Vi and Tally had come clean and admitted the tonic was a harmless concoction of seltzer water and herbs and the reason for the nausea was likely that she was pregnant. And so she had been. With twins. Seven and a half months later, she'd given birth to their sons Grayson and Graham. The boys were three now and she was nearly seven month's pregnant again. This time, no tonic had been needed.

More and more, physicians were discovering the mind's influence over the body. Because Sam *knew* he was having heart problems, he was unwittingly creating them. In her first examination, she'd been able to detect no malfunction of the heart and yet his pulse and blood pressure were too high. Because his father died at the same age, he had convinced himself that he would as well. But she'd just proved that if he believed the tonic was working, it would work.

Hopefully, it would work.

Chapter Two

Philadelphia, PA
Monday, July 2, 1888

The afternoon was muggy and overcast as Viola Ripley rode in a cab to the attorney's office on Willow Street. Doctor Jack Werthing, her friend Charity's brother and a friend in his own right had recommended the attorney, a man named Cecil Lawrence. Apparently, Mister Lawrence was not only well thought of, but he also occasionally took pro bono cases for a worthy cause.

The cab passed three young ladies walking arm in arm, giggling about something. Vi was reminded of herself, Charity and Tally during their years at The Women's Medical College.

She recalled an evening spent in the common room of the dormitory as they quizzed one another for an exam. Tally, rebel that she was, had produced a bottle of port, despite the ban on alcohol on campus. Still, they felt capable of being discreet – until everything became uproariously funny. It was the result of a combination of exhaustion and inebriation which they attempted to find just the right word for.

"Inebriaustion," Tally suggested, slurring the word.

"Exhaus—" Charity began slowly, trying to combine the words differently. The long pause that followed when she couldn't come up with one was cause for more hilarity. That was when a disapproving classmate came to see what the racket was about. Deborah Whitledge. "I should have known it would be you three," she stated nastily. "Charity and … the charity cases."

While Charity gasped with offense, Tally found it so amusing, all of them ended up erupting in fresh peals of laughter. Deborah was humorless and often bitter but, truth be told, it wasn't a bad description. Their amusement exasperated Deborah, who glowered before storming out, no doubt to get the hall monitor.

"We're in trouble now," Charity said.

"Who?" Tally asked. "You, Charity? Or we charity cases?" she asked, gesturing to each of them as she asked. "Although that's not really fair to Vi since her family has money."

"For all the good that does me," Vi returned.

Vi smiled at the bittersweet memory and focused her attention on the homes of tree-lined Willow Street. It was shady and green here. Very pleasant. When the cab stopped, she paid the driver, and started toward the house. It appeared Mr. Lawrence's office was in his home.

The brass nameplate to the side of the door read C. B. Lawrence, Esquire. She used the knocker, and the door was promptly opened by a well-dressed gentleman in his mid-fifties.

"Dr. Ripley?" he said politely.

"Yes. Hello."

"Please come in."

"Thank you." She stepped into a foyer full of substantial mahogany pieces and a lingering scent of lemon oil. Judging by the masculine feel of the place, she suspected Mr. Lawrence was a bachelor. A woman would have decorated with a lighter hand if she'd had a choice in the matter. But perhaps the office was his domain alone. "I'm not sure if Dr. Werthing is meeting us here or not," she began.

"I don't believe so. He already met with Mr. Lawrence."

"Oh." She blinked in surprise. "So you're not—"

He looked puzzled.

"I thought you were Mr. Lawrence."

"No, Dr. Ripley," a male voice said behind her.

She turned to a man of thirty or so who stood in the open doorway to an office. He was clean shaven with brown hair. He was not what she would call handsome, but he was attractive. He wore a charcoal-gray suit, an immaculate white wingtip collared shirt and a tie of sapphire blue.

"That would be me," he said with a bow of his head. "This is Mr. Cavanaugh," he said with a gesture to the older gentleman. "My clerk, whom I would be lost without."

"I'm pleased to meet you," she said, looking from one to the other. She felt more self-conscious than before. And she had felt plenty self-conscious. She was not accustomed to meeting with attorneys.

"Please, come in," Lawrence said, stepping aside.

She did, clutching her reticule.

"Please make yourself comfortable," he said as he followed. "May we offer you something to drink?"

"No, thank you." She sat in one of the tall armchairs in front of his desk as he walked around and took his seat behind it. She was aware that Cavanaugh quietly closed the door behind them.

"Dr. Werthing provided a brief overview of the case," he began, "but I would like to hear more about the unfortunate woman in question."

"Of course."

"Before you begin, I will tell you what I told Dr. Werthing. I am interested in the law, not politics. I have no political ambitions or constraints whatsoever. I will have no issue with taking the case and fighting for this woman's freedom if what was suggested by Doctor Werthing is true."

"Which was what exactly?"

"That a lady's husband has had her locked away under false pretenses in order to control her estate. Does that sum it up?"

She blinked. "Yes. Most succinctly."

He smiled. "Would you start at the beginning and share the events from your perspective?"

"Certainly. The lady's name is Louisa Heyer. She was an Edgerton, and they are an affluent family. She came into the

16

hospital with an inflamed appendix, and we had to remove it. While she was recovering, she shared that she'd been unwell on and off for weeks." She paused. "She grew to suspect her husband was trying to poison her."

"Why did she think so?"

"She'd hardly had a sick day in her life, but then began suffering a burning of the throat and stomach followed by nausea and other unpleasant symptoms after meals that—"

"What?" he urged when she faltered.

"That her husband could have had a hand in."

"*Could* have had a hand in," he repeated.

She nodded. "There were times where she would come into the dining room for a meal and find him already there and seated. The first course was also waiting. He'd ordered it to be set out before she was there."

"I see. And this was unusual."

"Yes. I should mention they've been married less than two years and there is a small fortune at stake that she inherited. I do realize this is all conjecture and circumstantial."

He smiled. "Spoken like an attorney."

There was something about his manner and his smile, perhaps the crow's feet at the edges of his eyes that she found appealing. "Honestly, I didn't know what to think of her, at first," she admitted. "She is a quiet woman. Her nature is reserved, even shy, and it was difficult for her to confide what she did. There was a … humiliation factor in it."

He nodded his understanding.

"But once she'd done it, it was as if she needed to talk. She spoke of a whirlwind engagement and a marriage that happened far too quickly. She's in her mid-thirties, so old in terms of just being married. She said he changed once they were married. He would be cold and removed for weeks at a time, frequently absent from the house, and then suddenly he'd seem passionate, declaring a great love for her. They'd dine in restaurants and attend the theatre, all at his arranging. She said it felt as if he was putting on a show."

17

Cecil rose, walked to a sideboard and poured two glasses of water from a pitcher. "Did she say how they met?"

"I don't believe so."

He returned and set the waters down for each of them. "Go on."

"She claimed that her every instinct warned he was trying to harm her. Possibly to kill her. She asked if there were some way of discovering if she had been poisoned."

He cocked his head, a curious look on his face. "Is there?"

"No. Not that I know of. Testing of tissue and blood can be done post-mortem, but the science is not well developed enough. Philadelphia General has a microscopist and only a few years ago, they created a laboratory for clinical microscopy and bacteriology. Pasteur, Koch and a few others are making amazing breakthroughs, but the science is simply not there yet."

"But you believed Mrs. Heyer."

"I found her fear compelling," she said haltingly. "Yes, I grew to believe her. She was genuine; I'm certain of it. And her husband didn't show up for days after the surgery, which was odd."

"Very. If he was in town."

"He was. He sent a few notes with excuses. I observed how tense they made her when they arrived, but once she'd read whatever excuse he'd given for his continued absence, she relaxed. She didn't want him there."

"*Hmm.* What does he do for a living?"

"He's an attorney."

"Oh?"

She nodded. "Blakely Heyer?"

"I haven't heard of him. But, please, continue. He must have finally shown himself."

"Yes. He showed himself in every conceivable way," she said wryly. "One afternoon, he came and insisted on leaving with her, despite the fact that she had not been released. Her incision still needed days of observation."

"You told him this, I assume?"

"I wasn't on duty at the time, but my colleague told him. Emphatically. But he insisted. He and his driver physically removed Louisa. My colleague, who is also my dearest friend, said Mrs. Heyer looked seemed witless."

"It's not a very appealing picture of the man."

"In my opinion, he is odious. I went to the Heyer home the next morning to check on her, but he refused to allow it. I was shown in only to be shown out."

"Why? Did he say?"

"He claimed it was her wish not to see me and he added that their family doctor had things well in hand."

Cecil Lawrence leaned forward, elbows on the desk, with a thoughtful expression. "Is it possible she didn't wish to see you again?" he asked gently. "Perhaps out of embarrassment given what she'd shared?"

"Possible, yes. But it is not what my instinct tells me." She paused. "In the hospital, she asked me if I knew what grounds were open to ladies for divorce."

"Did she? And what did you tell her?"

"I told her I didn't know," she said with a shrug, "but that I would find out. I said I believed it wasn't as difficult as it once was."

"That's true, but it is still not easy. Cruelty can be grounds, but it has to be proven. There is no divorce granted without fault."

"One spouse is trying to murder the other ought to be grounds."

"Indeed. For divorce, for prison, possibly for execution. But, again, it must be proven. How did you come to see her again? Did she seek you out?"

"No. It was nothing but luck and coincidence. The colleague I mentioned, Dr. Covington, we call her Tally, works one day a week in the female ward of the asylum. More than a month after Mrs. Heyer left the hospital, Tally saw her there. She thought it was her and records confirmed it."

"You're talking about Pennsylvania's Asylum for the Insane?"

"Yes."

"Kirkbrides' Hospital?"

"Yes, they do still call it that."

"Go on."

"I couldn't believe it. I went to the asylum to see for myself and I found her so medicated, she couldn't comprehend I was there. I asked a nurse what she'd been given and why she was there at all, but I was met with a stone wall. That nurse consulted with another who consulted with a doctor, and before long, I was asked to leave and told not to disturb the patient again."

"On what grounds?"

"On the grounds that she is the private patient of Doctor Leroy Backman, and that I had no business inquiring into her care. Care," she scoffed. "They dared to call it that. Dr. Backman is a knight of the first order of … superciliousness and pomposity."

He gave a single nod and a pursing of the lips. "Now, is that an official knighthood?"

She nearly laughed. "The subject tends to get my back up."

"I can see that."

She reached for her water and sipped. "I'd never been thrown out of a hospital before. It was embarrassing, but that's just silly pride." She set the glass down. "The important thing is that Mrs. Heyer is not doing well. Doctor Covington looks in on her weekly, but there is little she can do."

"Her husband committed her. Correct?"

"Yes."

"For what reason? What was Dr. Backman's diagnosis?"

"Insanity due to the suppression of menses."

Mr. Lawrence colored with embarrassment. "I had no idea there was such a thing."

"Most of us feel there is not. There are many logical reasons for the cessation of menses and none of them cause insanity. That isn't to say that you couldn't find a dozen cases of women

20

who have been diagnosed with it and locked away in various asylums in this city alone."

He looked troubled. "Is this Doctor Backman well thought of? Outside the circles of the Order of Superciliousness and Pomposity, that is?"

"He isn't badly thought of," she admitted reluctantly. "If ignorance and arrogance were reasons for losing one's medical license, we would have a much larger pool of female physicians."

Cecil Lawrence leaned back in his chair and smiled. "I will say that the charge of insanity seems a stretch when she seemed perfectly sane to you not long ago. Especially given her concerns in regard to her husband. But, to be honest, I'm not certain what I can do. I'll look into it, if you wish. Research precisely what his rights are, and hers. See if there are any similar cases. But my initial reaction is there's likely little I can do."

She was sorely disappointed. He seemed so sympathetic.

"I could make time to see her tomorrow."

Her heart leapt. "Oh, yes. Please do."

"Will I need permission to get in?"

"Tally can meet you there. She'll take you in."

He reached for a leather notebook and opened it to his calendar. "Would eleven o'clock be too early?"

"I'm sure that will be perfect."

"Do you have the Heyer's address, as well?"

"Not with me, but their home is on Spruce Street."

"Society Hill," he said.

"Yes. It was her home. It's very near Third. It has a red door with an oversized doorknocker engraved with an H."

He jotted down the information. "Where may I reach you to let you know what I discover?"

There was enough interest in his expression that she blushed as she opened her reticule and retrieved a card she had prepared. She handed it over. "It's very kind of you," she said gratefully.

"Not at all."

"But it is. Most successful attorneys don't accept pro bono work, do they?"

He blinked in surprise. "Pro bono?"

Yet more heat rushed to her face. "Oh, I thought—"

"Dr. Werthing offered to pick up the expense, if there is any. Was that not what you understood?"

She felt foolish for not guessing as much. "No, but that's very like him. His sister is one of my dearest friends. She's also a physician."

"I didn't realize there were so many female physicians these days."

"Did I make it sound so? No, there are not so many of us. It's still too steep of an uphill battle."

"It must be quite a passion then."

"It is. As I'm sure the law is to you." She rose and offered her hand. "Thank you, Mr. Lawrence."

He stood and met the handshake with a firm, warm clasp. "It was my pleasure, Dr. Ripley. I'll let you know what I find."

He seemed so very kind and sincere. She couldn't help liking him.

He released her hand. "I'll see you to the door."

Chapter Three

The asylum was an impressive looking facility at 44th Street and Haverford that sat on a campus of more than a hundred acres. It was said to be dedicated to the humane treatment of the inmates, and Cecil hoped it was so.

Having not been there before, he mistakenly went to the Department for Males first. The granite portico of the building was magnificent with a dome ceiling more than a hundred feet above. Facing outward from the building was a sweeping view of the city and the rivers beyond.

The entrance to the Female Department, when he found it, was less grand but still imposing. As he walked up the wide steps toward the tall pillars of its portico, he suspected the tall, attractive lady there was waiting for him. He was about to issue a greeting when she beat him to it.

"Mr. Lawrence?"

"Yes. And you must be Dr. Covington," he returned, offering his hand which was instantly met with hers. "Thank you for meeting me on such short notice."

"I'm happy to do it," she said, moving toward the doors. "Vi is covering for me."

Vi. The nickname gave him a warm feeling. He tried to do a quick double step to reach the doors first, but she was ahead of him and didn't wait to have it opened for her. Lady physicians seemed to be more about efficiency than propriety, although Viola Ripley had not seemed so.

"I'm sorry to report she's been medicated to the point where she's insensible today," Dr. Covington stated. "You'll be able to see her, as in lay eyes on her, but little else."

"I see." He started to ask the reason for such a large dosage. Had she been violent or disruptive? But he held his tongue as he followed her through wide corridors, glancing into rooms they passed. Most patients sat, occupied with one thing or another. It was a clean place with only a faint antiseptic odor, probably carbolic. Nurses wore dark gray uniforms with lighter gray aprons. None of them asked his business, but he was observed circumspectly.

Dr. Covington, walking with a businesslike step, turned into a room. "This is her," she said. She went to a dozing woman and took her pulse before jostling her a bit to rouse her. "Louisa?"

The woman's eyes fluttered.

"It's Dr. Covington. Can you wake?"

Mrs. Heyer made a breathy utterance, but if it was a word or words, Cecil could not tell.

"Let's sit you up," Dr. Covington said. "There is someone I'd like you to meet." She eased the woman forward and arranged pillows so that she was not fully reclined when she was settled back.

Mrs. Heyer's eyes moved back and forth as if trying to get her bearings. A line of drool slowly snaked from the corner of her mouth.

"Louisa, do you know what day it is?"

The woman didn't reply.

"It's Tuesday," Tally said soothingly. She took a cloth from the table and gently wiped away the drool. "This is Mr. Lawrence. He would like to help you."

Cecil took a few steps forward. Her gaze found his and he sensed her desperation. Goosebumps rose on his skin. "Hello, Mrs. Heyer."

She moaned softly and tried to form a word but couldn't manage it.

Tally covered the lady's hand with her own. "It's all right. Don't be distressed. I'll return shortly and we'll talk."

Cecil felt uniquely off balance as he followed Tally from the room again. "What is she being medicated with?" he asked when they walked side by side. "And why?"

"Chloral hydrate. To render her helpless, of course."

He felt horribly uncomfortable. It was very likely he'd just been shown a grave injustice, but he was a lawyer, not a miracle worker. They exited the front doors, and he turned back to face her. "Why was she declared insane? I know what the diagnosis was, but what did she do to get labeled as such? Surely, a person can't be called a lunatic and committed for no reason."

She considered him. "We think that's precisely what happened."

"Dr. Covington, I'm an attorney, bound to and by the constraints of the law. What I saw back there was disturbing to say the least. Especially in light of her concerns about her husband and the fact that she seemed normal only a few months ago. Or, at least, that was Doctor Ripley's opinion."

"It's not just her opinion," Dr. Covington spoke up. "I imagine you could find half a dozen witnesses to the fact."

"My point is, I'm not sure what I can do," he said. She looked annoyed and he understood that, but he had to be honest and candid. He could only work with facts and within the boundaries of the law. "We need to know what basis they had for the committal."

"But her husband could say anything, couldn't he? He could say she tore her clothes off and ran naked in the street brandishing an ax and threatening to cut people's heads off."

"But there should be proof of it. Witnesses to it."

"And if there is none? Can you do something then? We would like to have her removed from here and taken off the medication so that she can have a clear enough mind to tell you her side of the story. As it is, she can't even do that."

"I've never had a case like this. I'll need to research how much latitude we have. But a husband has rights over—"

"His wife's body and mind?" she interrupted hotly. "What a despicable concept. What the man wants is her money and possessions, but he'll destroy her body and mind to get it."

"I'm not the enemy, Dr. Covington."

"I know that," she relinquished. "I'm sorry, but it is infuriating to witness such a vile, disgusting wrong. For him to do something so heinous and get away with impunity makes me sick."

"I understand your feelings. And share them."

She studied him. "Do you?"

"Yes. As I said, I don't have my bearings on this yet, but I'll find out what I can."

"Thank you."

"What was your impression of Mrs. Heyer when you initially met her?"

"I didn't spend the time with her that Vi did. I know she had anxiety and some melancholy, but she'd nearly died with a ruptured appendix, and then there was the fact that she believed her husband wished her harm." Tally made a sweeping open arm gesture. "And here we are."

"Could the appendix have ruptured because of poison?" he asked.

"I don't think so, but even if it was, it couldn't be proven."

He wondered what else to ask. "Have you looked at her records?"

"Yes."

"And there was nothing about behavior on her part to get her committed?"

"No. There was a copy of the commitment form signed by Dr. Backman and Blakely Heyer and it had a date, diagnosis and prescribed treatment."

"I see."

"If you'll excuse me, I should get back to the hospital after I see Louisa again."

"Of course. Thank you again for meeting me."

"I hope you can do something to help her."

"So do I."

That evening, the setting sun cast Cecil's office in soft orange light as he perused a brief. At the sound of a light knock, he looked up to see Cavanaugh.

"If there's nothing else, sir?" his clerk asked.

"There is one thing. Do you happen to recall the name of the private investigator for the opposing side on the Cobb case? The one who worked against us rather brilliantly."

"The criminal, you mean," Cavanaugh said with a curl of his lip.

Cecil grinned. The investigator had uncovered information that had damned his case and it was highly probable that the man had gained the information illicitly, something he hadn't seemed the least bit ashamed of. Although, the loss had chaffed at the time, Cecil had since considered hiring him a time or two. Cavanaugh, on the other hand, had been heartily offended by the investigator. In his opinion, not only did truth matter, but so did one's methods.

"Are you thinking of hiring the rogue?" the older man inquired.

"I am."

Cavanaugh donned an expression of disapproval but supplied the name. "Kassel."

"That's right! Kassel. Tom Kassel. Thank you, Cavanaugh. Have a good evening."

"You as well, sir."

Cecil leaned back in his leather chair and tapped his pen against the desk absentmindedly. He listened to the front door open and close. A moment later, he heard the lock being set. "Now how to find you, Tom Kassel," he murmured.

Chapter Four

Saturday, July 7

Between his height of six feet, four inches, thick sandy-brown hair and a handsome face, Tom Kassel was difficult not to notice, which made it bewildering how he continually and surreptitiously got into places he didn't belong to discover things others wished to remain hidden.

The attorney who'd hired Kassel on the Cobb case provided the address of the boarding house where Kassel resided. It was on Cottman Avenue in the northeast neighborhood of Tacony. Cecil found it to be a neat, quiet place, moderate in size, although dwarfed by the church that stood next to it on a corner. Kassel wasn't in when he called, so Cecil left a note with the housekeeper. Kassel promptly replied by post offering to meet him Saturday at seven at The Ivory Lion.

The pub was an establishment like many others of its kind with a bar of dark wood and dozens of filled tables. It had a friendly, distinctly neighborhood feel and there was an enticing aroma of freshly cooked meat pies. Cecil walked through and spotted Kassel in a back booth watching him, as relaxed as could be.

"Counselor," Kassel greeted when Cecil reached him.

"Mr. Kassel," Cecil returned. He scooted into the seat across from him. "I appreciate you meeting me."

"Glad to. Join me in a drink?"

There was a half-full pitcher of ale with a clean glass beside it. "Thank you."

Tom poured, slid the glass to him and then lifted his own glass. "I can hardly wait to hear this."

Cecil took a drink of the amber ale. "That's good."

Tom nodded. "They also have an excellent pork pie if you're hungry. I'm going to have one."

"I am hungry, actually."

Tom looked up, made eye contact with someone and held up two fingers.

"Are you currently available for hire?" Cecil asked.

"Depends on the case, I suppose. What sort of job is it?"

"Investigating whether a man committed his wife to an insane asylum unjustifiably in order to gain control of her fortune."

Kassel made a face. "How grim."

"Yes, it is. The lady's physician, well, former physician, who is also a lady, came to me, believing it's so. She, the doctor, that is, cannot afford to pursue the case, but a well-heeled friend of hers has agreed to foot the bill if indeed there is a case. That's what I need to determine." He paused. "May I be so blunt as to inquire what you charge?"

"It varies. On a short term job, I usually charge two fifty an hour."

Cecil nearly choked. "Two dollars and fifty cents? An hour? I just had work done on my home and the bricklayer made three and a half dollars for the entire day!"

"I'm not a bricklayer."

Cecil wondered if Kassel was pulling his leg. "Who can pay that?" Cecil asked testily.

"Parties who want to win and who *can* afford to pursue cases. Not to be glib."

Cecil shook his head in astonishment. "I fear I've wasted your time."

"Maybe not," Kassel said. "I'm intrigued."

"Intrigued enough to cut your rates to something more affordable?"

Kassel grinned. "My main client is a large insurance firm. I would have to work your job around whatever might come up with them … should we come to a meeting of the minds regarding my rate."

"You're being perfectly serious? About your rate?"

"I never joke about money. Not mine, anyway." He took another drink. "But you're here and food is coming." He shrugged. "Tell me more."

Kassel had a point. "All right. Over the years, I have done some pro-bono work for hospitals and other civic organizations when I felt the cause was merited. I'd worked with Dr. Jack Werthing before, which is why he thought of me, I suppose. He contacted me, briefly explained the case and said that a Dr. Viola Ripley would provide more information, which she did."

"What's she like?"

"She's … lovely. Not that it has anything to do with it."

Tom gave an unconcerned wave, but a smile tugged at the corners of his lips.

"Dr. Ripley had treated Ms. Heyer for a ruptured appendix." Cecil took a folded piece of paper from his pocket. "Here are the salient points from our conversation." He passed it over. "If you care to see. I did not know you cost two fifty an hour when I wrote it."

Tom lifted a brow. "I fear you're going to have nightmares over it tonight."

"I may!"

Tom grinned as he opened the paper and looked it over. "The lady's husband is an attorney."

"Yes. He doesn't appear to have a thriving practice. He's only been in town some four or five years, but that's time enough to build a decent practice if you work at it. But, getting back to the story, I went the day after my meeting with Dr. Ripley to see the patient."

"At the asylum," Tom said as he read it. He looked up. "At least it's the best of them. None of the patients are chained, at least."

"True, but the lady has been drugged to mindlessness. I was thinking of speaking with her husband, but I can't compel him to provide answers."

"Plus, you risk alerting him that you may be onto him if there is wrongdoing involved. In my opinion, the better way to proceed is to quietly discern if there's fire causing the smoke."

Cecil found himself enjoying the conversation. "Where there's smoke, there is fire," Cecil rejoined. "What other kind of smoke is there?"

"What if it's fog and not smoke? Things can appear one way and be another."

Cecil bobbed his head, taking the point. He took a drink. "How would one go about finding out the truth of the matter? In a clandestine way?"

"How would …one?" Tom said, tapping his chest on the last word.

Cecil grinned.

"One would ingratiate one's way into the Heyer household to start," Tom replied mischievously.

"How *do* you manage to do what you do? How do you unearth secrets?"

Tom poured the last of the ale into their glasses. "If I told you my secrets, what's to keep you from getting into my line of work and putting me out of business?"

Cecil laughed. "My practice keeps me busy enough. I'm simply curious. And oddly fascinated."

Tom held out his hands as if in concession. "I'm oddly fascinating. Almost everyone says so."

Piping hot food arrived and it looked as delicious as it smelled. "I wish I could hire you this very minute," Cecil said when the barmaid had walked on. "But I have to get permission and your cost is high."

"But you're beginning to see why."

"Perhaps I am." Cecil cut into the crisp crust of the pie and his mouth watered as steam poured out. "I can take facts and work with them. I can interpret the law and argue with passion.

But how to get those facts when they're well hidden, that's the quandary."

"It is. By the way, have you ever determined what you cost an hour?"

"I don't charge by the hour."

"It's not difficult to figure out though. You should do it. Put it all in context."

"*Hmm*. Maybe I will." He tasted the pie and it was delicious.

Midway through the meal, Tom sat back. "Why don't I sniff around a bit? If your lady doctor is right and Mrs. Heyer has been wrongly incarcerated, she'll be grateful when we get her out and she can pay me."

"I like your optimism. *When* we get her out and not if."

"But if I think it is fog and not smoke, I'll let you know that, too."

"I'd appreciate that," Cecil said sincerely.

Kassel nodded. "It will be a pro bono hour or two of my time."

"An hour or two," Cecil repeated wryly. "You are confident."

"I am that."

Chapter Five

Tom left the tavern and took a cab to the Wyble residence on Locust Street near Rittenhouse Square where a dinner party was well under way. The party was the reason he was there, despite that he'd had his supper, plus which he was not invited.

Henry and Zilda Wyble would have called him a stranger, although he had gotten to know them in the last few weeks. His principal client, Citywide Insurance Company, had paid a handsome sum to the Wybles to cover their loss on a stolen ruby choker over a year ago and now a diamond brooch with a value of nine hundred dollars had been reported stolen.

"It will not do," his contact at Citywide, RT Coble, had declared, enunciating each word for emphasis. "Find out what you can." Translation: Prove one or both of them are lying because I'm damned sure of it and I want this claim made null and void.

When a claim or series of claims came to RT's attention and something about it seemed fishy, he brought Tom in on it. Odorific was the word RT used, although the word did not appear in Webster's Dictionary. Tom had checked.

In this case, he had been presented with a good deal of facts. Henry Wyble had made a small fortune in textiles. He was nearing sixty and in excellent health. There had been a few financial setbacks because of questionable investments over the last several years, but nothing catastrophic. His wife, ten years his junior, was an attractive enough although perpetually frowning woman. They'd had two children, a son and daughter. The daughter had long since died of an undisclosed illness at age fifteen and the son was grown and married with a child and home of his own.

Fourteen months ago, a ruby choker went missing from the Wyble's twenty-eight room home. Upon discovery of the theft, Henry Wyble flew into a rage. He finally calmed and made a determination of who was likely guilty. As he saw it, and his wife had agreed, there were two possibilities, her maids, naturally. After all, her jewelry was kept in a locked teakwood box that few had access to.

Both maids had tearfully denied it, but he fired them both without reference, effectively preventing them from securing another reputable place of employment. One of the terminated maids was relatively new, but Elizabeth Lee, they'd called her Betty, had been Mrs. Wyble's personal maid for more than eight years.

The insurance claim had been paid. However, now a diamond brooch was missing. According to the statement Mrs. Wyble made in regard to the matter, the brooch had been fastened to a long, fringed shawl worn to the ballet the night before the day Mrs. Wyble realized the brooch was gone. It was possible, she admitted, that it might have gone missing there. Perhaps when she slipped off the shawl, although it would have had to be an exceedingly clever thief.

Unbeknownst to the Wybles, Tom had observed the interview from behind an ingenious, not yet patented invention called a transparent mirror. It appeared to be a dark, antique mirror on the side in RT's office, but a person standing on the opposite side of it could see right through it as if were a window. Observing a person while they gave a statement revealed a great deal. Tom could almost always tell if they were sincere, lying or telling a partial truth.

In this case, he strongly suspected Zilda Wyble was not being truthful. As the interview progressed, he was more and more certain of it. He was bothered by the level of detail she offered. Who cared what her shawl looked like? He was bothered by the possibilities she offered for the theft. His guess was that she had hidden or sold her jewels. The brooch had been a gift from her grandmother before her wedding, the back of it engraved with her initials, so it seemed likely that the insurance settlement would either be given to her or she would have a replacement made for it.

As to her husband's involvement, Tom had doubts. The fury the man flew into upon discovering the original theft had been less than admirable, but genuine. If Tom's assumption was right, the jewelry would not be languishing in Mr. Wyble's safe. It wouldn't be anywhere he was likely to find it.

Tom had discreetly queried members of the Wyble's senior staff, all of whom believed the dismissed maids were innocent, especially Betty Lee. No one believed her capable of such a shameful act, but that was as far as they would go. They needed their jobs and weren't about to risk their livelihoods to assist him in a more in-depth investigation.

His best bet for gaining that assistance was Mrs. Wyble's new personal maid, an unmarried woman named Harriet Whitman. The angle he used with her was simple self-preservation since she was easy to blame. She was already nervous, having been questioned by her employers and the police. He understood and sympathized, he told her, especially after what happened to Betty Lee despite long years of faithful service. Betty had no history of poor, much less criminal,l behavior and she had been sent packing without a reference.

"But what can I do?" Harriet asked with tears brimming in her eyes.

He hesitated and glanced around the secluded courtyard he'd selected for its location and privacy before turning his gaze back to her. "May I share something which must be kept in strict confidence?"

She nodded frantically.

"I believe it's not missing at all," he confided.

She balked. "But w-why would they say—"

"For the insurance settlement." He certainly wouldn't disclose all the facts, but he needed to have her frightened enough that she would get him into the house to search. "I'm a very good detective, Harriet. Give me the opportunity and I will make sure this does not get pinned on you."

It had required coaxing and reassurances, but, in the end, Harriet had come through. First, she'd drawn a crude but accurate map of the home, identifying various rooms. Then, he'd been covertly let into the house when the Wybles were away on a weekend excursion. No one in the house was aware as he conducted a thorough and systematic search, even managing to locate, open and look through the safe in Wyble's study. It held certificates and bearer bonds and an antique pocket watch, but no jewelry belonging to his wife.

Tonight would likely be his last opportunity. His plan was to concentrate his efforts on two rooms, Mrs. Wyble's bedroom and the bedroom of the deceased daughter, which was kept locked and off limits except for a cursory monthly cleaning. He'd already spent time searching Mrs. Wyble's bedroom, so he would start in the other. If he was the guilty party and determined to stash a piece of jewelry, that's where he'd do it.

Tom was dropped off a few blocks away from Wyble's home and walked the rest of the way, casually ducking around to the back when he reached it. The house was lit up because of the dinner party and three carriages were lined up in front. Hopefully the party would be boisterous and require the full attention of hosts and staff alike. At the door that led to the cellar, he glanced around, saw no one and slipped inside. *Thank you, sweet Harriet.* Unbolting the door had been her most important responsibility of the evening.

He allowed his eyes to adjust to the darkness of the dank cellar before carefully finding his way across it to the narrow staircase and up to the door leading to the home's back hallway. He opened it slowly and heard laughter and voices. *Good. Let's keep it lively.* He shut the door silently and softly stepped to the back staircase frequented by the staff. He climbed to the second floor and peeked out. No one was in sight as he crossed the hall to the correct room and picked the lock. Harriet did not have access to that key.

He entered the room, closed the door behind him and locked it again. As he waited for his eyes to adjust, he slipped off his shoes. He lit a lamp and turned it low to provide just enough light for the search and then put a blanket at the base of the door to prevent any light from showing through the bottom. Heavy curtains were drawn across the windows, so his light would not be noticed there. He never took being an intruder lightly.

His process was to mentally cordon off a room in sections and then search it from top to bottom. Every plank in the floor was studied for a loose board. He looked under the bed and under the mattress. In pillows and pillowcases. He checked behind every hanging picture. Wardrobes and drawers were looked through as were hatboxes and inside shoes and boots. In this case, most the clothing and accoutrements were gone. Objects of décor had been left, vases and porcelain figurines and a gold-plated brush and mirror. Shelves held keepsakes of childhood such as dolls and books. He looked over each one.

Nearly an hour had passed when he concluded he'd been wrong. He'd looked everywhere. There was still the attic to go through more carefully, but where else? He turned a slow circle to make certain he'd covered every inch of the room. His gaze slid over the bedside table, wardrobe, free-standing shelf and then there was the door. On another wall was a skirted vanity table with a stool and a chair and end table with a lamp. On the outside wall were two windows. A petite desk and chair was positioned between the windows and in the corner was an ornamental screen concealing a potty chair. Then there was the wall with the bed. He'd covered it all.

He cursed under his breath and went to turn out the lamp, but then turned back toward the privy corner with a curious gaze. It was the only area he'd given a perfunctory look. He carried the lamp with him to be absolutely sure. Stepping behind the screen, he saw there was nothing but an elaborate antique wooden chair with a lid. Opening the lid, revealed the porcelain pot underneath. There was a small drawer at the base of the chair, so he squatted and pulled it out to reveal a narrow drawer containing squares of cotton cloth.

He reached around back and ran his hand over the chair top to bottom. It was solid except for a crack near the base. As if a drawer was there. But the drawer he'd opened in front had been of narrow depth, only some six inches. He stood and pulled the chair out carefully and bent to investigate what he'd felt. He experienced a rush of adrenalin because there *was* a drawer there, one without a handle. His pulse raced as he tried to finagle it out. It took wedging his pocketknife in for leverage before he got the bit of clearance he needed to open the door.

Inside the drawer were bundles wrapped in flannel. He reached down for one and it had the right feel. He unwrapped it to see a necklace or rather a choker with three strands of pearls. He'd found it. He had found the stash. He'd been right. Not only was Zilda Wyble a liar and a thief, she was the worst kind in his book, one who did it for reasons other than survival. She'd watched her maids blamed and punished for her actions.

He loaded his pockets with every last bundle, five of them, enjoying the weight of each as he did. He imagined Zilda's face when she discovered her booty was gone and he enjoyed that, too. He pushed the chair back as it had been. Before he left, he looked around the room to make sure there was no evidence that anyone had been there. Satisfied, he felt the flush of victory, but he was not in the clear yet. His exit would be even more cautiously approached than his entry.

Back at home, Tom unloaded his pockets and set the bundles on the table in his kitchen. He poured himself a drink and then sat and unwrapped them one by one, taking his time. Next to the pearl choker went a large silver locket. He opened it to see grainy photographs on each side, one side a man and the other a woman. It wasn't the Wybles. The third bundle he opened was a diamond brooch. He turned it and saw ZD engraved on the back. He didn't know what Zilda's maiden name had been, but this was it. The supposedly stolen brooch. He held it up to see what a nine-hundred-dollar pin looked like. The frivolity of it disgusted him. There were plenty of families who lived on nine hundred dollars a year and plenty more who didn't earn that much.

Why had she done it?

He set the brooch down and took a drink before unwrapping what had to be the ruby choker from the first supposed theft, although the jewels were more pink than the red he'd been expecting. He picked up the final bundle, untied and unwrapped it to reveal a green gem surrounded by silver filigree encrusted with small diamonds and attached to a long straight pin some six inches long. On back were tiny, sharp hooks. A hat pin? It must be. A large, bejeweled hat pin.

He stretched his legs out and reached for his drink. Tomorrow, he'd send a note to RT. The returned brooch would delight him. He would receive a nice bonus for the recovery, and so would Tom. Now he could lend a hand to Cecil Lawrence on his case. A win-win-win, he thought. Even Mr. Wyble would be satisfied. Only Zilda would be vexed. How he wished he could see that!

Chapter Six

Tuesday, July 10th

RT Coble stood looking out one of the windows in his office, his hands clasped behind his back, his legs slightly apart.

"I'm here," Tom said as he stopped in the doorway.

RT turned to face him with a scowl. With his thick mustache and dark hair parted in the middle and slicked back, he reminded Tom of politician turned cowboy Teddy Roosevelt. He'd seen Roosevelt in action as a state assemblyman of New York

"You're late and they were early," RT stated accusingly.

RT's tone irritated him, but Tom took a moment to reply so that it wouldn't show. He'd worked long and hard to control his temper. It had cost him too much throughout his life and he was determined that it would cost no more. "That is because the carriage in front of me hit a boy who was running from some other boys. The driver tried to miss him and, in doing so, he careened into milk wagon. It was quite a mess."

RT instantly relinquished his agitation. "Was the boy all right?"

Tom grunted. "Looked like a broken arm. Hopefully, he'll be fine. The police arrived quickly."

RT started toward him. "So what have you got? I hope it's worthwhile because the Wybles are unhappily cooling their heels in the lobby."

Tom shrugged. "It's a grand lobby. A fine place to wait."

"Get to it, man. Your note was vague. What does 'I found it' mean? You found the answer? You found the brooch? You found the man who fenced it? What?"

"Hold out your hand."

RT donned a comical, almost afraid to believe something so wonderful expression, and held out his hand.

Tom placed the brooch in it.

RT huffed in astonishment. He brought it closer to study it. "Is this really it?"

"Turn it over."

RT did and saw the initials. He then jerked his head up and stared at Tom. "How?" he whispered.

"There's no one else here," Tom whispered back. "Why are you whispering?"

RT grinned. "Did you find it at a pawn shop?"

"No."

"A shady jeweler?"

Tom shook his head.

RT blinked and suddenly wore an expression of disappointment. "Was it the maid?"

"No. In fact, she proved to be invaluable."

"What do you mean? Where was it?"

"In the house. Well hidden."

RT's jaw dropped. "Then how dih—" He stopped himself, paused as he considered. "How—"

It was amusing. RT wanted to hear but he couldn't afford to know. It was a dance they always began, but never finished.

"You got into the house?" RT whispered again. "Or did the maid search?"

Tom was impressed. RT didn't usually go so far as to ask. "Do you really want to know?"

RT's head went side to side. "Yes. No." He looked at the brooch again and shook his head. Looking back up, he asked, "Was it him or her or both?"

"My guess is her."

RT chuckled. "How will I explain having it?"

Tom shrugged. "Say that you hired a private detective whom you had heard good things about and *voila!* Tell them the man did not say where he found it, but your guess is a pawn shop where the thief must have hocked it as they usually do."

41

RT nodded, satisfied with the story. "It's got her initials. They can't deny it's hers."

"May I watch?"

"Indeed, you may. Be my guest. I'm going to go get them." RT cheerfully left the office while slipping the brooch into his jacket pocket.

"So?" Henry Wyble asked when they were seated. "What have you found out?"

Tom felt sure RT had made his apologies for keeping them waiting, although it hadn't lessoned Mr. Wyble's annoyance. Tom watched behind the transparent mirror with his arms crossed and a loose fist pressed to slightly smiling lips.

"It's excellent news," RT replied. "The brooch was found."

"Found?" Henry repeated. He smiled with delight. "Where was it?"

Tom watched Zilda's face. At the announcement it had been found, she'd drawn back in cool surprise, because she didn't believe it. Why would she when she knew how well concealed it was?

"I cannot say," RT replied. "I simply don't know."

"What do you mean?"

"We were having no luck with our normal inquiries, so I hired a fellow, a private investigator. I heard he was good …although unconventional, and I thought why not try every avenue?" He pulled out the brooch from his pocket and put in on the desk between the Wyble's.

Zilda gasped. Her eyes grew wide. She reached for it, but her husband was faster, picking it up and turning it over. He smiled jubilantly and handed it to her. "Here it is!"

She couldn't tear her eyes from it. Then she looked at RT with dark suspicion.

"We're so pleased to be able to return it to you," RT said, looking from one to the other. "However, I must recommend that you look into better security measures for your home."

"You think we were burgled then?" Henry Wyble asked. His earlier annoyance had vanished.

"I think this was the work of a highly devious thief. I would hate for there to be a third occurrence, because the policy would come up for review and very likely be cancelled due to the irregularity."

Henry huffed, but it was more in surprise than anger. "I thought it was the maid the first time." He looked at his wife who was still staring at RT with disbelief. "We both did."

"If you will write out a receipt," RT said, sliding a blank paper to Henry. "You only need to say 'brooch returned' and sign it. Oh, and add the date."

"Gladly." Henry began writing.

"Who was the investigator?" Zilda asked stiffly. "We'd be very interested in meeting him. To thank him."

"I'll happily pass the request on when I next see him," RT said pleasantly. "His name is Thomas Allen, but he is not the easiest man to locate. The nature of his business and all."

Henry set the pen back in its holder, having finished the note. "I would be very interested to learn how he went about hunting it down. I wonder if the police were called in."

"I've encouraged it," RT replied. "They should be called in. As I said, this was a loathsome, devious thief with no regard for decency."

Tom chuckled at RT's sly enjoyment and Zilda Wyble's pinched expression.

Henry was nodding. "If it was pawned, the pawn shop owner should have records. If not, he should be arrested for complicity."

"I agree. I'll keep you informed as to what I find out."

"Thank you." Henry stood and looked at his wife, who also stood. Shakily. "Are you all right, dear?" he asked solicitously as he took hold of her arm.

"Yes, of course," she replied unhappily, turning to go.

Tom could have done a jig. Oh, for the privilege of being a fly on the wall of the daughter's room when Zilda Wyble got

43

home and found the opportunity to check her stash. He would have paid good money to see that.

When the Wyble's were gone, RT turned to the mirror and straightened his tie. "I must say I enjoyed that," he said with a smile.

Tom stepped out from the closet like room that adjoined RT's office. "Thomas Allen, eh?"

"I didn't add your surname. If you wish to, you can still catch them. I believe they are not moving very quickly. The shock and all."

The men laughed.

Chapter Seven

The delicate bells on the door of Forrester's Fine Jewelry tinkled as Tom stepped inside. It was not the fanciest jewelry shop in town by a long shot, but it was presentable enough. It had been passed father to son to nephew, and it was the nephew, Paul Doggett, that Tom had a working relationship with.

"May I help you, sir?" a man asked on approach.

Tom didn't recognize him. "I'm here to see Mr. Doggett. The name is Kassel."

"I'll see if he's here."

"He's here," Tom said with a disarming smile. "We're associates. Oh, Doggett," he called, since there was no one else in the shop.

A privacy curtain in back of the shop was yanked open and Doggett waved him through. "It's fine. This one never makes an appointment," he added with a wry expression.

"I never know when I'll be in the neighborhood," Tom replied.

Doggett stepped back to let him through and then yanked the curtain back in place before following Tom into his cluttered office. "What have you got?" Doggett asked.

"A few things." Tom reached into his pocket and pulled out the locket.

Doggett looked at it and shrugged, not terribly impressed. "I'll take it, but it doesn't set my hair on fire."

"And this," Tom said, handing over the pin. "A hat pin, if I'm not mistaken."

"Yes," Doggett said, more interested than before. He took it, went and sat at his desk and reached for his magnifying glass. "It's a theatre hat pin."

45

"Why is it called that?"

Doggett turned it over and pointed to the small hook on back. "This hooks into the end of a seat at the theatre. So a lady can conveniently hang her hat." He studied the pin through the magnifying glass. "Nice."

"Yes," Tom agreed. "That's an emerald." He had no idea if it was or not, but he was hopeful and tried to sound certain.

Paul Doggett looked at him with a droll expression. "Thank you," he replied in a flat voice. "Saves me time."

Tom grinned. "What do you think it's worth?"

"What do I tell you every time? A thing is worth—"

"What someone will pay," Tom finished for him. "Why do I ask?"

"Why indeed?"

"There are also two chokers." He handed him the pearl choker.

"I suppose I'll need to go to New York to sell them?"

Tom shrugged. "No one is looking."

"You're saying they are not reported stolen?"

"As if I'd handle stolen merchandise! What do you take me for? Now, this one," he said, retrieving the ruby choker and laying it on the desk, "*was* reported stolen a few years ago. It wasn't found, because it really wasn't stolen, but the insurance company paid on it."

Paul set down the pearl necklace and picked up the ruby. "Wasn't stolen," he murmured, "and yet here it is." He looked up at Tom. "And it's too small for your neck."

"I know or I wouldn't be parting with it."

Paul Doggett chuckled. "The usual arrangement?"

"Yes. Except for that one," Tom said, pointing at the ruby choker. Whatever can be fetched for that is to find its way to," he paused to retrieve a note card from his pocket. "This lady." He handed the card over. "There is a message written there for her, as well."

Doggett, a man of forty-eight, adjusted his spectacles so he could read it. "'From someone who knows what was unjustly

taken from you, in hopes that it makes up for part of your loss.'"
He looked up at Tom. "There's a story here."

"Yes, there is."

"Why don't I buy it from you now and you can take the money to the lady yourself?"

"What? For a fraction of its worth?"

Paul pulled a wounded expression. "Ye of little faith. How you wound me. I'll pay fair wholesale." He glanced at it. "Six hundred."

"I'm an investigator," Tom said dryly. "I know what the owners paid for it."

"They paid retail, I pay wholesale. I have to make something on it, too."

"Nine hundred," Tom said.

"I'll be lucky to sell it for nine hundred!"

"You'll sell it for more than that. I'll take eight hundred and we'll be good."

"Seven hundred and not a penny more," Doggett replied crossly.

Tom glowered and leaned forward. "Seven hundred dollars and *ten cents*," he said enunciating with exaggeration.

Doggett tried to match his expression but couldn't help giving in to the tickle of amusement he felt. "Always have to have the last word," he said with a shake of his head. "Wait here. I'll get your money."

<u>Chapter Eight</u>

At the Sylvan Street address he'd been given for Betty Lee stood a quaint, white-washed home on the city's west side near the Zoological Garden. It had a picket fence and neat beds of flowers. He knocked on the door, but no one answered. He wanted to be done with this particular affair, so he decided to wait a bit. He walked back to the nondescript Phaeton he'd rented that morning and petted the horse's neck. He strolled the street for a quarter of an hour until he saw a lady walking toward him toting sturdy burlap carrying bags, probably groceries. He started toward her. "Mrs. Lee?"

She stopped, clearly surprised. "Yes. I'm Elizabeth Lee."

"My name is Tom Kassel. May I take a few minutes of your time? I was hoping to speak with you."

"What about?" she asked meekly.

She was early to mid-thirties, slender and plain with an aura of resigned wariness, as if she expected the worst of life. Had she always been like that, he wondered, or had the Wybles done the damage? "It's nothing bad," he assured her. "I'd rather talk in private, though. Your front porch will do."

She glanced around and then nodded.

"May I carry those?" he asked.

She relinquished one of the bags. "We'll go to the back porch," she said when they neared the house.

He followed her to a comfortable, well-shaded back porch, where she invited him to sit. He transferred the bag to her and she set them near the back door. "Your home is lovely," he said, taking a seat on one of the rocking chairs. "This is pleasant back here."

"Thank you. It's my aunt's home. She's not well."

48

"I'm sorry."

"She's almost ninety," she said as she sat. "And I'm here to care for her now. She's been a blessing for me and I'm trying to be one for her."

"I'm sure you are."

"What is this about, Mr. Kassel?"

He licked his lips, suddenly uncomfortable. He hadn't planned out exactly what he was going to say, nor had he thought it would be a difficult as it suddenly was. "I know what happened with the Wybles," he said hesitantly.

She looked as though she'd been struck.

"I mean that I know the truth," he added. "I know you didn't do anything to deserve what happened to you."

She looked away from him, her mouth ajar. A tear ran down her face and she quickly wiped it away.

"I know," he continued, "and so does everyone else."

She looked back at him, full of anguish. "Not the Wybles," she said in a tremulous voice. "They think I took it."

"No one took it, Mrs. Lee. You were ...used."

Her face filled with confusion. "What?"

"Mr. Wyble probably thought you took it when he dismissed you. Although he dismissed another maid at the same time. He couldn't have thought you both took it."

"I thought that Mrs. Wyble would know I couldn't have done it. I thought she would speak up for me."

He nodded slowly. "I know, but she's not a good nor honest person, Mrs. Lee."

"It's Miss. I was never married," she said tiredly. "I lived my life in service. It was my life. I thought it would be my life and I was content with it." She sighed softly. "One day everything was fine. The next, I was cast out with only two hundred and eighteen dollars saved. I'm not a spendthrift, but I'd helped care for my mother, you see."

Tom loathed Zilda Wyble more with each passing second. He loathed Blakely Heyer, as well. He hated all bullies who mistreated others because they could and because it benefitted them.

"I had nowhere to go except here."

"What about your mother?"

"She lives with my sister and her family, but there's no room for me." She lowered her head to swipe beneath her nose discreetly. "I was so ashamed. I couldn't bear to tell them what happened." She took a breath and exhaled and then looked back at him. "Would you care for some tea? Or cider? We have apple cider or hard peach cider. That's Aunt Dorothy's favorite."

He hadn't planned on staying, but he felt the need to linger for a bit. "Cider sounds delicious. The non-hard variety. I've still got work."

She stood.

"But before you go." He also stood and reached into his pocket. "I came to give you this," he said, pulling out a thick envelope. "Since you're going in, you might want to put it somewhere safe."

She was puzzled as she took it in hand. She glanced at him and then looked inside the envelope. She drew in a sharp breath and sat back down again. Her eyes were wide. "What is this?"

"Compensation for what you went through."

"I don't understand."

He also sat again. "The ruby choker that was supposedly stolen—"

She nodded.

"It was never stolen. It was never missing. Not until I took it very recently."

"You took it," she repeated.

He nodded. "Yes, ma'am. And sold it. And that's the money that came from it. It's in repayment for what was done to you."

She was at a loss for words.

"No one knows except you and I," he continued. "I'm not telling anyone else and I hope that you won't either. If you do, I'll have to deny it." He smiled wryly.

She looked down at the money and then back up at him. "Why would you do this? Why would you care?"

"I hate injustice. I detest anyone, man or woman, who thinks they can get away with hurting other people because it benefits them."

She swallowed. "She did that? Claimed it was stolen when it wasn't'?"

He nodded. "She did."

"But why?"

"I don't know," he replied with a shake of his head. "If she hadn't done it again and I hadn't been asked to investigate the matter, I would never have learned the truth."

"Something else went missing? Or she said it did when it didn't?"

"Yes."

"I don't know what to say."

"You don't have to say anything. I almost left that envelope with a note, but that didn't feel quite right."

"I'm glad you didn't." She swallowed. "Do you not think it's wrong to keep it?"

"I think it's absolutely right to keep it," he declared passionately. "Maybe I have a skewed sense of right and wrong, but I think it's completely right for you to keep and use it. You were owed that and more for what was done."

"I would never have made this much," she admitted. "Not even half of it."

"That's not the point. It was not just a salary that was taken from you, was it?"

"No. It was my dignity and reputation." She straightened her posture and then rose. "I'll get that cider"

When she'd gone inside, it occurred to him that the encounter had lightened his heart. When the door opened again, it wasn't Betty but her aunt that appeared. The old lady was bent with age, but her eyes sparkled with intelligence and wit. He stood and she came to him and offered her hand. "I'm Aunt Dorothy."

"Tom Kassel."

"Not Robin Hood?"

He laughed. "No."

Betty stepped back out with a tray. "Aunt Dorothy, I would have helped you out."

"Oh, bosh. I can put one foot in front of the other. I will have one of those, though," she said as she walked to a chair and sat.

Betty served her first and then Tom, grinning at him conspiratorially.

"My niece just shared the most entertaining story I've heard in many a day," Dorothy said.

Betty looked at Tom apologetically. "I won't tell anyone else," she said.

He nodded, believing her.

"When she came here the day it happened," Dorothy continued, "she had no color in her face. I said I'm the old lady. Why do you look all gray and withered? She told me, all right. I wanted to take my walking stick to those people's heads."

"I understand," he said.

"I told her I would not tolerate one word about *her* feeling ashamed. It was them who needed to feel ashamed. Of course, I knew they wouldn't. People like them never do."

"I don't know what I would have done without her," Betty said, looking at her aunt with affection.

"I feel the same," Dorothy said, holding up her glass to her at her niece in a salute. She sipped and looked at Tom. "She's cleaned this place up and made it pretty again. Hadn't looked this good in twenty-five years. And when I go to my everlasting peace, the house will be hers and she can turn it into a little boarding house and make her way just fine. That's our plan. It's a good one, don't you think?"

"I do," Tom replied.

Dorothy sat back and began rocking. The mischievous glint in her eye was still there. "You always go around rescuing damsels in distress, Robin?"

He grinned. "No, ma'am. Although recently, there have been a few instances."

"Oh, tell us," Dorothy urged, slapping the arm of her chair. "You just don't know how you're making my day."

Betty looked sheepish, although she was grinning, too.

"I'd have to swear you to secrecy and use false names," he said, charmed by the ladies.

Dorothy looked at Betty. "Honey, go fetch a little kitchen knife and we'll do a little blood oath with Robin here."

He laughed. "That won't be necessary."

<u>Chapter Nine</u>

An hour later, Tom drove by the Heyer home as a man walked out the front door, possibly Blakely Heyer. He was the right age, mid-thirties, sharply attired, and he was coming from the home as if he owned it. If it was him, it was a stroke of good luck. Tom had only planned to locate the home before he began surveilling Heyer in the morning. Tom pulled over and twisted around to peer out the small window behind him. The man was climbing into a waiting carriage which then headed his way.

Tom drove on, managed a U-turn at the next street and started back in the opposite direction just in time to see the occupants of the carriage as it passed. There was a woman driving, a very attractive woman. Judging by the pair's closeness in the carriage and their animated conversation, they seemed intimately associated. Tom considered following them, but instead he parked and went back to the house. It wasn't a front door conversation that he needed to have, so he made his way to the back of the home and knocked on the door.

After a minute, he knocked again. A shapely, middle-aged woman opened it. She wore a plain gown and a no-nonsense look about her. "Yes?" she asked curtly.

"Good afternoon. I'd like to speak with Mrs. Heyer."

A crease deepened between the lady's brows. "Mrs. Heyer is away, at present."

"May I ask where?"

A look of distaste crossed her face. "May I ask who you are to inquire such a thing?"

"A friend."

"I don't think so," she retorted. "I have known her for many years and I do not know you."

"Do you think you know all her friends?"

"I either know them or know of them and there has been no mention of anyone like—" her gaze flicked up and down him, "—you."

"You know what I'm like?" he asked worriedly.

She saw he was teasing, and the corners of her mouth twitched. "As I said, she's not available," she repeated. "Good day to you." She started to close the door.

"I know she's not available," he replied. "She's in the asylum."

The woman jerked the door further open before leveling an angry gaze at him. "How dare you say that!"

"I dare because it's the truth."

Her face was flushed. "Who are you?"

"My name is Tom Kassel. I am an agent of inquiry."

"What, pray tell, Mr. Kassel, is an agent of inquiry?" she asked scornfully.

"Would it possible to have this conversation inside? If I'm not mistaken, Mr. Heyer left a short time ago."

Clearly, she didn't know what to make of him. "Why would we do that? What is it you want?"

"I'm working on behalf of a concerned party who feels Mrs. Heyer has been unjustly committed to the asylum."

"What party?" she asked suspiciously.

"I hope you understand, I cannot divulge too much. If word got back to Mr. Heyer—"

She stepped back and gestured him in. Glancing sideways, she said, "Put out the tea, Mabel."

Tom stepped into a corridor that led to a kitchen. Upon the lady's impatient gesture, he went into the kitchen where Mabel the cook was standing and listening. She was a woman of sixty or so with a well-cushioned squarish build. He nodded to her, and she gave him a dour once-over. "Tom Kassel, eh? Sounds like a made-up name to me."

"It's not."

She stepped forward and offered her hand. "I'm Anderson. Mabel Anderson."

He shook her hand. "Mrs. Anderson. A pleasure."

"I heard what you said," she stated. "If it's not true, if you're working for *him*, I'll poison your tea."

"Mabel," the first lady scolded mildly. "Don't be ridiculous. He'd be long gone by the time we discovered he lied to us."

He looked over at the first lady knowing more was coming.

"Then we'd have to find another way to get even," she said with a straight face.

"I didn't get your name," he said pleasantly.

"My name is Mrs. Georgina Yardley and I am the housekeeper. My friends call me Gina. You may call me Mrs. Yardley. Now, who is the interested party you spoke of?"

"Mrs. Yardley, I'm here to help Mrs. Heyer if I can, which is not without risk. What if your loyalty is to Mr. Heyer and he gets wind of my investigation? It could worsen the situation for Mrs. Heyer."

"How is that possible when the scoundrel has her locked away? How does it get worse than that?"

"Oh, it could get worse," he stated darkly. "It could get much worse. At the moment, she is overmedicated, but she is in a quality facility." He saw the ladies react to the statement. "As I told you, an interested party is concerned that she's been committed unjustly."

"She has!"

"If that can be proven, perhaps we have a chance of getting her out."

"Sit," Anderson said as she turned to see to the refreshments.

Tom sat at a well-worn table with six chairs around it. "I need information."

"Regarding what?" Gina Yardley asked.

"Everything. I need to know about this household and about Mrs. Heyer. I don't yet know what I'm looking for, so I need to learn everything I can. Why don't we start with what you know of Blakely Heyer."

Gina Yardley sat catty-corner from him. "He came from New York, I believe it was in '82 or '83, but that's all I know of his past. They met three years ago about this time of year."

"How did they meet?"

She thought back. "It was an art exhibition. The works of William Morris Hunt. Louisa has three or four of his paintings."

"And then there was a whirlwind romance, I understand?"

"That's a good way to describe it, I suppose. She's never done a foolish thing in her life except for marry that man. He's a charlatan."

"Do you know where he was going this afternoon?"

"No, I do not. We do not ask and he does not tell."

"Would it surprise you if I told you he was picked up in a carriage driven by a lady?"

She scoffed. "Nothing would surprise me about that man."

"You say he's from New York. The city, I suppose?"

She shrugged. "I believe so."

"Did he have a law practice there?"

"I assume so."

"How would you describe the Heyers' relationship?"

"He made her miserable for the most part," she replied in a resigned voice. "He was up then down. Pleasant and then surly. He would disappear for days at a time. Then he'd be back with flowers, swearing he'd be a better husband. It's almost as if he wanted to keep her off-balance. Never sure what to expect."

"Did he ever say where he went during these absences?"

"Not that I know of."

Anderson put a tray on the table and sat. The tray held a pretty china tea pot, cups, saucers and plates, a pitcher of milk and a bowl of sugar cubes, plus thick slices of cake that smelled delicious. "Help yourself," she added.

He did. "Thank you."

"His absences," Gina continued. "They made Louisa miserable at first, but eventually they came to be a relief. For all of us."

"We hoped he wouldn't come back," Anderson stated. She handed Gina a cup.

"Tell me about the household." Tom took a bite of the cake. It was rich and delicious.

"I can tell you it's not as it was," Gina said bitterly. "Before him, there were four of us. Louisa, us and my son."

"Your son?"

"Yes. William. He's sixteen." She glanced away if steeling herself. "He'll be seventeen next week."

"Is he still here?"

"No. Blakely Heyer saw to that."

"Accused the boy of theft," Anderson said, her eyes hard with indignation. "That man stashed his cufflinks in William's room and then made a row about them missing."

"My boy is no thief," Gina declared. "But Blakely Heyer scared him half to death. Said he'd see him locked up for it."

"Then he went and lied to us," Mable Anderson interjected. "Lied right out his lying teeth with his lying tongue. He claimed that he discovered the theft and so William ran off. But Janie overheard the whole thing."

"Who is Janie?"

"The new maid he hired. A pretty thing. He's got designs on her, but I'll stick him in his worthless gizzard before I see him violate that girl."

Tom couldn't help liking the feisty Mabel Anderson. "Is she still here?"

Both women nodded.

"We didn't want her at first," Anderson said. "But she's one of us now."

"Where is she?"

"Upstairs," Gina replied. "Cleaning his room. She's scared of him, so she does it when he's gone."

"Scared of what?"

"What Mable said. He's a lecher."

"But he hasn't hurt her?"

"No. He sends chills up her spine with the way he watches her and the things he says and the occasional touch to her back or arm. But no. He hasn't forced himself on her."

"She knows to call out if he tries any funny business," Mabel said.

"May I speak with her?"

Mabel leaned forward, frowning suspiciously. "How do we know you're on the up and up? You could be here judging our loyalty on his behalf. Not that he won't fire us the minute he can get away with it because he will."

Gina nodded slowly. "Who is the concerned party you mentioned?"

He hesitated.

She lifted her chin. "You will not get a single word more from us until you say."

"Fair enough," he relented. "When Mrs. Heyer went to The Women's Hospital for her appendix, she confided in her doctor."

"The lady doctor," Gina said quickly. "Dr. Ripley."

"Yes."

"She came here afterwards. Tried to see Louisa."

"I know. She was turned away and told not to come back."

Gina nodded. "I tried to catch her when she left, but she was gone. She's the concerned party?"

"Yes."

The women glanced at one another and then Gina rose. "I'll get Jane."

"Is there a photograph of Mr. Heyer I could take with me?" he asked her.

"Yes. There's one in Louisa's room. I'll get it."

"What if he notices it's gone?" Anderson asked.

Gina shrugged. "Perhaps William snatched it as well," she said, her voice thick with sarcasm. "Being the incorrigible thief that he is." She walked off.

Tom looked at Mabel Anderson who was studying him warily.

"I believe you," she said gravely.

"I believe you, too," he replied with the same gravity.

She chortled and the tension was broken.

"We can't get in that place to see her," she said. "We're not on an approved list. Have you seen her?"

"No, but my associate has. Dr. Ripley and a friend of hers, who is also a doctor, are doing their best to keep an eye on her. Unfortunately, another doctor has control over her medications." He paused. "What happened to get her taken away? Was there an incident?"

"No. Of course not. It was all quiet. Like a sneak thief. We didn't know a thing until after it was done."

"You're certain there was no episode?"

"Louisa didn't have episodes. She's a lady."

"What did Heyer say afterwards to explain her absence?"

She guffawed with disgust. "He said she'd grown … what was the word he used? Means sad. Despondent," she exclaimed, remembering it. "Yeah. He said she was despondent. To the point he was worried she'd take her own life. What rubbish! I've known her all her life, Tom Kassel. The only one thinking about taking her life was *him*. I'd swear my life on it."

Tom heard footsteps and rose. He turned to see Gina carrying a framed photograph, and a pretty fair-haired young woman he judged to be about eighteen. She looked apprehensive. "I'm Tom Kassel," he said to her.

She bobbed a curtsy. "I'm Jane, sir."

"Pleased to meet you, Jane. I work as an investigator and I'd like to help Mrs. Heyer if I can. Will you speak with me?"

"I didn't know her well," Jane replied with a slow shrug. "But I did like her."

"Sit down, dear," Gina said to her. "I'll get a cup for you."

"I'm not finished with his room," Jane fretted.

"We'll finish it together. Don't worry. It'll get done."

Jane came and sat next to Mabel.

"It's all right," Anderson said, reaching over to pat her hand.

"What's your last name, Jane?" Tom asked.

"Behr. Jane Behr. Rhymes with Jane Eyre, I know."

He smiled. "Get teased about that?"

She nodded and shrugged. "I don't mind. I like her. Although she's a better person than me. She's forever thinking about what's right and proper."

"And what about you?" he asked lightly.

"Oh, I would have stayed with Mr. Rochester," she replied earnestly.

He chuckled. "I imagine many ladies would have. When were you hired here?"

"It's been eight weeks, sir."

He nodded. "Where were you before that?"

"I was the parlor maid for Mrs. Stanton, who is an older lady. When she took a fall, it scared everyone, so she moved in with her son and his family. They said it was time. Then I saw this position advertised."

"For a front parlor maid," Gina Yardley said with a wry expression as she put a cup in front of Jane. She handed Tom the photograph of Heyer having removed it from the frame. "As if we need one. But he's one to put on airs."

Mable poured Jane some tea and brought the tray closer to her. "Don't be shy," she said to the girl.

"What did you overhear between Mr. Heyer and William?" Tom asked Jane. "The altercation."

"Mr. Heyer doesn't know I heard it," Jane replied worriedly.

"And we'll keep it that way," he assured her. "Just tell me about it … as if you were telling a story."

She thought back. "It was in here in the kitchen that they had words. I'd brought things down for the laundry."

"We send laundry out for washing," Gina interjected. "But we organize it in the workroom to the left of where you walked in. She was in there."

"I heard William say something," Jane continued. "Loud. That's not like him. He said, 'I didn't do it!' They must have had words upstairs and then one of them followed the other down."

Tom nodded.

"Then Mr. Heyer said, 'I say you did. They were found in your room. What do you think the police will say?'"

Gina ducked her head, a pained expression on her face.

"Then William said, 'But I'm the one who found them and brought them to you.' Then Mr. Heyer said, 'After you got cold feet, I imagine.' Then William said what would he need fancy cufflinks for, and Mr. Heyer said he was probably planning on selling them. It went on like that until Mr. Heyer said he was going to go fetch the police. William was upset. He swore he didn't take them. He swore to God. Mr. Heyer said he was going to get the police and that if William had any sense, he'd clear out before they got back and he would stay gone. It would either be that or jail."

Tom looked at Gina. "Where were you at this time?"

"I take Tuesday afternoons off. Which is why it happened when it did."

"So you were away from the house?"

"Yes. I put flowers on the graves of my husband and parents."

"And you?" he asked Mrs. Anderson.

"Gone to the market as I do that time of day."

Tom looked back at Gina. "What did Heyer say to you when you got back to explain William's absence?"

"He said he discovered his gold cufflinks missing so he went to William, suspecting him. He claimed they had words and that he threatened to search every inch of my son's room. Then William turned defiant and came out with them. Thrust them at him." She huffed and rolled her eyes. "Then Heyer said he had half a mind to get the police involved and that's when my son pushed him and ran. Ran from the house. Ran away."

Tom nodded slowly. "Have you heard from William since?"

Gina's eyes filled. She shook her head.

"How long ago was this?"

"Three months," Mrs. Anderson spoke up. "It was the tenth of April. Not long after Louisa was taken."

"Five days later," Gina said. "It was a dreadful week."

"So William knew about Louisa being taken?"

"No," Gina replied. "I didn't tell him. We said she'd taken a holiday."

"We hoped she'd be home soon," Mabel added.

"Do you have any idea where William would have gone?" he asked Gina.

Gina dabbed at her eyes and nose with a hanky. "No and I've thought of little else. Racked my brain. Asked his friends. To no avail. He had very little money. We have no other family."

"I'm sorry," Tom said. "I know how difficult not knowing is."

She nodded.

"Do you happen to have a photograph of him?"

She looked at him sharply with hope suddenly burning in her eyes. "Why do you ask?"

"I could ask around. If I could borrow it?"

Gina Yardley's guard had been dropped enough that a sob escaped her. Embarrassed and without a word, she left the room. Jane looked down at the table, tears in her eyes.

"You can stop in for tea and cake anytime you want," Mrs. Anderson said to him with a knowing nod. "You're a good man."

He looked stricken. "Oh, Mrs. Anderson, please do not spread that rumor. It would ruin me."

She laughed heartily and Jane grinned, too. "We won't tell a soul," Mabel replied. "I'll tell you this, Tom Kassel, William is a good boy. He's got a fine mind. Got good marks in school. He would never be one in trouble with the law. Never."

"You've seen him grow up," he commented.

She nodded. "From five years of age when they came here. I saw him lose his baby teeth. I was here the day he got his scar," she said, taking her finger in a diagonal line from the left edge of her lips to her jaw line. I never thought of that as good luck, but it's how you can know you've found the right lad if you come across him."

"How did he get the scar?"

"Fell and hit a sharp edge just right. Bled like there was no tomorrow."

"Can you do me a favor and check on her?" He gestured upstairs. "I think I upset her."

She drew her bulk up from the chair. "I'll check on her."

Tom waited until he heard her climb midway up the stairs. He noticed that Jane looked wary. "Is there anything else you can tell me?" he asked quietly.

She glanced at the door and then looked back at him, conflicted and possibly embarrassed.

"Anything that would shed light on Blakely Heyer? Or William?"

Her blush increased.

"You liked William?"

"How do you mean?" she asked stammering a bit. "Of course, I liked him. Like him. I hope he'll come back. Mabel is right. He should have a good future. Mr. Heyer should not be able to take that from him."

"Did William like you, too?"

She looked away with a sigh and reluctantly nodded.

"Did Mr. Heyer know William had feelings for you? And that those feelings might be reciprocated?" He heard returning footsteps and knew she did, too. She looked at him and nodded. "I think so," she said quietly. "He looks at me so odd."

"Mr. Heyer?"

She nodded.

"Be careful of him," he warned.

"I will. I won't let him touch me. My family needs the money, but—"

Georgina Yardley came back in with the photograph of her son. She was composed again and provided a list of names and addresses of William's friends that he might have turned to, despite the fact she'd had no luck with them.

When Tom left with the list and photographs, he was feeling increasingly foolish. He wasn't even getting paid for this job and what was he doing but digging in deeper and deeper.

Yes, please, let me go rescue your son.

Then again, he might end up getting paid and he did feel something was rotten in the state of Denmark. His next step would be to get the scoop on Blakely Heyer's character and his past. Which meant writing to Reggie Glass, his cohort in New York. He'd do that as soon as he got home. He'd also send Cecil Lawrence a note letting him know he suspected they were dealing with fire rather than fog.

Chapter Ten

Wednesday, July 11

The girl was emaciated and dehydrated. She was suffering from cholera, the same disease that had claimed the life of her brother only days ago. The grandmother who had brought her in to the hospital was bony and distraught. "The sickness just came on," she said. "Both of them. Sick out both ends. Couldn't stop it."

Vi started an Intravenous infusion of Ringers Lactate Solution on the girl. Grandmother and granddaughter were as filthy as anyone she'd seen. Their clothes were soiled, their hair hadn't been washed in months, and they smelled to the point of making her feel nauseated. Dirt lined the sides of the girls face and beneath her ears. It was caked beneath her fingernails. She was probably beyond saving, but the infusion brought back some color into her pallid face.

A nurse walked in and blinked in surprise to see Vi. "I thought you'd gone," she said.

Vi's shift had ended, and she could have gone. She should have. "Will you clean her up as best you can?" she asked the nurse. "And continue the solution."

"Of course, Doctor."

Vi looked at the grandmother who looked ashamed. Vi was certain the conditions these people lived in were deplorable and yet the old woman was probably doing the best she could. "I believe your granddaughter has cholera."

The old woman moaned in dismay. "I feared it," she admitted in a tremulous voice.

66

"Your water source is probably contaminated. Either that or it became contaminated before it was consumed. Do not continue drinking it as you have been." She paused because she felt ill. It was everything she could do not to put her hand in front of her mouth and nose. "The children's parents?"

The old woman shook her head. "Gone. Drink took her and then he took off. Left me with the two of them. Not that they was a bother 'ceptin there's never enough food to go around." She looked at the girl sorrowfully.

Vi had to leave the room. "I'll be back," she said as she made her escape. She walked on to the next corridor and stopped to rest against the wall until the nausea passed. Of all the physicians she knew, she had the weakest stomach. It was pathetic that she had never outgrown it.

She walked on, pausing to look into the room of a seventy-year-old man she'd treated earlier. He had a failing heart and he'd developed pneumonia. He was propped up in bed and asleep, his mouth hanging open, the wheezing audible from where she stood. It was only a matter of time. The best they could do was to keep him as comfortable as possible.

Several young women passed her. Medical students from The Women's Medical College, her alma mater. Some of them looked excited, a few looked apprehensive. One petite, dark-haired young woman caught her eye. It was the way she held herself and the nervous expression on her face. She reminded Vi of her younger self. On a whim, she followed the group into the surgical theatre.

The students went to the row of reserved seats. Vi hung back near the door. The room was mostly filled, and Dr. Franklin Arnett was speaking from the stage below. The patient, a middle-aged woman who was badly jaundiced, lay unconscious on the operating table. An anesthetist stood close by, and Dr. Clara Reed, as well, to assist as needed. Clara was in her late thirties with a stoic face and a deliberate manor. She possessed a razor-sharp wit which took everyone by surprise when they first discovered it. It wasn't expected from someone as serious as she.

"Welcome ladies of the medical college," Arnett greeted. "I was just explaining the patient is a forty-two-year-old female with advanced Bright's disease. No treatment has proven effective and so we are poised to conduct a more radical approach. I say radical, but nephrectomy ... I hope you all know that is the surgical removal of a kidney," he said to a tittering of laughter, "has been a well-established and often successful operation for nearly a decade. Partial nephrectomy has also had some success and has been increasingly performed in the last year or so."

Vi crossed her arms and leaned against the wall.

"Today I will open up the patient and examine the kidney on her right side for possible removal as it's thought to be the more diseased organ. As you all know, a human being can exist with only one kidney. If any of you did not know that, please leave."

Again, there was some laughter. Vi didn't feel so inclined.

He took a scalpel in hand and uncovered the patient's naked body. Vi clearly recalled the first time she'd witnessed a patient's unveiling before surgery. Seeing a human being laid bare and vulnerable before surgery was nothing like reading about it or even seeing illustrations in a textbook.

She looked at the medical students and knew what some of them were feeling by the expressions on their faces and the tension in their bodies, especially the young woman she'd noticed earlier.

"The incision begins below the rib cage," he said as he cut.

Several eager observers in the theatre stood to see the operation better. A line of blood followed the scalpel and Clara blotted it with clean rags. One of the female students turned away sharply and blew out a breath. The young woman next to her whispered something to her before taking hold of her hand.

Vi had been similarly affected once. She'd been a wholly different person then, young and tender, trying to measure up and be strong. She wanted to be more like Tally and Charity who were not daunted by anything or affected by the sight of an open cavity or an oozing sore or what seemed a fountain of blood.

68

"The incision will be approximately six inches on this patient," Arnett said. "There are several layers of muscle to cut through."

Vi thought back on Louisa Heyer's surgery when her appendix had nearly ruptured. They'd been fortunate to get to it in time. She could have easily died that day. Then again, the poor woman was languishing in a drugged stupor in an asylum. Would it have been better for her to die of a ruptured appendix? Vi cringed at the unbidden thought. What was wrong with her? Too often of late she was either exhausted or numb or thinking dark and cynical thoughts.

More audience members stood and craned their necks to better observe the operation, but Vi quietly left the room. She wasn't sure why she'd stepped in.

Chapter Eleven

Thursday, July 12

Tally walked into the second-floor physician's lobby and found Vi slumped in a chair. Vi had been on duty since six that morning, but she didn't usually look quite so peaked at this mid-afternoon hour. "There you are. Are you all right?"

"Three more scarlet fever cases today," Vi replied. "A two-year-old, a five-year-old and a fourteen-year-old girl who I think has developed diphtheria. Not only that," she said quietly, despite the fact that there were just the two of them in the room. "But she was with child."

Fourteen! Tally recalled herself at fourteen. She'd been a determined scrapper, but still an innocent girl. Not quite a child, but not yet a woman by a long shot. "What do you mean she *was* with child? Did the girl die?"

"No, not yet, but there's no fetal movement or heartbeat. The girl said the babe was moving until she got sick. I don't think she'll live much longer." Vi heaved a sigh. "I'm so tired. I'm saying everything all wrong."

"No, you're not. Saying everything all wrong, I mean. Of course, you're tired. You've been at it for nine hours. Are you still going to Dr. Keen's lecture?"

Dr. William Williams Keen was the hospital's professor of surgery, but he rarely did lectures. He had removed a brain tumor last year and the patient had lived. "I should. I know it will be fascinating." She rolled her shoulders and slowly stretched her neck. "I need a strong cup of tea."

"Good idea. With a shot of brandy in it. By the way, this came for you," Tally said, pulling a letter from her pocket. She handed it over. "So, let's go. You'll have tea or coffee and something sweet to eat and then we'll attend the lecture."

Vi gave her a look. "How would you feel about carrying me there?"

Tally gestured to the floor. "Lay down and I'll drag you by a leg. That way you can rest, and we can provide a bit of entertainment to everyone we pass." That earned a chuckle. Vi rose and the two of them left the lobby. "I saw Louisa Heyer today," Tally said as they walked. "I was able to intervene with the afternoon's dosage."

"Were you? Good!"

Tally nodded. "I said I would give it and I did. I gave it a good toss into the chamber pot." That drew another smile from Vi, but the letter drew a more interesting reaction once Vi noticed it was from Cecil Lawrence, Esq. It was apparent that Vi liked the man. Tally found it a bit disconcerting, but that was only selfishness on her part talking.

Most of their friends were married and had children, and now Vi seemed smitten, having met Cecil Lawrence only once. Sadly, it seemed destined that she, Thelma Anne Covington, would end up the only unmarried one of the lot. It wasn't cause for grief, exactly, but it wasn't cause for celebration either.

She'd always assumed she and her closest friends were too unconventional for marriage. Typically, men were not drawn to professional women, much less doctors who worked ten and twelve hour stretches at a time only to end up too exhausted to do anything but sleep until it was time for the next shift or emergency.

It was a passion for healing that sustained them, but did it completely fulfill them? She didn't usually admit it, but the answer was no. Fortunately, it was easy enough to ignore the thought when they kept as busy as they did, but having friends fall in love and having children reawakened a yearning and a certain, private loneliness. "I can hardly wait to get better acquainted with your Mr. Lawrence."

"He is not my Mr. Lawrence."

"Oh, Viola," Tally said in a sing-song voice.

"What?"

"You just blushed."

"I did not!"

"You did so."

They rounded a bend to a new hall and Vi scanned the letter. "He wants to take me to dinner. To talk about the case."

"To talk about the case," Tally said suggestively. "Yes, that should be done over dinner. With a fine wine and a violin playing. Where has he proposed to take you?"

"Bookbinders."

"Ooh, how nice." She frowned. "He isn't talking about tonight, is he?"

"No. Tomorrow night."

"That's good. You can cut tomorrow short and get pretty for your ... discussion of the case."

Viola sighed. "That will depend on Betina Morris."

"Who?"

"The fourteen-year-old. Her temperature was 104 and her throat is severely swollen. There is thick membrane in her esophagus."

"What are you treating her with?"

"A distillation of sweet spirit of nitre, acetate of ammonia and laudanum. She's been isolated and we're trying to bring down the fever."

Tally nodded. "And what will you wear to your meeting with Mr. Lawrence?" she asked just as soberly.

Vi grinned at the teasing. "He wants to know whether I would prefer to meet him there or have him pick me up. What do you think?"

"That I'm jealous. But it's good to see you animated again. You're suddenly full of vigor."

"Because I'm looking forward to the lecture," Vi rejoined.

"*Mm-hmm,*" Tally murmured.

<u>Chapter Twelve</u>

Friday, July 13th

As Vi followed the maître d' to the table where Cecil Lawrence waited, she wondered if it was obvious how much thought and effort she'd put into her appearance. Her cap-sleeved gown, which had never been worn before, was deep indigo with a fringe of lighter lace at the moderately plunging neckline as if to draw the eye there. And, as if to assure it, she'd worn her favorite necklace with multiple pendants of small amethysts and sapphires dangling from it. Her gloves were elbow length, and her hair was drawn back into a soft roll that had taken a half hour to perfect. She'd even put a fine veil of rouge on her cheeks and lips.

It had been far too long since she'd had a proper evening out with a gentleman, and she was nervous. He might have nothing but a discussion of the case in mind. If that was the case, how foolish did she look? A diner with a mustache and dramatic sideburns gave her an appreciative once-over, which was equally flattering and disconcerting. She noticed Cecil rise from a corner table he had probably paid handsomely for. He looked handsome in a fashionably cut suit and a tie of green.

"Good evening," he said when they reached the table.

"Good evening, Mr. Lawrence."

The maître d' pulled back her chair for her and she sat, as did Cecil.

"I ordered a bottle of champagne," Cecil said. "But I'll order something different if you prefer."

"No, I love champagne."

The maître d' poured a glass for her and informed them he'd send the waiter. As he walked away, Cecil smiled and lifted his glass to her. "I've been looking forward to this."

She picked up her glass and touched it to his. "So have I." They sipped and it was delicious. It had been ages since she'd enjoyed good champagne.

"How was your day?" he asked eagerly.

She hesitated. "It was not the easiest day. I lost a patient. A fourteen-year-old girl."

He grew somber. "I'm sorry."

She set down her glass and began removing a glove beneath the table. "Diphtheria. It was too far progressed."

"I can imagine how difficult that must be."

"Yes." She smiled wanly. "I imagine you've lost a case before."

He drew back with a frown. "Never!"

She smiled and then laughed lightly at his answering smile.

"Of course, I have," he said.

"One you cared about and the verdict felt unjust?"

"Yes."

"I suppose it's somewhat the same."

"But I've only been involved with a few capital cases. Matters of life and death are terribly wearing. After all, if it goes badly—"

"Have you had that happen?"

"No one executed. A friend of mine represented Richard Riggs three years ago and I consulted on the case. I believed it was self-defense, so his conviction was a bitter pill."

She nodded and sipped her champagne. The trial had been a widely publicized sensation, so she knew the story. Riggs was a dashing man, a laborer, who married a rather notorious beauty who believed her husband to be dead after a long absence. The husband, a man by the name of Manny Westbrook, was a rogue, by all accounts. When he suddenly reappeared, there was trouble. Riggs and Westbrook fought and Westbrook was killed.

Riggs claimed it was self-defense and public sympathy was with him, but he was convicted and later hanged.

"But that is a gloomy subject," he added.

It was, indeed. "On a different subject," she said. "I made a point of seeing Louisa today."

"Oh?"

She nodded. "She was more cognizant than the last time I saw her. She didn't do much talking, but I think she understood most of what I was saying. Unfortunately, I got quite a stare-down from a nurse and then a doctor came in to ask my business. I fear I may be banned from visiting before long."

"They should not be allowed to ban the visit of a friend."

"I imagine they would claim I'm causing her distress. My aim is just the opposite, but Dr. Backman and Blakely Heyer will not want me anywhere near her. If they catch wind of it—"

He nodded. "I brought a private investigator in to look into the situation, if only briefly."

She felt her breath catch. "Oh?"

"The first few hours are pro bono out of the goodness of his heart. I'll tell you all about it, but shall we look at the menu first?"

"Yes," she said agreeably. It was such a relief to have him as an ally. She picked up the menu.

"We could start with an appetizer," he suggested. "They have a platter of raw and baked oysters, if you like them."

"I do. Very much."

"And I highly recommend nesselrode for dessert. Have you had it?"

"Not for ages," she replied excitedly. It was a rich, delicious frozen custard confection with hazelnuts and currants and vanilla and cognac. She made her entrée choice, baked sole with vegetables, and they ordered before returning to the topic at hand.

"The detective's name is Kassel," he said. "Tom Kassel. He is someone who worked for the opposing side in a case I had several months ago. It's because of what he uncovered that their side won."

"Ah." She sipped her champagne.

"His methods may not always be on the up and up, but he gets results, so I contacted him to see what he could do and what it would cost. It's too much, but we had an enjoyable dinner and a good conversation and he agreed to nose around a bit."

"That's wonderful."

"I don't know what he's done thus far, but he sent a note saying we should stay the course and that he's looking into Blakely Heyer."

"I am so relieved. I've felt quite alone in this. Naturally, Tally would do anything to help, but there is so little we can do."

He nodded. "Perhaps we can all meet soon and discuss what's been learned."

"I'd like that. I look forward to meeting Mr. Kassel and expressing my thanks, even if his assistance amounts to no more than a few hours."

"What would your thoughts be on me seeing Dr. Backman?"

She resisted an urge to immediately shake her head. "What would you say?"

"That there are parties who feel Mrs. Heyer's interests are not being well served. Although *not* due to negligence on his part," he added comically.

"Of course not," she played along. "As if there could be."

"It'll be important that he not get defensive. Perhaps, by then, I might learn something about Heyer that will throw his character into enough doubt that Dr. Backman may begin thinking of protecting his own reputation."

"Doctor Backman is an arrogant man. You would need to be very careful with any mention of his reputation."

"I'd gathered as much. It's just not anyone who can get into the royal order of pomposity and superciliousness."

She laughed. "No, it is not."

"But if he knows Louisa is being watched by concerned parties and that there is unease as to her diagnosis, he might be more disposed to taking a more conservative approach in regard to her medication."

It didn't feel like the right course of action to her. "There is a risk."

"I know. What if he is insulted and tells Blakely Heyer? They could ban all visitors or move her to a worse place. Somewhere we couldn't reach her."

"Precisely. Or what if he increases her medication? There is grave danger in that. It could mean convulsions, heart arrhythmia or even coma."

"So much hinges on how responsibly Dr. Backman tended Louisa in the first place. What did he base the diagnosis on? Was it after an event of some sort and a thorough examination or did he base the diagnosis strictly on what Blakely Heyer told him? We're at a disadvantage not having all the answers." He paused. "I'll see what Kassel has come up with and confer with you before we do anything."

She nodded in agreement. The idea seemed too risky without knowing more.

He reached for his glass again. "I hope it's not too forward to say how lovely you look this evening."

She murmured her thanks and felt her face flush. Luckily, the oyster platter arrived and the waiter refilled their glasses which gave her the moments she needed to regain her composure. When they'd helped themselves to the selections they wanted, she said, "My mother sent the gown at the beginning of the summer and I hadn't had the opportunity to wear it before this evening."

"She chose well. Are you close to your family?"

"No." She saw that her reply had surprised him. "We were until my medical training came between us."

"Oh?"

She'd taken a bite, so she was forced to wait to reply.

"You don't need to tell me, if you don't wish. I'm interested, but I don't want to pry."

"I don't mind telling you." She sipped her champagne, thinking of how to begin. She hadn't talked about her family in a long while. "As a girl, I went to a boarding school, Linden Hall, and my family was proud of my achievements. My parents said I could continue on at Pennsylvania Female College if I wished, but I knew then that I wanted to pursue medicine so I asked to attend the Women's Medical College. My father refused. He declared it was no path for a properly brought up girl and my mother agreed. The choice of pursuing higher education for a year or two was mine, they said, but they would not pay for medical school. End of subject."

He nodded slowly. "I see."

"Except it wasn't the end of the subject as far as I was concerned. I went to my grandmother, my father's mother, Nona, we called her, and she wholeheartedly agreed to support me. My father was highly displeased with her and me, but I didn't care, and Nona was unyielding." She smiled, but then it dimmed. "Unfortunately, she suffered a stroke midway through my second year of school."

"I'm sorry."

She looked down and toyed with an oyster on her plate. "She never recovered." She looked up at him and shrugged. "My father stopped the support, thinking I would be stopped at that point."

"That was wrong of him," he said quietly.

"I thought so. We became estranged because of it. And it didn't stop me because the college had a scholarship program."

"Oh?"

She nodded. "In exchange for our schooling …my schooling," she corrected herself. "I said we because Tally was also on scholarship."

"Ah."

"Anyway, in exchange for the completion of our medical training, we agreed to work for The Women's Hospital for less than we would have made for a set amount of time. Three years.

Three years of JASP. An acronym for Just Above Starvation Pay. We came up with that; they didn't."

He chuckled.

"Of course, we've continued our employment beyond the obligation."

"But you never mended relations with your parents?"

She shook her head. "No. They have tried in the last few years, especially my mother. I've rejected their attempts."

"You don't seem happy about that," he observed.

"It's an unhappy situation. I've begun to relent a bit by occasionally returning a note or accepting a gift. Sending a thank you card. The relationship can never be as it was, but it may be time to allow some healing to occur. It's difficult, though. I've built a wall of resentment. A fortress of it. It would be far easier to let it stand than tear it down."

He murmured his understanding. "Do you have siblings?"

"I do. An older brother, Michael. And he has a wonderful wife and two children, a girl and a boy."

"Are you close to them?"

"I love them, but we haven't spent the sort of time together that I would like. My work is demanding."

He reached for the bottle. "Was Michael supportive of your becoming a doctor?" he asked as he topped off their glasses.

"I don't think he disagreed with my parents," she said thoughtfully, "but he saw how badly I wanted to be a doctor. I think his vote, if he'd gotten one, would have been to have our parents pay for school, although, deep down, he believes I would be better off in a more traditional role."

"A wife and mother," Cecil said.

She nodded.

"Is that an aspiration?"

The question and the shy but intent expression on his face robbed her of breath and heat rushed to her face. She reached for her glass and feared her hand was trembling. "Of course," she managed. "One day."

"And would you keep working?"

It was astonishing they were having this conversation, but she didn't mind. "I don't know," she admitted. "You met Jack Werthing."

His expression grew puzzled, but he nodded.

"His sister, Charity, is my second closest friend in the world."

"And also a doctor," he recalled.

"Yes. Several years ago, she and her brother learned that a man had been shot in the head and was languishing in a coma."

He grimaced.

"It was an injury much like the one their father had sustained."

"Really?"

She nodded.

"Shot in the head does not seem survivable," he said.

"Their father did not survive it, but they learned a great deal trying to save him and felt compelled to go. They traveled all the way to Virginia to treat the man and they saved him."

"That's remarkable."

"It is. And, while Charity was there, she met a man who owns a ranch and a mine and several other businesses and they fell in love. They are blissfully married and have twin boys and she is expecting another."

He smiled. "A happy story."

"She couldn't be happier and she combines marriage and motherhood *and* keeps a part time practice." She paused and drank more champagne. She felt the effects and it was pleasing. "I can't imagine Tally giving up medicine when she finds the right man. But—"

He cocked his head, studying her closely.

"As for myself, I truly do not know."

"Things do change," he mused. "What you most want and need at one point in time may be very different at another time."

She nodded. "The workload has become a grind. My ambivalence may be nothing more than that, but I just don't know."

"Then I won't pressure you to decide tonight," he teased.

She laughed. "Thank you for this evening. I'm having a wonderful time."

"So am I. Thank you for sharing it with me."

Vi started up the sidewalk toward home after being dropped off by a cab. She and Tally had taken rooms at Mrs. Wolsey's boarding house after graduation and had never considered living anywhere else. The home on Cabot Street was close to the hospital and comfortable. Mrs. Collene Wolsey, widowed for more than twenty years, was attached to all her boarders and they to her.

Vi went into the house and walked through to the screened-in back porch where Tally was stretched out on a settee. "I wasn't sure you'd still be up," Vi said, setting her reticule on a table.

"It's too hot to sleep. Besides, I had to know how your evening went." She donned a sad face. "And now I do." She sighed dramatically.

"What?" Vi laughed crossing her arms.

Tally moaned. "I'll be the only old maid left in the world. It's hard enough to be an old maid, but to be the *only* one."

"You are so silly."

"And you are glowing."

"That's the moonlight."

"No, dearest, it's not." She looked off, pouting. "I'll only ever be old Aunt Tally, the maiden aunt." She looked at Vi again. "It would have been far better to be Vi and Tally, those fabulous doctor ladies who are also old maids."

Vi went to one of the cushioned wicker chairs and sat. "I had a lovely time and I am somewhat inebriated. *And* you are being silly."

Tally cocked her head and looked at her with great affection. "We know each other too well for pretense."

Vi felt her expression waver. "I only just met him," she offered sheepishly.

"I know."

"I don't want to read too much into anything."

Tally nodded. "I know."

"It does feel special," Vi admitted just above a whisper.

"I know," Tally whispered back. She grinned. "You realize it's Friday the thirteenth. If it went that well on Friday the thirteenth, it's a very good sign."

"Where did that superstition ever come from? The notion that Friday the thirteenth is bad luck?"

"I have no idea. I imagine it was several things going very, very wrong on a Friday that was also the thirteenth."

Vi leaned back against the worn cushion. "We talked about my family."

"Really?"

Vi nodded. "He was sympathetic." She paused before adding, "He asked if I had aspirations to be a wife and mother."

"Oh my."

"And if I would want to continue working when I had a family."

Tally chortled. "How much wine did you have?"

"Too much. We had champagne and then a Beaujolais. Oh, but it was so enjoyable."

"So what did you tell him about working after the two of you elope and have triplets … somewhere around next spring?"

Viola giggled, but then she sobered. "I told him the truth. That I don't know."

Confusion flickered on Tally's face. She swung her legs around.

"Being a doctor has been my life for so long," Vi continued. "To even think of doing anything else, with all I've given up feels …almost like a betrayal."

"Well, it's not," Tally stated. "You wanted it and you sacrificed for it. How many people have you helped? How many lives have you saved? If you choose to walk away tomorrow, all it will mean is that you are leaving one meaningful chapter behind for a different one."

Tears filled Viola's eyes. She leaned forward and clasped Tally's hand. "Thank you."

"There's nothing to thank me for. Things change," Tally said with a shrug.

"Cecil said the same thing."

"So then we think alike, which means he's brilliant and we'll be the best of friends. That's a good thing since I'll probably be living with you and him and the triplets."

Vi laughed. "I'm glad the heat has not wilted your sense of humor."

"I really do look forward to getting to know him better."

"I think it will be soon. They've learned things about the case they want to pass on."

"They?"

Vi nodded. "A detective is doing some digging on Blakely Heyer."

"A detective. How glamorous. I hope it amounts to something worthwhile."

"So do I."

"By the way, you look *very* pretty. I love the dress and glowing suits you."

Vi smiled warmly. "Thank you." She stood. "I've got to go to bed. I'm on in the morning."

"Night."

"Goodnight."

Vi went inside, leaving Tally feeling more alone than in some time.

Chapter Thirteen

Sunday, July 15th

A little before midnight, Tom went to the front door of the office of elderly attorney Matthew F. Penny and glanced around to make certain the coast was clear before he picked the lock and let himself in. Blakely Heyer leased a main-level room there. It was a smart move on Heyer's part since Penny had enjoyed a robust practice and the place had an air of established success about it. These days, Penny worked a few days a week when and as it suited him.

Tom found Heyer's office to the left of the lobby, picked that lock and slipped inside. After lighting a lamp, he saw the office was sparsely decorated with only a desk, chairs and a bookcase. There were paintings on the main walls, seascapes, plus there were small silhouettes of a man and woman to the side of the office door. The seascapes were probably Penny's since they matched the décor in the reception area.

There were few personal items in the office. There was a fountain pen in a marble base on the desk, a cut-glass ash tray, a small decorative box and a hunk of iron pyrite. Fool's gold. He picked it up. It was half the size of his palm and weighed a pound or so. He jiggled it as he walked to the bookshelves to peruse the contents, legal journals, an empty vase, a few wooden statues, and a sleek wood box. Inside the box was a dozen cigars of good quality. Taking one, he took a last glance around. Nothing spoke of a personality.

He rounded the desk and sat, accidentally kicking a wastepaper basket below the desk. He set the pyrite back in its place and found matches in the small box. Striking one, he lit the cigar, enjoyed a few puffs, and then went through the files in the left drawer. It appeared Heyer had only four clients at present. One case involved a dispute over ownership of a business, one was a patent application and two were wills being drawn up. Hardly a thriving practice.

He opened the top drawer to see a hairbrush, additional pens and pencils, a letter opener and a small mirror. The top side drawer had a box of his cards and a tray of other people's calling cards. There were a few folded handkerchiefs, a packet of headache powder and a leather-bound notebook. He flicked his ashes in the ashtray and sat back to peruse the contents of the notebook. It contained names and notes that meant nothing to him. The bottom drawer contained only paper and envelopes, and the wastepaper basket was empty. No great finds. Resigned, he got up to leave. He put the cigar ashes in an envelope, folded it and carried it with him.

He reached the door, but hesitated. He looked at the silhouettes. Was the male silhouette Heyer? Tom stepped closer to it, shoving the envelope into his pocket. It *was* him. Tom looked at the silhouette of the lady, but he didn't know what Louisa Heyer looked like. He took it off the wall to see it better in the light but felt something loose on back. He turned it to see another photograph stuck into the bottom frame. He pulled it out to study the half-body image of a pretty, highly posed woman in some sort of theatrical costume. Her hair was fair, and her shapely lips darkened. It was a delicate face with a cleft chin. She held a large fan of feathers and wore a low-cut bodice and bejeweled headband. She had to be an actress. Was she the woman in the carriage he'd seen with Heyer? He couldn't be sure.

He put the photograph back into place and turned the silhouette back around. The silhouette was of the actress. He saw it now. Was she Heyer's mistress? His reason for doing away with his wife?

~~~

The following day, Tom surveilled Heyer. The man arrived at his office at ten o'clock, had no appointments, and left at one for lunch which he ate alone in a nearby tavern. He returned to his office until a little after three o'clock when he took a cab to a stately brick home on Locust Street. Old money resided here. Tom waited, ate another sandwich and drank lukewarm water from his thermos. Such was the nature of surveillance. Heyer left the house at twenty till eight wearing a different suit and in the presence of the same lady Tom had seen driving the carriage. The same face in the silhouette. It was the actress. It had been a long, dull day, but it had finally yielded fruit.

Between the county deeds and records office and the research room of the four-year old library at Juniper and Locust, Tom had amassed a good deal of information by the afternoon of the following day. He'd also developed a strong suspicion that Heyer's story was deeper, darker and far more twisted than they'd supposed.

The woman he'd seen Heyer with was Lillian Oliver Holmes, the widow of Gerald Mason Holmes. She'd been twenty-six when she married Holmes almost four years ago. He had been 69. She was a native of Camden, New Jersey, although she'd made her home in Philadelphia for the last five years. Roughly, the same amount of time Heyer had been here. The theatrical photograph he'd seen made him wonder if she had been pursuing the stage in New York before moving here.

Gerald Holmes had met a violent end in September of '85 after a mugging in which Mrs. Holmes was also injured. He'd been robbed and stabbed to death. Her injuries were not detailed in the newspaper account.

Gerald was survived by two married daughters. Tom made a note of their names and addresses. It was time he stopped kidding himself about nosing around for a few days to see if there was misconduct afoot. There was and he was most definitely on the case, something Cecil Lawrence needed to know and damn well appreciate.

<u>Chapter Fourteen</u>

At three-thirty in the afternoon, Tom knocked on one of the eight-foot oak doors of the Smith residence, home to one of Holmes' daughters. A maid answered the door. Tom introduced himself as he offered his card. "I'm hoping to speak with Mrs. Smith on a matter relating to her late father."

There was a moment of awkward surprise from the maid. She glanced down at the card before looking back at him. "If you'll step in, I'll see if she's available."

"Thank you." He stepped into a large foyer.

She shut the door behind him. "If you'll wait here."

As she hurried off, he looked around. There was a filled umbrella stand, an elaborate coat rack, empty at present, a circular oriental carpet and decorative tables with lamps and flower arrangements.

The walls were papered, narrow white and yellow stripes on a crimson background, although one hardly noticed it for the scores of portraits and landscapes upon them. On either side of the foyer were closed pocket doors. An imposing staircase wound up and around, and a hallway led to the area in back where the maid had gone and now returned followed by a lady, presumably Mrs. Ellen Holmes Smith, the elder of Gerald Holmes daughters.

"I'm Mrs. Smith," the lady said as she stepped around the maid in a smooth, well-practiced dance.

He judged her to be forty or so. Her dark hair was swept up revealing an angular face. She was slender with a look of intelligence in her brown eyes. She was not a pretty woman, but something about her face was strangely appealing. Her skirt and blouse were casual enough for the assumption she had not been going out or expecting callers. "I'm sorry to intrude, Mrs. Smith," he began. "However, I need information on Lillian Oliver Holmes. I was hoping you could help me."

She stiffened at the mention of the name. "What is this in regard to?"

He hesitated. "I am limited in what I can say at this point, but the welfare of a lady, whom you do not know, is in jeopardy. There is a man at the heart of it, a scoundrel, if my instincts can be trusted, and I have reason to wonder if your former stepmother—"

"Please do not call her that," she snapped.

He inclined his head slightly. "I apologize for offending you."

She seemed to mentally check herself and then looked at the maid. "We'll be in the drawing room. Please bring tea." Mrs. Smith then turned and led the way. She didn't speak again until they stood in a formal drawing room. "Do have a seat, Mr. Kassel, and tell me what this is about."

He went to a floral settee and sat. She took a seat opposite him on its twin. "It seems possible that Mrs. Holmes—" he began.

"If you would refer to her as Lillian Oliver, I would appreciate it," she interrupted. "I realize it is not factual, but I cannot bear to hear that woman referred to with my father's name."

He nodded. "The reason I'm here is that Lillian Oliver appears to be in a close relationship with the man I mentioned earlier."

"I am not surprised by that," she said without expression.

"This man has committed his wife to an asylum," he said somberly. "Unjustly. Or so some of us believe."

She flinched. "That is monstrous."

"Yes, it is."

"What is it you want from me?"

"I'm simply gathering information. What you know about her. Where she's from. How did she meet your father?"

She looked baffled. "What could that have to do with this man?"

"I don't know yet. Perhaps nothing at all. But he moved here from New York City some five years ago."

Her eyes flashed. "So did she."

"Exactly. I am wondering if they were associated before coming here," he said carefully. She rubbed her arms as if suddenly chilled, although the room, like every other room in every other house in every part of the city, was too warm. At least this house faced southward and was blocked from the sun's afternoon assault. There was also a ceiling fan whirling above them. The feel of moving air was always a relief.

"We disliked her from the first," she admitted. "She is ten years younger than me, five years younger than my sister. It was disgusting. Phony. She was after his money. But he allowed himself to be swept in by her. He knew how we felt and he disliked making us unhappy, but he was happy with her. Or so he said," she added with a light shrug. "We met for tea one afternoon, Clarice and Papa and I. Clarice is my younger sister."

He nodded.

"I won't say the conversation got heated exactly, but he saw how strongly we despised her. Perhaps for the first time. He wanted to know why." She sighed and shook her head. "My father was a wonderful man who had made a very good living. He'd been a wonderful husband to my mother for twenty-six years until her death. He would have never forsaken her. He was also a model father. He was always reasonable and even-tempered. He could drive us to distraction because he'd be too rational, almost amused at a dilemma that had one or all of us upset." She smiled sadly. "I can hardly believe how much I miss that now."

He understood the remnants of her mourning.

"But that day at tea, he asked if it was our inheritance that we were worried about. And he asked it calmly and with tender concern." She huffed. "Clarice and I are both well set. That wasn't the point at all. We were worried for him, not us. But I …

91

I didn't know how to voice my concern. Our concerns." She frowned, even now struggling to put her feelings into words. "It felt to us like she had infiltrated our lives and infected them." She paused while considering him. "You think I'm being melodramatic, I imagine."

"I don't actually," he replied.

A wistful smile crossed her lips. "Do you know what he did?"

"What?"

"He began to take stock. That's what he called it. He began writing us letters every week and sending us the most precious mementos. Things he wanted us to have. The first was a Fabergé egg I'd always loved. Clarice got a silver music box she'd adored. He passed on Mama's jewelry that we hadn't already been given. There was an engraved silver tray and much more."

Tears filled her eyes and she had to take a minute to regain control. She pulled a handkerchief from her pocket and dabbed the corner of her eyes and beneath her nose. "He saw how much his notes and gifts meant to us and we, in turn, saw how much our happiness meant to him. After all, when something has meaning, a memory attached to it, you want it to mean something to someone else. I'll do the same with my own children one day."

He wished he didn't feel as moved as he did. He was after facts that might help Louisa Heyer and that was all.

"I asked Papa once if *she* knew he was gifting us with these things. He said she did not know, nor was he going to tell her or change his mind about what he wanted us to have. Of course, he didn't change his mind about her either. We suffered through a few family get togethers during holidays, but mostly we avoided one another. Lillian and us, I mean to say. In the end, we had to accept that it was his life. She was what he wanted and he wasn't dotty. Without question, she had seduced him, but he knew that. He simply decided to enjoy it. In all fairness, I believe she treated him well. He seemed content."

He nodded slowly, before addressing the most difficult subject. "I know about the attack in the park," he said carefully. "I'm very sorry."

She looked down at the handkerchief in her lap, her face a mask of pain. "It was no way for his life to end."

"You're right. And she was also injured?"

"Yes. She was struck multiple times, I believe. There was a cut and swollen goose egg on her forehead," she said, gesturing to her own forehead. "We saw her the day after the attack and she seemed devastated. We called on her once after the funeral and she still seemed distraught. I felt sorry for her, but there was nothing for us to build a relationship on. And my feeling of sympathy did not outlast my resentment of her. It may not be fair, but I still feel that, if not for her, we'd still have him."

He tried to remain impassive, although he agreed with the sentiment. "If you happen to think of anything else, will you contact me?"

"I will. Was I any help to you?"

"You helped form a picture of her. Which is what I asked. Thank you."

"Perhaps not everyone will be as uncharitable in their assessment of her, but I don't know anyone who knows her. She is not part of our circle or any circle that I know of. The neighbors tell me she is private and not open to neighborhood socializing. They barely speak in the street while passing. She also began replacing the staff directly after the funeral. Or just outright dismissing them. She let Stine go, father's butler, and did not bring on a new one. Stine had been in service with papa for almost thirty years."

"Did she provide him a reference?"

"Yes. As did I. But it's difficult to make such a big change at a late stage in life. It was the same with the cook and the housekeeper. I don't know any of her help, now."

"I won't keep you any further. Thank you, again." He stood and she did the same. They started out and had just made it to the door as the tea cart was being wheeled in.

93

"Oh, tea," she said. "Would you care to stay?"

The maid lifted the lids off silver trays revealing a lovely spread of cucumber sandwiches and slices of rum cake if his nose could be trusted. It was tempting, but he never wanted to overstay his need. "It looks wonderful, but I should be going," he replied regretfully.

She accepted his refusal with grace and led the way back to the foyer. He was about to step through the door when she spoke again. "Mr. Kassel?"

He turned back to her. "Yes?"

"I don't imagine that it matters, but my father left us our full inheritance."

He waited, sensing more was coming.

"Lillian was bequeathed a life tenancy in the house and some money, but we got most everything. He split it evenly between my sister and myself. We only learned of it after the funeral and so did she. She went very pale. So much so that we thought she might faint. I am quite certain it was not what she was expecting."

"Who was his attorney?" he asked curiously.

"George Hammond of Hammond and Hargrove. He was Papa's attorney since I can remember. Why?"

"Just wondering." He tipped his hat to her. "Thank you again for your time. Good afternoon, Mrs. Smith."

"Good afternoon, Mr. Kassel. Good luck," she said meaningfully.

<u>Chapter Fifteen</u>

Sitting. She was sitting in a chair in her room. Someone had just helped her there. She was sitting. In a chair. In a room. Three parts. Three parts that made one whole. Or did it? Louisa looked around, not using her neck, just her eyes and even that made her dizzy. If only someone would stop everything from moving. Having her eyes closed was no better than having them open. It made no difference. She could do nothing. She was being held down and poisoned, and the poison was making the world quake and wave.

Faces sometimes loomed at her, their distorted lips moving as they spoke. If the face wasn't too horrifying as it changed shape, she tried to catch on, to understand the words. Occasionally, she did and it made her ache. She'd been sent away to this terrible place, this vile existence to languish until the poison finished her.

The bulging, looming faces reminded her of the fish in The Fish House at the London Zoo she'd visited as a child. Like the crowd of onlookers around her, she'd been fascinated by the tropical fish and sea creatures behind walls of glass. Watching them was mesmerizing. She'd wondered if the fish were aware of being ogled. Now, she knew the answer. She might as well be one of them. Being watched and moved and handled while having no control was grotesque. If only she could make someone understand, but her words and thoughts were disjointed, like tiny, cruelly jagged pieces to a puzzle. She was no longer capable of forming them correctly.

Someone, a female, stepped in front of her. The woman's skirt brushed her knee before she bent closer and Louisa saw it was the lovely tall doctor who helped her sometimes.

"Hello," the doctor said.

Could she even form the word hello to say it back? She tried.

"I'm glad to see you sitting." The doctor pulled up another chair and sat. "I brought something for you." She had something wrapped in her hands. She unwrapped it to reveal a roll. The lady tore a piece off and brought it to her lips. "It's delicious. Try it."

Louisa opened her mouth and felt the pressure as a soft hunk was shoved inside. She closed her mouth and tried to chew. Was she chewing? There was no taste to it.

"Please, hang on, Louisa," the doctor said quietly. "I know how alone you must feel, but there are people working to free you. Some of us know how badly you've been treated. Do you understand?"

Louisa nodded, although it made the room spin more madly than before. The next thing she knew she'd toppled forward enough that the doctor caught her. And held her. Thank God she held her.

Chapter Sixteen

Blakely Heyer stepped purposefully into the Philadelphia National Bank and went to one of the dozen clerks who sat in six by ten foot cubicles. They seemed like cages to him. Each was open in back, but the sides were solid and there was only a window in front for customer interaction and it was partially barred.

"May I help you, sir?" the clerk asked.

"Yes. I wish to make a withdrawal. My wife has an account here."

"Is your wife with you?"

"No. She's not well at present."

"I'm sorry to hear that, sir. Do you have a withdrawal request or a cheque with you that she's signed?"

"No," Blake said testily.

"A letter or any sort of documentation? Are you … you are not on the account, is that correct?"

"I'm not on this one, no."

"Perhaps you could withdraw from one you are on, sir," the clerk suggested.

Blake shifted on his feet, aware of looking like a fool. "There is not one at this bank and yet here I am. I wish to leave here with cash in hand from my wife's account. Our account. What's hers is mine."

"I am sorry, but we are restricted by regulations. Both the National Banking act and state laws stipulate that—"

"Get your supervisor," Blake hissed. A man glanced over from the next station as if he were some sort of criminal, and another customer now waited behind him. Heat was prickling up his body, torturing his neck which was undoubtedly turning red. "This is outrageous."

"May I ask your wife's name, sir?"

"Louisa Heyer," he bit out. "She was an Edgerton before we married."

The clerk quickly left his cage. Blake heard a woman huff behind him and ignored it. He felt a tap on the shoulder, so there was little choice but to turn to the well-dressed lady in a flattish hat positioned at an angle. She must have been exceedingly proud of how it sat, judging by how stiffly she held her head.

"Should I choose another window?" she asked with a sneer of distaste.

"Yes, madam. I believe you should."

She huffed again.

"It's inconvenient, I know," he said. "I wish that incompetence was not to be born," he said loftily. "But alas."

She made a breathy sound and gave a lift of a brow that conveyed marked skepticism and marched on.

He turned back around feeling like an utter spectacle. *Damn them.* They would pay for humiliating him. He would close her account and move it elsewhere. By God, he would! He felt another tap on the shoulder and turned to see an older man in a fine suit. Behind him was the clerk.

"You are married to Louisa Edgerton?" the man asked.

"Louisa Edgerton Heyer. Yes. I am Blakely Heyer. Attorney at law."

"Heyer, of course. Forgive me. I knew that she married. I've seen her a few times since then." He extended his hand and Blake shook it. "I'm Noel Reay. I've acted as Louisa's fiduciary for years. All her life, actually. I assisted all the Edgertons."

Blake tipped his head in acknowledgement.

"How is she?" Reay asked.

"Not well, I'm sorry to say."

"I am sorry to hear it," the man said with a suddenly grave expression. "Is she ill?"

"She is. And I am taking care of our affairs so she can convalesce without worry. I'm sure you can appreciate that."

"Louisa's always enjoyed the best of health," the man fretted. "May I ask the nature of her illness?"

"We're keeping it private," Blakely replied more quietly. "But I can tell you her doctor feels it's nothing that a nice, long rest cannot cure."

"I'm glad to hear that. I can assure you, sir, that I certainly understand and appreciate the bounds of propriety and privacy. As I've said, I am and have been her fiduciary for the whole of her life. The very nature of my work is private and confidential. Our customers' best interest are what we care about."

"I'm glad to hear it. You can assist me, then?"

"Certainly. I'm happy to. As soon as Louisa provides authorization. As an attorney, I feel certain you understand our legal position."

Blakely was livid but determined not to show it. "Is there a specific form you need filled out?" he asked stiffly.

"There is a form I can provide, but a letter will also do, if that's easier. I know Louisa's handwriting from years of experience, so as soon as we're assured that it's her wish, again, a legal requirement, I'll see the thing done. I can come to her, as well. I'd be only too glad to. Is she at home?"

"She is not, at the moment. I'll take the form," he stated coldly. "I must say, I would have hoped for more cooperation than this, given our long standing with this bank."

"You mean … the Edgerton's long standing," the man asked with a curious glint in his eye. Was he enjoying the exchange? Reay turned to the clerk without waiting for a reply. "Get Mr. Heyer the form, will you?"

"Yes, sir." The man scurried away.

Reay turned back. "Please give Louisa my regards," Reay said. Then he inclined his head briefly and walked away.

Chapter Seventeen

In a second-floor drawing room, favored in the summer because the window placement transported as much of a breeze as the atmosphere allowed, Lillian sat at an ornate desk while Blakely stood peering over her shoulder.

"It's too tight on the end," he complained. "More of a loop here," he said, pointing at part of the signature she was practicing. She let out a huff of frustration, and he took the hint and walked to the sideboard to make himself another drink.

"Why can't you get her to sign it?" she asked testily.

"I already told you. I tried. She's incapable."

"Why not ask for her medication to be lightened so that she can do it?"

He turned with a drink in hand and looked at her. She was impatient and quickly growing churlish, but she was so beautiful. Her fair haired curled naturally around her face. She had a small cleft in her chin which was unusual for a woman, but he adored it. She was flushed from the heat, but even that looked good on her. Her amber blouse was low cut showing delicious cleavage, but he needed to keep his mind on the task at hand. "I don't have the authority to have her medication changed. I suppose I could ask the doctor to do it, but I'm sure it will cost more and the place is already costing an arm and a leg."

She leaned back, looking put out with him. "Well, it's *her* arm and leg, isn't it?"

He bit his tongue to keep from snapping at her. "Once we get this done," he said in the most patient tone he could muster, "we can move ahead. I'll have her moved to the state hospital at Harrisburg and that will be that. She won't last a year there."

Lillian rolled her eyes. "Even if I get the signature right, won't you need a witness or something?"

"That's easy enough to get. Everything is available for a price. You know that." Still, she looked truculent. "Do you want another drink?"

"No."

"Then if you please—"

She puffed with displeasure again but leaned forward to make another attempt.

"When this is done," he placated, "perhaps we'll go to Italy for a month or two. Get away."

She looked at him. "Not to be crude, but is there not a faster, easier way this could be done? Can she not be …suffocated?" When he didn't reply, she added, "It would be kinder."

He walked over and sat in front of the desk. "Darling, everything has been done for the sake of appearance. The appearance of perfect propriety. She's in the best place, which means she is watched carefully. I haven't come this far to end up hanged for murder. Have you?"

Her jaw dropped momentarily. "I haven't committed murder," she whispered harshly. He gave her a look and it proved to be too much. She rose abruptly and started to the door "I'm going to have a bath," she said as she went. "Do not follow me."

"Yes, yes," he murmured when she was gone. "By all means. Have a bath." He reached for the paper she'd been practicing on and looked it over before crumpling it and tossing it over his shoulder.

Chapter Eighteen

Thursday, July 19

"What can I get you to drink?" Cecil asked Tom Kassel who'd just arrived. Fortunately, Cavanaugh had already gone for the day. The clerk was efficient and dependable, but he was also opinionated and set in his ways. He would always do his job and do it well, but he might not be particularly pleasant to Tom whom he referred to as 'the criminal.'

"Whiskey is good," Tom replied. "Or whatever you're having."

"I have a better idea. I was just given a bottle of fifteen-year-old Mackinlay by a pleased client."

Tom's brows lifted. "Must have been an impressive victory."

Cecil grinned. "It was, if I do say so myself. Let's crack it open."

"Excellent. Maybe afterwards we can go for some dinner."

"I can't," Cecil said as he went to the small sideboard to fix the drinks. "I have court in the morning and I have to finish my summation. But I have roast beef the cook made yesterday. I was going to have a sandwich for supper. You can join me, if it appeals," he added as he handed Tom one of the squatty lead crystal glasses with a healthy shot of scotch.

"It does. Thank you." Tom lifted his glass to Cecil and then sipped. "You have a cook?" he asked as Cecil went back to his seat.

"I have a lady that comes in twice a week to clean and cook. I couldn't do without her."

"This scotch is excellent," Tom commented.

"It is, isn't it?"

"Is it an interesting case you're working on for the morning?"

"No, but we should win. Since you are not working for the opposing side," he added with a wry smile. He noticed the look of satisfaction on Tom's face. "Is that expression on your face because of the compliment or because you've learned something?"

"Yes."

Cecil laughed.

"I'll let you read the telegram for yourself," Tom said, reaching into his inner jacket pocket. "I just received it."

Cecil took it and read. In a matter of seconds, he jerked slightly and glanced up at Tom with a dubious expression. "Disbarred?"

Tom nodded. "Blakely Heyer is a scoundrel, cheat and liar."

"So he came here and set up shop again. And met Louisa Edgerton."

"And there is something about the woman Heyer is carrying on with."

"What do you mean?"

"There is something seedy about the two of them. And maybe worse. I sent her name and a description to a fellow detective in New York yesterday to learn what I could. I believe she may have been an actress there."

"The simple fact that he is carrying on with a woman in light of what's happened with his wife is seedy, but what else is there?"

"Do you think it could be coincidence that Heyer and the actress moved here about the same time from the same place and met future spouses who would then meet with calamity and or death, leaving them with small fortunes?"

Cecil took a moment to reply. "Rather strains the bounds of probability, doesn't it?"

Tom nodded. "I would say so."

"I can't imagine how we'd prove it."

Tom took a sip. "Step by step."

"Oh," Cecil said, remembering something. "There's a dinner party at Dr. Werthing's home on Sunday and we've been invited and asked to provide an update. Cecil slid the invitation over. "Dr Werthing is the man who's offered to foot the bill."

"I recall."

"His daughter is getting married and so his sister is coming into town for it. Dr. Ripley and Dr. Covington are close friends of hers."

"I'd be delighted to join. I must say I'm particularly curious about Dr. Ripley."

"I can't imagine why," Cecil returned, although a smile played on his lips.

"Let's just say you have a certain look about you."

"Do I?"

"You do. I'm trained to observe and analyze. Have you been in love before this?"

"I didn't say I was in love. If you'll remember, I just met the lady."

"Yes, and she's hardly crossed your mind since," Tom said drolly.

"No," Cecil replied.

Tom cocked his head and donned a doleful expression.

"I mean ... no, I haven't been in love before. There was a lady I courted and seriously considered marrying."

"What happened with her?"

"Nothing. I just couldn't take those final steps. There was nothing wrong with her. I couldn't say a single bad thing about her. But—" He rose to get the bottle. "You know the strong man game at traveling fairs?" he asked as he came back.

Tom grinned quizzically. "Yes."

Cecil refilled their glasses. "It seems to me that love should feel like that. That bell ringing when the hit is strong enough."

Tom chuckled. "And the lady didn't ring your bell."

"It wasn't her. It's that *we* didn't ring the bell. On paper, she's perfect. Had someone drawn her picture and described her

104

to me and then asked if I could fall for her, I would have said yes. Absolutely. But I didn't. I simply didn't."

"I understand."

"Do you?"

"Of course. And you're right. When it's the right strike, the bell rings."

"Spoken like a man who's heard it for himself."

Tom nodded.

"So what happened? Where is she?"

"Heaven."

Cecil's smile vanished. "Are you serious?" he asked haltingly.

"I wish I wasn't."

"I'm sorry."

"So am I. But I had her in my life. Which means I always have her. Her memory. The love of her. There was a time I wondered if it would have been better not to have met her and loved her and married her."

"You were married," Cecil breathed. He felt terrible. He'd been teasing. They'd both been teasing earlier, but this was no laughing matter. "I'm truly sorry if I made light of—"

Tom waved it off. "You didn't. I'm fine. Enough time has gone by that I can just be glad we had one another."

"How long ago was this?"

"Eight years. She was murdered."

"Oh, my God! Tom!"

Tom nodded, understanding the shock Cecil felt. "It changed me. It changed everything, but here I am. I have survived it and we are working to free Mrs. Heyer." He finished his drink in a gulp. "So let's come up with ideas. I'll tell you what I've learned and what I think and you let me know if you can see another path."

Tom nodded, but he felt so badly.

"May I?" Tom said, pointing to the scotch.

"Of course."

"It really is all right, Cecil," Tom said consolingly. "I don't have that many close friends, but the ones I have all know. I don't talk about it much, but nor do I try to keep it a secret."

Cecil felt moved that Tom was already considering him a friend. He'd been feeling the same. Maybe it was a lesser strongman game where friendship was concerned, but there was still a sort of bell ring when kindred spirits hit.

Chapter Nineteen

Friday, July 20th
Green Valley, VA

Charity woke for the third time and decided to get up. She'd had trouble sleeping because there was no getting comfortable. Between being hot and huge and an aching back and the baby kicking, she tossed and turned for too much of the night. Now, she rose slowly and put on a robe over her gown. She walked to the window and looked out at the view she knew and loved. Seasoned trees and green lawn as far as the eye could see. Beyond them were mountains. Their ranch, The Triple H, was over a thousand acres. She didn't know it inch by inch like her husband did, but she knew it well.

She got ready for the day and went to the schoolroom. Before she reached it, she heard her sons singing the ABC song. The letters were right, more or less, until they reached the twelfth, which they dubbed 'ellabiddowee' no matter how clearly their twenty-three-year-old governess, Veronica, pronounced it while pointing out L, M, N, O and P as she did so.

"Mommy," Gray called, charging at her when he saw her.

She scooped him up and hugged him and then bent to do the same to Graham. They were so beautiful. They filled her heart completely, just as they did their father's. They were fraternal, born five minutes apart. Grayson, the first born, favored her, while Graham favored Greg, although in temperament it was the opposite. Gray was the leader and the instigator, Graham the easier going, milder natured child.

"We're going on a pony ride later," Gray said excitedly.

"You are?"

Both boys nodded. "Daddy said," Graham said.

She pressed a kiss to his head. "That will be fun, won't it?"

"How are you feeling?" Veronica asked her. She was a plain young woman, but as dear as could be.

"It was not the easiest night," Charity replied. "But they aren't, these days."

"I'm sure not," Veronica said sympathetically. "When do you and Mr. Howerton leave?"

"The train leaves at three."

"I want to go on the train," Gray said, pulling a pout.

"And when you're older, you will," Charity replied. "Not on this trip, though. It's too long and too hot." She grinned at his continued pout and stood.

"Let's get back to work," Veronica cheerfully said to the boys. "We're learning the letter M today," she said to Charity.

"M." Charity nodded. "*Mmmm.* Marvelous."

"And also M for Mommy," Veronica said.

"M for mouse," Graham said.

She stroked his cheek. "That's right."

"M for mouse," Gray repeated, "and ...mommy."

She smiled and nodded. "Yes. Good!"

The boys happily turned and went toward their table. Charity saw papers laid out with pictures of mice and mountains and men. She gave Veronica a smile and left to finish packing.

Chapter Twenty

A distant church bell struck four times as William Yardley walked dazedly from the steel mill to a triangular patch of shade jutting beyond the brick wall of another building. He carried a tin cup of water and an apple. He reached the building and slid down the wall feeling sick from the heat. There were many who would have complained about the heat of the mid-July day, but it was sheer delight in comparison to the heat of the building.

He closed his eyes and savored the feeling of a softly tickling breeze in his sweated-through clothing. When strength allowed, he lifted the apple to his mouth and took a bite. Two men stood a few feet away engaged in conversation, also on their break. One was smoking and the smell of the tobacco drifted to him along with their voices.

"True as can be," one insisted. "The man was oiling the machine."

"The ore crushing machine?"

"Yeah."

"And his shirt got grabbed?"

"Some part of his clothes got tangled in the cogs and dragged him in."

"It makes me sick to think about."

"As it should. The newspaper said he was mangled out of all semblance of humanity. His flesh ended up stuck on the cogs."

William leaned his head back against the brick wall and tried not to listen. He'd heard about the horrific accident and at least a dozen others. Only a month ago, a boiler explosion in this very factory had taken the lives of three men. Working was a daily risk, but it was better not to think about it when you needed the pay to survive.

109

Four facts, he challenged himself. It was a game he played, trying to recall facts that his teachers had claimed were important back in his other life when things had been easy. He hadn't realized how good it had been in a clean home with his mother and school and friends and enough food. How he missed Mable's food. He even missed school. Six months ago, he would have scoffed at the notion.

Four facts. He thought of random words. Today, he was up to the letter M.

Monrovia.

Monrovia is the capital of Liberia. Not that it mattered. Who would ever be impressed by his knowing it? But that wasn't the point. Another word, another fact. Any letter. Any word.

Epoch.

An epoch is a notable period of time.

Such as what?

Such as the Pre-Revolutionary War era.

And what was a cause of the Revolutionary War?

Wanting freedom from oppression. He'd wanted freedom or he thought he had. Now he wanted just the opposite. He wanted to go home, but that lying sack of shit Heyer had made it impossible. All because he'd kissed Jane. He hadn't known the master of the house was spying on them at the time. He was stuck in hell because he'd kissed a pretty girl. Although Jane was more than just pretty. She was kind and good. He liked everything about her. What did she think now? Did she believe he was a thief? Did any of them believe it?

He heard distant thunder and looked up at the sky as it darkened. Maybe it would storm and cool off. That would be good. There wasn't enough air flow at the flophouse he lodged at, but a cooler temperature would make it more bearable.

The gossiping men trudged back to work, and he knew it was time for him, too. Back to his eleven-hour day toiling as a boilermaker's assistant. It's not what he should have been, but prison would be worse. Although this life was a sort of prison.

Chapter Twenty-One

Noel Reay lifted the metal arm of the door knocker and brought it soundly down, sneering at the **H** engraved upon it. Louisa had always been a woman of modest, conservative taste, so how in the world had she ended up marrying a peacock like Heyer? The door was opened by the housekeeper who inquired whether she could help him. "Good afternoon," he returned. "I'm hoping to see Louisa if she's home," he replied pleasantly.

"I'm sorry, sir, she's not."

There had been the briefest of hesitations before she said it and there was something in her expression. A certain wariness mixed with ... what? "Is she well?" he blurted worriedly.

The woman drew back and then opened the door and gestured him inward.

He stepped in, realizing how tactless the question must have seemed. She shut the door behind him. "The reason I ask is that I saw her husband a few days ago at the bank." He reached into his inside jacket pocket for his card case. "My apologies. I'm Noel Reay, Louisa's banker of many years."

"Oh!"

He extracted a card and handed it over. "I should have thought to present that. As I said, I saw her husband at the bank and he said she was not well. I was surprised to hear it since she's always enjoyed excellent health as did both her parents until their seventies." The housekeeper looked uncomfortable, as if she had bad news. "Is it true? Is she not well?"

"She is—"

He found himself leaning in as she hesitated.

"I'm sorry to say this, but she is in an asylum. For the insane."

111

He laughed. Then his smile vanished. "You're not serious?"

"I am."

"Insane," he repeated. "Louisa? Louisa Edgerton … insane?"

"I am not saying she is, sir. She is certainly not. I am telling you she has been put in the Pennsylvania Hospital for Nervous Disorders."

He was aghast. "For what possible reason?"

"We believe her husband is behind it."

He exhaled strongly. "I had a bad feeling. But this! I cannot believe what I've just heard. I'm sorry, what is your name?"

"Georgina Yardley. I am the housekeeper."

"When did all this happen, Mrs. Yardley?"

"It's been three and a half months now. She was put there on April fifth. We learned about it the next day, a Friday."

"Good God," he said under his breath.

"It was the strangest thing. She'd been here and fine … or relatively fine, and then she was just gone."

"What do you mean *relatively* fine?"

"I mean that she wasn't happy. It wasn't a happy marriage."

"I imagine not," he snapped. "I'm sorry," he immediately apologized. "That was rude of me."

"It's fine," she said.

"Just the shock. I cannot believe what I'm hearing."

"You said he came to the bank?"

"Yes. He wanted to withdraw some funds from her account." He sniffed. "I was not able to assist him without her authorization."

Georgina Yardley smiled to hear it.

"I instantly had a bad feeling, but I thought it was because he was in some sort of debt. He seemed the type. I didn't believe for a moment that Louisa was really ill. But to learn this! The accusation that she is mentally unstable is preposterous and despicable."

"There is an effort being made to rectify the matter," she said quietly. "Of course, that needs to remain strictly confidential."

"Who is behind it and how can I help?"

"Well, for one thing," another voice said.

He turned to see a plump cook behind him looking decidedly impatient.

"You could come into the kitchen where I can hear without straining myself," she said.

"Mr. Reay," Georgina Yardley said. "This is Mrs. Anderson."

"Mable," the cook said, extending her hand.

He shook it.

"Come sit a spell and we'll tell you all about it."

"All right," he agreed.

"Tell you this much," Mable said as she walked. "Louisa is not without friends, even if her real friends haven't been able to see her in that place."

<u>Chapter Twenty-Two</u>

Sunday, July 22

At 3:15 in the afternoon, Tally washed up as best she could at the sink in the doctor's lounge. She wetted a rag and put it to the back of her neck, sighing with relief. She'd worked nonstop from seven that morning, not even stopping for lunch. She was expected at the Werthing's this evening and she needed a bath and a rest before changing. She tossed the damp rag in the soiled bin and started for the door.

Her last patient had been a woman of twenty-nine with three children at home. Carolyn Levine had come in for the delivery of twins after her water had broken. She'd given birth to all the others at home but, since she was having twins, she'd decided to have them in the hospital. When the first twin made his appearance, he was healthy. Tally looked him over before handing him to a nurse. "What's his name?" she asked.

"Frank," Carolyn replied tiredly. "He's our first boy. Oh, and these have to be the last. Can't you give me something for that?"

"Advice," Tally replied wryly as she felt to determine the position of the second baby. There had been some fear the babe was breech, but it was not. If it had been, it had turned on its own.

"What advice is that?" Carolyn played along. "Don't let my husband near me again?" Carolyn groaned and began to pant with another contraction.

"You can let him as near as you want. To a point," Tally said meaningfully.

The woman barked a short laugh and then cried out. A short time later, the second sac broke and labor began anew. Minutes

114

later, the girl twin came into the world. Her name was Amanda, Carolyn said. A third baby emerged not a minute later. She was a surprise and a tiny thing, not even two pounds. She was slightly blue and so still that Tally thought she was stillborn, but there was a faint heartbeat. Mrs. Levine looked mortified. She was exhausted, almost all emotion wrung from her, and she hadn't planned on a third baby. She hadn't even considered the possibility of it.

Tally took the infant to a table to better observe her, but the heartbeat had stopped. There was nothing to be done. She wrapped the babe in a blanket and turned back to Carolyn wondering if she wanted to see her or hold her.

Carolyn shook her head. "Take it away," she uttered.

Tally handed the swaddled baby to one of the nurses. "Do you want to give her a name?" she asked the mother gently.

Carolyn Levine shook her head again and looked away as if to deny the child's presence.

The nurse glanced at Tally and took the baby from the room with a quiet step. Tally left a short time later and saw the nurse with Mr. Levine. The middle-aged man was holding the tiny body of his deceased child. "Mr. Levine," Tally said, stepping up to him.

"So there was three of them," he marveled.

Tally nodded. "The good news is that your new son and daughter are perfectly healthy. They're both close to five pounds with good lungs."

"Yes," he replied. He looked down at the baby in his arms. She was the size of a doll. She looked like a doll. "Praise be. And we've three more girls at home." He reluctantly handed the baby back to the nurse. "Can I collect her later to bury her proper-like? I'd like the reverend to say a few words over her."

"Of course," Tally said. "Of course, you may."

The nurse, with lowered head, left with the child.

"Fern," the man said as he watched them go. He looked at Tally. "I had a younger sister named Fern. She died early, too."

He looked off after the retreating nurse and tears filled his eyes. "Poor little mite. Never stood a chance, did she?"

Tally touched his arm and walked away. Tears threatened, but she willed them away. A certain pressure remained in her chest, but she would will it away too. When she reached the ground floor of the hospital, the level of noise and activity was perplexing. Bloodied people were straggling in and there were wounded sitting in chairs and lying on cots. She caught the eye of an attendant, a large boned woman who usually collected soiled linens and dealt with bedpans. "What's happened?" Tally asked.

"Bad accident in Grays Ferry. The ironwork come off the back of a tenement. Balconies, railings, stairs. All of it. People fell and the iron crushed them below."

"Dr. Covington," Dr. Walter Nunn called, pointing down the corridor. "Check that boy, will you?"

Tally put herself in motion. The boy, perhaps twelve years of age, was sitting in a chair, staring straight ahead. Tally realized he was dead before she reached him. The left side of his skull was bloodied and misshapen. How had he even made it this far? She closed his eyes and looked around for an attendant to get him moved, but there wasn't one available. The morgue would soon be filled beyond capacity.

A man was being helped in by two other men, one of his legs badly broken. She started toward them, but another doctor reached them first. She segued to an unconscious woman lying on a cot, whose breathing was shallow and severely labored. At least one of her lungs was punctured. Tally bent to examine her and quickly determined her ribs were shattered.

"Tally," someone called. She looked up to see Doctor Anna Unger shake her head. "Broken back," she said quietly. "Too many internal injuries."

In other words, move on and help someone that can be saved. But she couldn't. Not yet. Tally pulled out her scope to listen to the heartbeat of the woman who looked to be in her mid-twenties. The heartbeat was weak and irregular. The woman was

116

dying. Tally started to straighten, but she felt the woman touch her arm. It shocked her, but the woman's eyes had opened, and her gaze was fixed on Tally's. The woman's expression was peaceful and *knowing*. Then her eyes went vacant and her hand slipped off Tally's arm.

Tally closed the woman's eyes and laid a hand on her shoulder before moving on. Dr. Unger had a screaming girl with multiple fractures to deal with.

Tally had lost track of time and patients when she realized the situation was finally in hand. The injured were all being treated. She sighed heavily and started for the door but stopped when she noticed the woman who had died flanked by an older man and another woman close to her age. Given the resemblance, the woman had to be a sister.

Tally was drawn to them. "I'm sorry for your loss," she said when she reached them.

Grief lay heavy on them. "She knew," the woman said. "She knew she was going to die. She's said it for a going on a year now ever since her husband was killed on the docks. She said she knew she'd be following him shortly. That she was just waiting on something."

The older man ducked his head and his shoulders repeatedly heaved as emotion overtook him.

"I told her to stop saying it," the woman continued in a thick voice. "I thought it was her grief talking and she wasn't doing herself any good thinking it. You don't get on with living that way. She was as healthy as me." The woman wiped her face with a handkerchief. "She'd just get this look of pity like she was feeling sorry for me. It made no sense." She shuddered. "Who could have guessed the floor would drop out from underneath her and send her to her death like that?"

Tally nodded sadly. She nearly walked off, except for a strange prickling of curiosity. "She said she was waiting on something?"

"Aye," the man said. "It didn't make a bit a' sense," he added with a lyrical Irish accent. "Nah even to her." He pulled out a soiled handkerchief from his pocket and wiped his face. "My Wanda had good sense. Even as a wee one. She didn't talk nonsense. But this … it were nonsense like."

The woman took hold of her father's arm for support. "She claimed she was waiting on a fern to arrive," she said.

Tally felt her breath catch.

"I asked why," the woman continued. "Why on earth would you be waiting on a fern? She didn't know. Other than she needed to bring it home with her." She shrugged and shook her head. "It made no sense."

"Miss?" the man said to Tally, noticing whatever expression was on her face. "You look like you just saw a ghost."

"I'm fine," Tally said at once. "It's just—" They were watching her, waiting. "I'm a doctor."

The man nodded. "Aye."

"We saw you helpin' the injured and such," the woman said.

"Yes, well, I helped with a delivery earlier," Tally said haltingly. "A woman having twins. That is, they were expecting twins."

"Did something go wrong?" the woman asked warily.

Tally shook her head. "Not with the twins. But there was a third babe. A girl. She was tiny and weak and …died shortly after birth. The mother … couldn't cope. It was the father who gave the baby a name, the same name of his sister who had also died early in life."

"What was the name?" the father asked with a puzzled frown sensing there was a point to the story.

Tally's eyes filled. She tried to blink them away, but it had been a long, draining day. She couldn't speak for a few moments. "Fern," she finally managed.

The man and woman stared at her in awe. "This was today?" the woman stammered.

Tally nodded. "Not long before I encountered your sister." She glanced down at the still face on the table. There was a beauty in it she hadn't noticed before. "I was with Wanda when she passed."

"Fern," the man repeated. Tears slid down his face.

His daughter turned to him and they embraced.

"Thank you, Miss," the man said to Tally.

Tally walked away. Tears let loose as she made for the door, but she wiped them away and kept walking.

Chapter Twenty-Three

Charity paced in the foyer, waiting for Vi and Tally to arrive. At seven twenty, Viola arrived alone. The women laughed and hugged before Vi drew back to better look at her friend. "So do you think there is only one this time?" she teased, looking down at Charity's protruding middle.

"Yes. This time, I'm carrying my girl."

"I'm delighted to hear it! And what does her father think?"

"That it's another boy," Charity said with a shrug. "One of us will be proven right and … he'll learn to live with it."

Vi laughed.

"Good evening, Viola," Alma Werthing said, stopping a few feet away with her hands folded primly in front of her waist.

"Hello, Alma. It's nice to see you again. How are wedding preparations going?"

"Quite well, thank you. I was just going into the salon to join the others."

Charity looked at Vi. "Will you take a stroll in the garden before we follow?"

Vi smiled. "That would be lovely."

Charity glanced at Alma, who inclined her head in acknowledgement. The pair of friends started off. "Where's Tally?" Charity asked when they were beyond Alma's earshot.

"There was some sort of accident that caused pandemonium at the hospital. She sent a note telling me to go on. Hopefully, she won't be too late, but—"

"It's fine," Charity assured her. "No one understands better than we all do."

"Other than Alma, you mean?"

Charity grinned.

"Vi," Jack Werthing called, hurrying to catch up to them. "Alma said you'd arrived."

"Hello, Jack," Vi said with a smile.

"Mr. Lawrence and the investigator are here."

Vi's smile vanished with a small gasp. "Oh?"

"I wanted them to come a bit early, because I hadn't yet made any sort of recompense."

Vi cocked her head. "Is that necessary with pro bono work?"

He ducked his head a moment. "About that."

"Yes. About that. You are so generous and kind and I am grateful."

"You were passionate about the matter so I knew there must be something to it. And if that was the case, it was worth pursuing. I thought it might be easier for you to accept if—"

"It was pro bono," she supplied.

"Ironically, although it didn't start out that way, it may have turned into it. Mr. Lawrence informed me this evening that he doesn't have an invoice for me and he may not. You see, he found this detective, Mr. Kassel, who has gotten caught up in the case with no guarantee of pay and … well, I think they've become good friends and they are both convinced of wrongdoing and want to see the situation righted."

Charity noticed the telling expressions crossing Vi's face.

"Cecil suggested we could keep the arrangement between us," Jack added. "I believe he said we *could* keep it, not that we *should* keep it, so, I feel a bit of latitude in sharing it with you."

Vi nodded. "Thank you."

"He's a good man," Jack said, stepping back. "We're all in the salon whenever you care to join us."

"We'll be there soon," Charity said.

When he'd turned and left, Charity gave Vi a look. "What is it with this Mr. Lawrence? I'm tempted to run into the salon this minute."

Vi grabbed her. "You will not!"

Charity laughed. "As if you could stop me. I'm three times bigger."

"I'll tell you all about it *out* of doors."

Cecil found the dynamics of the couples in the room interesting. They'd gathered for drinks in the salon of Dr. Werthing's residence, an imposing home that had passed father to son for generations. Neither Dr. Jack Werthing nor his sister, Dr. Charity Howerton, seemed adversely affected by the wealth they'd been born to. If anything, wealth had brought out the best of them. As the two of them shared amusing stories, the affection and camaraderie between them was clear to see.

The Werthing marriage seemed solid, but less than idyllic. Cecil suspected Alma Werthing felt some resentment for her sister-in-law but was trying to mask it. Perhaps she resented their intrusion this evening when the sole focus should have been on their soon-to-be married daughter, although the bride to be was out for the evening. Had Doctor and Mrs. Werthing once been madly in love? He couldn't quite picture it.

Gregory and Charity Howerton were the opposite. They were still madly in love. He was a successful businessman and rancher who could have been plucked from Cecil's idea of the old west. He was confident and comfortable in his skin, and he adored his wife and young sons.

When the doorbell rang, Charity Howerton rose and excused herself, anxious to see Tally.

In the foyer, Charity hurried toward Tally who'd been admitted by a new maid, and the two embraced. "Hello!"

"Hello," Tally returned.

Charity pulled away. "Are you all right? Vi said there was a catastrophe of some sort."

"I'm tired, but fine. But look at you. You look wonderful."

"I feel large. And roastingly hot and usually uncomfortable. But, except for that, I'm perfectly well and happy."

"Are the boys here?"

"No, we didn't bring them, and Jack has not stopped complaining about it yet. We thought it would be too difficult with the heat and my condition. Besides, it is Alexandra's wedding and it didn't seem right to add to the chaos. I think it's what Jack misses but, for once in our lives, Alma agrees with me," she added in a whisper.

Tally grinned.

"Come on," Charity said cheerfully, linking arms with her and starting toward the salon. "I have to share you with everyone else. Hopefully the three of us can get together by ourselves tomorrow or the next day."

"Yes. We need to. Real girl talk."

"Indeed we do. Vi and Cecil Lawrence? When did that happen?"

"Oh, five minutes ago," Tally replied breezily. "It might as well have been."

"I like him," Charity said.

"So do I. And so does she."

When they turned into the room, the men stood.

"Tally," Jack greeted. "Welcome."

"Hello. I'm sorry I'm late." Her gaze stopped on the handsome man who had to be the detective before she pointedly looked away.

"Don't think a thing about it," Charity assured her.

"Yes," Alma agreed dryly. "I'm certain it couldn't be helped. Life and death and all."

Tally caught the look of exasperation on Charity's face.

Gregory Howerton came forward to shake her hand. "Good to see you. How are you, Tally?"

"I'm fine, thank you. It's good to see you. How was your trip?"

"Quiet without the boys."

"Tally," Jack said, "I believe you know Mr. Lawrence."

"Yes." She looked at him and he bowed his head. "Hello."

"Good evening," Cecil replied. "It's nice to see you again."

"And you."

123

"And this is Tom Kassel," Jack said.

"Dr. Covington," Tom said with a bow of his head.

"Good evening," she returned.

"Let's get you some refreshment," Jack said. "What will you have?"

Tally glanced at the drink in Jack's hand. "One of those will do beautifully."

"Then I'll make it," Jack offered. "I'm convinced no one makes it better."

"Whiskey and soda is so complicated," Charity teased.

"It's the ratio," Jack teased back. "And the stirring."

Tally moved to a chair opposite Vi and everyone sat again. Tally tried not to look at Tom Kassel, at least not when he was looking at her. He was handsome in a flashy sort of way. He was well dressed, especially for a detective, which she had always aligned with a policeman in her mind. His attire, however, suggested a more lucrative career. He was entirely too handsome, which meant he would be full of himself, sure that every female would fall at his feet, something *she* would never do in a million years.

"Vi mentioned there was an accident?" Jack said as he returned to Tally with her drink.

"A bad one, I'm afraid. The fire escape scaffolding collapsed off a tenement in Grays Ferry."

"Oh, no," Charity exclaimed.

Tally nodded grimly "The whole framework."

"How high was the building?" Jack asked.

"Six floors."

Alma grimaced. Her shoulders rounded inward. "That makes me feel ill."

"How many were injured?" Viola asked.

"I don't know because they were taken to various hospitals. A lot. Because of the heat, there were too many people on the landings. The entire structure came loose and collapsed."

"Six floors," Cecil murmured. "Can you imagine how frightening it was when they realized what was happening."

Tally nodded. "It also injured or killed anyone on the ground beneath it and some in an adjoining building, as well."

Vi gave her a look of empathy tinged with guiltiness that she'd gone home early. Tally returned a look conveying that was silly. There had been no way to know it would happen.

"Was this near thirty-fourth?" Tom asked.

"I believe so," Tally replied.

"The Forgotten Bottom, they call it," Tom remarked.

"Every city has one," Gregory Howerton said.

"That's one of the advantages to living in Green Valley, isn't it?" Vi asked Gregory and Charity, attempting to lighten the conversation.

Gregory shrugged. "Poverty exists everywhere. We have mining camps no better than slums. None of mine, of course."

"I think I'll see about dinner," Alma said, rising imperiously. "And perhaps, when I return, we could discuss something more pleasant than gruesome injuries and slums."

Charity and Jack exchanged a look as Alma left the room. "So," Jack said to Cecil. "What have you learned about Mrs. Heyer?"

Cecil looked at the Howertons. "Do you know about the case?"

Charity nodded. "Jack filled us in. Is it as diabolical as it appears?"

"It may be. Tom looked into it and discovered disturbing information." He looked at Tom.

"First of all," Tom took over, "There was no behavior on Louisa Heyer's part to suggest mental illness, much less insanity. If there were any signs of madness, it seemed to have happened solely in her husband's company."

"Isn't that convenient?" Tally remarked.

"The house was hers," Tom continued. "And the staff was all hired by her except for a parlour maid. They all detest him. That alone doesn't mean anything, but it is telling. So is the fact that none of them knew she was being committed. They were only told afterwards and the reason they were given was that she was so melancholy, Mr. Heyer was concerned she'd do herself in. The cook said that was nonsense. That the only one thinking of doing away with her was him."

"She said that?" Viola breathed.

"She did. Blakely Heyer disrupted the household, even chasing off the sixteen-year-old son of the housekeeper on false pretenses. I'm not sure why, but my gut says it has to do with the pretty young maid he hired. I think Blakely Heyer wants his own way and he's going to have it, no matter what he has to do to get it."

"What happened to the boy?" Charity asked.

"I'm trying to locate him. For his sake and his mother's."

"Is there other family he might have gone to?" Vi asked.

"No. No family and his friends don't know where he went. My guess is he found work and he's laying low. Heyer threatened to call in the law over a theft he said the boy committed."

"A theft of money?" Gregory asked.

"No. A pair of cufflinks. William found them in his room and brought them to Heyer who then accused him of stealing them. William denied it, but Heyer claimed he was alerting the police if the boy didn't take off and stay away. By the way, this was not the story Heyer told the boy's mother when she returned later that day. They knew the truth because the new maid overheard the confrontation and passed it on."

Charity shook her head. "This Heyer sounds like a vile man."

"You haven't heard it all yet," Tom said. "The man has been in a long-term affair. He moved here from New York and so did the lady, an actress, arriving approximately at the same time. The lady then married an older gentleman of significant means, only he was killed in a mugging, leaving her a wealthy widow." He paused as that sunk in. "His family thinks of her what the Heyer staff thinks of him."

"That, of course," Cecil spoke up, "is opinion and innuendo, but Tom also learned Heyer was disbarred in New York."

"Disbarred?" Vi repeated. "Can you get disbarred in one state and simply start again in another?"

Cecil replied. "Disbarment in one state is usually grounds for disbarment in another. But it has to be discovered."

"Why did he get disbarred?" Gregory asked Tom.

"He attempted to defraud an old man by having him sign a bogus will on what was thought to be his death bed."

Greg barked a short laugh. "What, leaving himself the old man's money?"

"Yes. Only the man recovered. You can imagine how livid he was at the discovery. He brought charges."

"This is excellent information," Vi said looking to Cecil. "What can we do with it?"

"I'm not sure," Cecil admitted. "I thought about bringing all this information to the doctor who made the diagnosis of insanity. I have felt more and more certain the diagnosis was based on whatever nonsense Heyer claimed. I thought perhaps when the doctor heard it all laid out, he might reconsider his position. Unfortunately, by all accounts, he is not the sort of man who will admit a mistake. In fact, when faced with the prospect, he's been known to dig in his heels even at the expense of a patient."

Vi nodded. "That I believe."

"So do I," Tally concurred.

"I cannot disagree," Jack added. "So what can we do?"

"We could go to Blakely Heyer with what we know and see if we can force his hand," Cecil suggested. "Get him to sign for her release."

"And then what?" Tally asked. "I wouldn't trust her to his care for a single minute!"

"I'm sure we're all in agreement on that," Tom said.

"There was a similar case in another state a few years ago," Cecil said. "That lady, who had been unjustly labeled insane and incarcerated, won her release and a divorce, but it took time. She was in an asylum for three years before a court ruled in her favor. And she had a lot of supporters."

127

"Louisa won't last three years," Vi stated. "Not with the medication they have her on. We have to get her out soon."

"Then go get her," Gregory said. "Seems obvious to me. Go get her, put her somewhere safe to recover and then go after Heyer."

"It's not that simple, Gregory," Jack replied.

Gregory grinned lopsidedly. "It may not be easy, but it is simple. She needs to be removed, so remove her."

Tally shook her head. "I admire the idea, but the asylum is a secure facility with limited visiting hours. A person can visit only if they are on an approved list."

"You're a doctor there," Gregory said. "Right?"

"Yes."

"Is there a back door of this new and very secure facility?"

Tally stared. "Sneak her out? Is that what you're suggesting?"

He shrugged. "That or take her out the front door. Are there guards?"

"Yes. They're called attendants, but yes."

"They armed?"

Cecil shook his head. "I, too, admire the thought, but I can't take part of anything illegal."

"It would be considered abduction," Charity said to her husband.

"You think Mrs. Heyer would call it that?" he asked her.

Alma stepped back into the room. "Dinner is ready," she announced.

"We'll be in momentarily, dear," Jack said.

Her expression was one of irritation, but also curiosity. She glanced around, wondering about the current topic of conversation.

"No, I do not," Charity replied to her husband. "But her removal has to be done in such a way that she can't be forced back."

Tally frowned as she thought about it. "Even if we could get her out, which I'm not at all sure we could, where would she go? She has to be cared for. She can't go home."

"She could come here," Jack offered.

"Absolutely not," Alma exclaimed. "Your daughter is getting married in less than a week!"

He huffed. "What does that have to do with—"

"May I speak with you," she hissed furiously. "Privately?" She turned on her heel and left the room. Jack rose with a resigned expression, excused himself and followed his wife.

"I know a place," Tom said in the wake of silence that followed.

"How could we do it?" Vi asked quietly.

"Why don't we go into dinner," Charity said as she rose. "Where we will discuss anything other than this. Then, afterwards, we can go for a carriage ride to discuss the matter. Just the five of us since you should not be part of it," she said to Cecil.

Greg stood. "Good idea. Except there will be four of us. The two of you need to stay behind. I should say the three of you," he said, glancing down at her swollen middle.

Charity gave him a wan smile. "Fine." She looked at Cecil with a droll look and a shrug. "Maybe a game of chess while they're occupied?"

"I'd be delighted," Cecil replied. "Resentful that they're having all the excitement but delighted."

Chapter Twenty-Four

By nine o'clock, a rescue plan was in motion. Tally entered the front entrance of the asylum with Vi trailing close behind. Tally didn't recognize the attendant at the desk.

"May I help you?" the man asked.

"I'm Dr. Covington, an attending. I was passing by and wanted to stop in and see about Mrs. Black's fever."

He looked down a list of authorized personnel. Finding it, he nodded and looked up at Vi.

"This is my associate," Tally explained before he could ask. "Here to consult. We won't be long."

"I'll need her to sign in," the man said.

"Certainly," Vi replied. She stepped up, signed in and then followed Tally. They passed a nurse who looked at them quizzically but didn't question them. "It's a different staff at night," Tally said.

They passed Louisa's room; it was dark and silent, and continued to Alberta Black's room. Hovering in the doorway, they looked in both directions and saw there was no one in the hall for the moment. They exchanged a glance and Vi hurried further on to the stairwell. She lifted her skirt and sailed down the stairs with a quiet step. The plan was for her to find a lower-level back door to open, and for Tally to stand watch and distract anyone who came along. They hoped a distraction wouldn't prove necessary, but Vi had no sooner disappeared from view, then a nurse rounded a corner and came toward Tally. Tally started toward her with a measured step. "Any problems this evening?" she asked the nurse, who seemed vaguely familiar. She was in her twenties with auburn hair, blue eyes and clear ivory skin.

"It's been mostly quiet," the nurse replied shyly.

"Good. I stopped by to check on Mrs. Black," Tally said, turning back to keep an eye on the stairwell.

The nurse blinked. "Mrs. Black?"

"She had a fever earlier, but it's passed. How is Miss Strickland?"

"They've got her restrained, as usual," the nurse reported sympathetically. "But she still finds a way to pull her hair out."

Tally nodded tightly.

"It's when she's alone or she gets agitated," the nurse added. "I try to sit with her until she sleeps. She enjoys being read to."

"That doesn't surprise me. She is well educated."

"You're Dr. Covington, aren't you?"

Tally smiled. "I am. I was just trying to remember your name."

"Rhodes. Nurse Rhodes. Alice," she added, blushing when she said it.

"Of course. You don't usually work nights, do you?"

"No, ma'am. I work an extra shift here and there where I can."

"Ah."

"Dr. Covington, I … I was wondering—"

"Yes?"

"Mrs. Dale is begging for more laudanum," the nurse said sheepishly. "Is that something you can authorize?"

"Mrs. Dale?"

"In room thirty. Syphilis. Final stages."

"Oh, yes. Yes, of course. Let's make her as comfortable as possible."

The nurse smiled with relief. "Thank you. I'll see to it." She walked on and went into the supply room.

A moment later, Vi peeked out from the stairwell. Tally frantically waved her onward. Vi stepped out and started toward Louisa's room and, a moment later, Tom followed. Tally's heart pounded. They would be in such trouble if they were caught. Gregory Howerton was now following Tom, looking as relaxed as if taking a Sunday stroll on his own land. Under less pressured circumstances, it might have been amusing. Perhaps one day, if they weren't caught tonight, it would be. Of course, Gregory Howerton wasn't risking his career in this rescue attempt. Then again, he had nothing to gain by helping either.

It was a relief when both men made it into Louisa's room without being seen. The hall was clear for the moment, but for how much longer? Tally walked on and caught up to Vi. "If we don't get caught," she whispered. "It will be a miracle."

"If we do," Vi said, "The blame will be mine. I did it behind your back. You knew nothing of it."

Tally gave her a sour look. As if she would let that happen.

"I mean it," Vi declared. "My life will change soon, anyway."

Tally blinked in surprise. Was Vi referring to Mr. Lawrence? The two of them were obviously smitten with one another, but it was a huge leap to say her life would soon change because of it. "Are you talking about—" she began but ended the question abruptly because Tom and Gregory were already stepping back through the door supporting Louisa Heyer between them. She was wearing nothing but a plain hospital gown, but time was of the essence.

"You go one way," Vi whispered, "I'll go the other."

Tally nodded and started to lead the awkward threesome toward the stairwell, but Vi grabbed her arm.

"I should go with them," Vi said fervently. "You shouldn't be seen with them."

"I would never let you take all the blame," Tally retorted, resuming the lead. She felt nauseous with nerves, but certain they were doing the right thing.

The men had made it to the stairwell and started down when Nurse Rhodes rounded the hall again. Tally sucked in a sharp breath not knowing if the nurse had seen them.

Alice Rhodes stopped a few feet away from her with a concerned expression on her face. "Are you all right?" the nurse asked.

"Yes, I'm fine." Oh, Lord! Her heart was beating so fast. She could hear it in her eardrums. "I wanted to say … you're an excellent nurse."

Tears sprung to the young woman's eyes. "Thank you."

"You know what's important and you care enough to see it done."

Alice looked shamefaced. "She shouldn't have to suffer as she is."

Was Alice talking about Mrs. Dale or Louisa Heyer? Had she seen her being removed?

"Doctor Nolan hardly ever sees her," Alice continued, "but when I ask about upping her pain medication, he says her dosage is sufficient. But he doesn't see her suffering. He doesn't know."

"Make the dosage what it needs to be. I'll sign off on it."

"I don't want to get you into trouble," the nurse fretted.

Tally smiled. "I too know what's important and care enough to see it done."

Alice nodded. "Thank you."

"Good night, Alice."

"Good night, Dr. Covington."

Tally turned and went to join Vi hoping that she hadn't gotten anyone into trouble. Herself included.

"Seemed too easy," Tom commented as they approached the door they had entered earlier, this time with Louisa between them.

"Let's not celebrate just yet," Gregory replied.

The smell of fragrant tobacco smoke hit as soon as the door was opened. A nurse, a heavy-set woman of at least fifty, sat on the steps, smoking a pipe. She narrowed her eyes at them but didn't move or speak.

"Let's go," Gregory urged.

In for a penny, in for a pound, Tom thought as they walked on.

"Fine night," Gregory said to the woman.

"Yeah? Fine night for what?"

He shrugged. "Taking a smoke or taking a walk." They were even with her now. He pulled out a neatly folded twenty-dollar bill from his pocket and offered it to her. "Or taking a moment to appreciate the good things in life."

She snatched the money with a deft hand. Of course, she could still yell and alert others, and all their effort would have been for nothing.

"This lady is not insane," Tom said to her. "Her husband had her put here to get to her money and so that he could carry on with another woman."

The nurse looked away and cocked her head, as if confused. "That's funny," she muttered. "I thought I heard something, but it can't be when I'm out here all by my lonesome."

The men quickly walked on, hoping the carriage was waiting just beyond the gate as they'd planned.

"Hope he goes straight to hell," the woman said behind them. The statement was followed by a low-pitched cackle. "Him and the floozy he's carrying on with."

It was a relief to see the carriage waiting when they cleared the gate. "Do you know Sylvan Street?" Tom asked the driver.

"Sure. Near where the big exhibition was," the man said. "I know it."

"There is a white house on Sylvan near forty-eighth. I've forgotten the number, but it's got a picket fence."

"Got it," the driver said.

From inside the carriage, Vi and Tally helped get Louisa secured between them. Gregory and Tom climbed in and the carriage started in motion. Louisa's balance was badly skewed, her breathing shallow and labored. Her hand, which Tally held, was cold and limp.

"Well, that was an interesting diversion," Greg commented. He was smiling. In the dark, his teeth were illuminated.

Tally's nerves were so on edge, she abruptly laughed. Their victory felt incredible. Intoxicating. Not that questions wouldn't be asked. She'd almost certainly get a visit from the police tomorrow, but that was then and they had Louisa with them now. "Where are we going?" she asked Tom.

"Aunt Dorothy's."

"Your aunt?"

"No. I met a lady named Betty Lee recently. She lives with and cares for her aunt, Aunt Dorothy, who is elderly, near ninety, I believe she said, but as spritely as they come. I feel certain they'll welcome Louisa."

Louisa moaned and laid her head against Vi's shoulder.

"We're taking you somewhere safe, Louisa," Vi said.

Tally felt a tightening of Louisa's grip, which was heartening.

"Thank you," Louisa muttered. The words were slurred, but understandable.

Tally met Vi's gaze and smiled. If worse came to worst, they might both have a big change in their future, but they would find a new path knowing they had done the right thing. They rode in silence for a while, each absorbed in their own thoughts.

"Betty Lee was also wronged by someone," Tom commented, breaking the silence.

Tally looked at him. "Is that how you came to meet her?"

"Yes."

"Your work sounds interesting," Gregory said.

"It can be," Tom replied. "It can also be excruciatingly dull. I spend a lot of time watching and waiting for something to happen."

"How was the lady wronged?" Tally asked.

"She was accused of something she didn't do. A theft. She was scapegoated and her employer knew it. Despite that, they fired her without providing a reference."

"What makes you think the employer knew it?" Tally challenged.

"Because the employer did what Betty was accused of."

Tally was baffled. "What does that mean? Something was stolen within the house?"

"Supposedly. Something belonging to the lady of the house."

"And her husband took it for some reason?"

"No. The lady herself was the culprit. She hid it away for some reason. The item wasn't really stolen; she merely claimed that it was."

"How strange," Vi replied. "Was it to get insurance money?"

"It's possible. The claim was paid."

"What makes you think the lady took it?" Tally asked.

"Because the same thing happened again. Another alleged theft of a piece of jewelry. I suspected she did it based on several things and … I proved it."

"How?" Tally was utterly bemused by the story and by Tom Kassel.

"Something illegal and possibly unethical. Let's just say I righted an old wrong to someone who hadn't deserved what happened to them."

Gregory chuckled. "I have a feeling I would approve."

Tom grinned.

"Well," Vi said, "we have just done something illegal, and I have no doubt it was the right thing."

Tally couldn't let the story go. "What did the lady say when she learned she'd been found out? What did her husband say?"

"I didn't confront them. They weren't my clients. I would have dearly loved to have been there when she made the full discovery."

Tally would have pushed for more, but Tom leaned out the window and banged on the cab.

"This is it," Tom said. The cab stopped. "Give me a moment to explain the situation," he said before climbing out.

Tally, Vi and Gregory watched as Tom went to the house and knocked on the door. A lady in a dressing robe answered the door and, in a matter of moments, she opened the door wide and Tom started back to the carriage with a smile that relieved all of them.

Gregory climbed out first and then they all helped to finagle Louisa out. Tom and Gregory walked with her cradled between them. They'd picked up her legs and were supporting her full weight.

"It's the first room to the right," a lady of perhaps thirty-five said to the men. Her hair was braided and hanging over one shoulder, her hands were clutched in front of her.

"We're sorry to disturb you," Vi said as she stepped in.

The lady shook her head. "Oh, no. It's fine. We're glad to help. Mr. Kassel told us about her."

Tally stuck out her hand. "Tally Covington."

The woman clasped her hand. "Elizabeth Lee. Betty," she amended.

"I'm Viola Ripley," Vi said. "I'll be looking in on her."

Betty nodded. "It's a pleasure to meet you both."

"It's a great pleasure to meet you," Vi said. "If you'll excuse me, I'll help settle her in."

"Of course."

"What can I do for her?" Betty asked when Vi had walked on.

"She's had a debilitating medication forced on her," Tally replied. "Until it gets out of her system, she'll sleep a great deal. But, as soon as possible, she needs to be up and eating, drinking and doing for herself. Normal things."

"It's a terrible thing that was done to her."

"Yes. It was."

The bedroom Vi entered was perhaps ten feet by ten feet, with a four-poster bed, bedside table and single dresser. There were two long windows on the outside wall. The windows were open, the curtains billowing softly in a breeze. In the daytime, there would be good light and fresh air.

Tom and Gregory left the room, having gotten Louisa into bed.

Vi sat on the edge of the bed and Louisa's gaze focused on her. "I know that everything feels strange," Vi said, "but that will go away. You'll be safe here."

"Thank you," Louisa whispered.

Vi smiled. She heard something and turned to see Tally and Betty standing in the doorway. She beckoned to Betty, who came closer. "Louisa, this is Betty Lee. Betty, this is Louisa."

"You're very welcome here, Louisa," Betty said.

Louisa murmured a thank you, but her eyes were closing. She had spent her reserves of strength.

"Does she need anything special to eat or drink?" Betty asked quietly.

"No," Vi replied as she stood. "She will probably have little appetite at first. I'd keep it to broth and soft foods for a few days. She should drink water and, when it's possible, she should get up. She'll be weak at first."

"I understand. We've got a bedpan."

"We can't thank you enough," Vi said.

"I'm glad to do it. I would do it for nothing. For her sake and for Mr. Kassel, but that other man just gave me this," she said, pulling a wad of bills from her pocket. "It's too much, but he wouldn't hear a refusal."

Tally turned and left.

"It's not too much," Vi said to Betty. "Your help is invaluable."

"We'll take care of her," Betty pledged.

A tall old lady appeared in the door in a nightgown and open robe. Her long gray hair was also in a braid. "Is that Robin Hood out front?" she asked.

Vi looked at Betty, surprised by the question, and saw that Betty was close to laughter. "Yes," Betty replied. "Viola, this is my Aunt Dorothy."

Vi extended her hand. "Viola Ripley," Vi said. "I'm a doctor at the Women's Hospital."

"A lady doctor," Dorothy said as they shook. "I'm impressed."

"Mr. Kassel has brought the lady he was telling us about," Betty explained to her aunt.

Dorothy glanced at Louisa. "Did he go and break her out of the madhouse?" Dorothy asked Vi with a look of delighted incredulity.

Vi's jaw nearly dropped. "Yes," she replied when she found her voice. "We all did."

"Good for you! I just adore Robin."

"Why do you call him Robin Hood?"

"Oh, that is a very great secret. But if you're a friend of his, tell him he can share it if he's a mind to." She looked at her niece. "Unless you object."

"Not at all," Betty said. "I think we all may be complicit, now."

"How wonderful," Aunt Dorothy exulted. "I've always wanted to be complicit."

<u>Chapter Twenty-Five</u>

At midnight, back in salon of the Werthing home, the group of seven conspirators had just polished off a third bottle of champagne in celebration, and another was opened. Tom and Tally had reenacted the events of the evening to the delight of Charity and Jack, including the story about Betty Lee.

"Are you sure you're fine with hearing all this?" Tom jested with Cecil when they were almost finished.

"I'm sorry. Did you say something?" Cecil asked. "I was in the other room and didn't hear a thing."

"That's true," Vi said. "I just saw him in the other room."

"I think it sounds marvelous," Charity exulted. "The whole thing. You should all be very proud of yourselves."

"I'm proud we didn't get caught," Tom said.

Gregory shrugged. "We would have explained that we are good Samaritans who found the lady wandering."

"I am so relieved that's she's out of that place," Vi blurted.

"Will she recover fully?" Tom asked.

"In time," Vi said. "I absolutely believe she will."

Tally nodded in agreement. "Although her odious husband still has control over her possessions and affairs."

"We'll find a way to free her," Cecil pledged.

"It occurs to me," Charity mused, "that you gentlemen have embraced a charity case or two."

Vi nearly choked on her champagne. Tally gave Charity a warning look, although most the men failed to notice.

"A worthy cause is good for the soul," Jack spoke up.

"Well, you can't make a living at it," Tom said. "But they can make life more meaningful."

"Yes," Charity said, enjoying herself immensely. "They do."

140

Vi gave Charity a look of reproach.

Tom quirked a brow. "I do believe there's an internal joke at play here."

"No, no, no," Charity said, trying to look earnest. "I'm only saying what a wonderful thing it is to take a charity case to heart."

"Who won the backgammon game?" Tally asked pointedly.

"You don't want to discuss worthy causes any further?" Charity asked.

"I think it's been covered."

"You really ought to share the joke," Tom urged.

"Cecil and I each won a game," Charity said sweetly, batting her eyes at Vi.

"How nice," Vi returned dryly.

Charity's eyes danced with merriment. "Isn't it?"

At quarter till two in the morning, Tally sat at her vanity after washing her face. She unpinned and brushed her hair. It had been an exceptionally long day and she saw the evidence of it in her reflection. She'd been powerless as she watched a woman die, she had helped rescue Louisa Heyer, and she'd been rude to Tom Kassel for no other reason than his too-obvious appeal. Her initial expression of disinterest might have passed for coolness after a particularly trying day, but he'd offered his arm on the way to dinner and she'd rejected it, saying that she hardly needed an escort.

What would it have hurt to have accepted? To be friendly? Unfazed, he'd offered her hand up in the carriage and she'd pointedly hesitated before grudgingly accepting the assistance. He had to think her terribly rude because she had been. Were her feelings toward Tom Kassel because of Pete? Tom reminded her of him. Both men had the same build and eye-catching handsomeness and self-assurance. However, having spent the evening in the presence of Tom, she knew there were far more differences than similarities to her childhood beau.

Pete had cared most about himself. He wanted an easy, traditional life with a passive wife. How either of them could have ever entertained the notion that they could be happily married was beyond her now. It seemed a million years ago, but she could still vividly recall their last encounter, perched comfortably in the shade of the giant oak on the May afternoon she'd completed her twelfth grade exams. Pete had left school three years before, at age sixteen, and begun work in a tin-plate factory with his father and brothers. He was content with it. It was what he'd expected of his life.

He was leaning against the tree with one knee pulled up watching her blow the white fluff off the aged dandelions she'd picked as they walked. "What are you wishing for?" he asked.

She shrugged. "Perfect marks." She picked up the last stalk and blew. "Adventure." She grinned. "Cake for dessert."

He grinned back at her. "It's time, you know."

"Time?"

"To marry," he said with a smile she would later think back on as glib.

Her smile vanished. What was he talking about? "I'm not finished with school."

His expression turned almost apologetic. "C'mon, Tal. You need to be. I should have said something before now, but I kept thinking you'd come to your senses."

She huffed. "My senses are just fine. Thank you. And, by the way, today is supposed to be a celebration."

He scoffed. "You don't even know if you passed your exams yet."

She rolled her eyes and gave him a look.

His expression soured and he pointedly looked toward the creek. "All right, yeah. You're smart." He looked at her again. "But you're full of yourself about it, too. You know?"

"Should I be sorry that I'm smart?"

"What you should do, is make up your mind. Do you want to go on and on with schooling forever or do you want to marry me? Because it's time I get married."

The statement stuck in her craw. "It's time *you* get married," she repeated slowly.

"You know what I mean," he snapped.

"Why is it so all-fired important *you* suddenly get married?"

"It just is. I want to have a family."

"I want have a family, too, but I also want to be a doctor."

"So be a doctor to our children," he said testily.

Why did this argument have to happen today? She wouldn't turn seventeen for three months yet.

"If not," he added with a shrug, "—then go be a doctor. And I'll go—"

"What? You'll go what?"

"I'll go get married. To someone else."

Was he being serious? "Who?"

"Does it matter?"

She got to her feet and took several steps away before turning back. She crossed her arms tightly. "Have you been courting someone else?"

"No," he replied. "Not really," he added a moment later with a definite note of guilt.

She exhaled in a rush. So much was clear all the sudden, most especially how ridiculous the idea of a life with him was. Still, tears pooled in her eyes. She resented it but, on second thought, why not let him see that he'd hurt her? They were the hurt feelings of a silly girl when it was time for adulthood. "I wish you luck with whoever she is," she said stiffly.

Her response had clearly surprised him. All sorts of expressions crossed his face. "Constance," he blurted. "Constance Redmond."

It was not even someone she knew. She wanted to say goodbye, but the words got caught in her throat. She whirled around and began the walk home.

"You're choosing this," he called.

She kept walking.

"I'd rather marry you. You know I would. Tally!"

She refused to turn back around and give him the satisfaction of seeing the tears stream down her face. He would think they meant regret. She didn't know exactly why her heart felt as broken as it did, but it was not because of regret.

She sighed and shook off the memory as she set down the brush. She regretted that she'd been rude to Tom, but there was nothing to be done about it now. She couldn't send a note apologizing. That would look like flirtation. "Learn your lesson," she said accusingly to her mirror image. *Don't be so quick to judge. When you do, you're made out to be a fool.*

She rose and headed to bed knowing that Cecil Lawrence and Vi were still together, probably either sitting on the porch or strolling hand in hand. He was a good man, a learned gentleman. She got into bed and turned out the lamp wondering if she was both happy for Vi and envious in equal measures? If so, she ought to be better than that.

"I should go," Cecil said. He and Vi were sitting on the screened-in porch, where they had been watching fireflies light up the yard. "Do you work tomorrow?"

She nodded. "I have a short shift. From ten to two."

"Then I really must go." He rose. "And let you get some sleep." She stood and their hands connected. "Would it be too imposing to suggest dinner tomorrow?"

She smiled. "Not at all."

"May I pick you up at seven?"

"I'd like that."

She walked him out to the front porch. "My mother sent a note today asking me to come for my father's birthday," she said.

"Oh?"

"I think I'd like to go," she added reluctantly.

"I'm sure it will mean a great deal to him."

"You know that we had quite a falling out."

"Yes."

"Not only has it never been mended, I wasn't certain I wanted it to. But … I will go to dinner. I can't swear that I want reconciliation, but I'm not sure that I don't."

"At least you're open to it. That's something."

"I was wondering, would you like to come with me?"

"I'd love to!"

She beamed a smile. "It's Thursday, the twenty-sixth."

"You'll have to help me think of something I can bring as a gift."

"That's not necessary."

"I insist. I may need to curry his favor one day," he added mischievously.

She ducked her head looking embarrassed but pleased. "It was a wonderful night," she said softly, looking back up at him again.

"Yes, it was." He reached for her hand and kissed it. Then he leaned forward and pressed a kiss to her cheek. She stayed close and the moment felt right so he kissed her lips. *More* was what he found himself wishing for. More time. More of her company. More kissing. And more. Fortunately, there was tomorrow. "Good night," he said, stepping back.

"Goodnight."

<u>Chapter Twenty-Six</u>

Monday, July 23

The desk sergeant looked up and beamed a smile as Tom walked through the front doors of the police department's ninth precinct the next day. "Thomas Kassel! You finally back to join us?"

"Not today," Tom returned with a grin. "I'm hoping to see Cass if he's around."

"He is," Lieutenant Casper Ketler said as he walked into the lobby tugging on his jacket. "Good timing on your part. I'm just headed out to see the aftermath of last night's riot. You want to go?"

"Sure." Tom gave a casual salute to the desk sergeant and followed Cass from the building. "What riot?"

"The usual nonsense in the bloody fifth," Cass replied. "I was asked to look in on it."

"Were you?"

Cass was Tom's closest friend and had been a brother in uniform. They'd worked so well together, they'd ended up as Special Officers in charge of investigations. 'Put Kassel and Ketler on it,' had become a common refrain in the ninth precinct and beyond. In the years since, Cass had risen to the role of a lieutenant and there was talk of a captaincy in his future. Tom had no doubt his friend would achieve the office in due time and no one was better suited. It was probable they would have risen the ranks together had everything not changed on a cold April morning eight years before.

"I'll go," Tom agreed. "And then you can buy me lunch."

"Aren't you the one making fistfuls of money? You buy lunch."

"Fistfuls is going a bit far, but I'll buy. In exchange for some information."

Cass grunted. "Always a trade-off. Did you drive?"

"I did," Tom said. "It's over here." They climbed in and started down the road before he asked, "How are the girls?"

"Hannah has taken to mimicking everything Mollie does. I'm not home five minutes before I hear, 'Stop 'peating me!' Daddy make her stop!"

"Poor man," Tom said with mock sympathy. "How do you bear it?"

"Laura keeps trying to impress upon Mollie that imitation is a compliment, but she's not having it."

Cass's daughters were five and three and Tom was their godfather. "They'll grow out of it."

"Not soon enough for us."

"Just watch. You'll miss it in a few years when they've moved on to some other trying phase."

"We shall see. So what information do you want?"

"There're two things. The first is I've been looking for a sixteen-year-old boy who was chased away by his mother's employer, a scoundrel by the name of Blakely Heyer. I don't know why he wanted the boy gone, but it may have been nothing more than lust over a pretty maid in the house."

"What? The maid and the boy liked one another?"

Tom nodded. "Anyway, Heyer threatened him, and the boy panicked. He was on foot when he left the home with very little money, so he's probably within a ten-mile radius. He would have had to find work. He didn't go to any of his friends. I checked. I also asked around the waterfront, but no one recognized him."

"Where did he start from?"

"Society Hill. Which, given the radius, hopefully puts him in your territory."

"Who hired you to help?"

"No one."

"Then why are you?"

"Kindness."

Cass shot him a look of suspicion.

"I stumbled onto the thing because the boy's mother is the housekeeper of another lady I'm trying to help because she was committed to an insane asylum when she's perfectly sane. Committed by her nefarious husband."

Cass shifted to face him. "That's a terrible accusation."

"It's a terrible thing."

"And nefarious is a ridiculous word."

"True. But I rather like it. I believe it fits the man to a T."

"Can you prove any of it?"

"We're working on it."

"Who is 'we're'?"

"A lawyer named Cecil Lawrence brought me in on it. Do you know him?"

"By reputation only. Good reputation."

Tom nodded. "He's got a strong moral compass. Cares more about people than money."

"And yet the two of you get along?" Cass teased.

Tom cracked a grin. "You should be proud of me. I may not even get compensated for this job."

"No!"

"Yet more shocking is that I don't even care at this point. Oh, I'd rather get paid. Don't get me wrong. But I want to see Heyer pay for what he's done even if I don't see a cent for it."

"What is the world coming to? But if you're rediscovering a hunger for justice, why not come back to work with us? The need has never been so great."

"You want to partner up again?"

"I'd love that, but as you well know, I'm on the political track now. For better or worse. Besides, you don't need a partner. And I'm serious, Tom. You've made a tidy sum, I'm sure. You should come back and let your skills be of real use to the city. Isn't it time?"

Tom didn't reply right away, but his friend's sentiment was affecting. "We would need to have a conversation before I would consider it."

Cass shook his head and waved a hand. "I know enough about New York."

"It's not that. What do you know about a fatal mugging in the park a few years ago when an older man was killed? His name was Gerald Holmes."

Cass thought back. "I believe the wife was attacked, too, although she wasn't badly hurt."

"That's right. That's the one."

"They didn't catch the man who did it."

"Can I get a look at the report?"

"That wasn't ours."

"I know. It was the seventh precinct. But they were less than cooperative when I went to them."

"Ah. Well, you probably contributed to some case being proved or not that failed to put them in the best light."

"It's possible."

"No doubt, you've burned a few bridges."

"I've burned lots of them. It's rarely a problem for long. I just find new ones. Or build them myself."

Cass chuckled. "Your self-confidence never fails to inspire."

"Thank you."

"I'm sure I can get hold of the report," Cass said. "But what are you hoping to learn?"

"Who did it and why."

Cass chortled. "If that was known, the man would have been arrested and hung."

Tom spotted a shady area on a side street and drove to it. He parked before turning to Cass who was watching him curiously. "Let's say you know that a certain person is guilty of a terrible crime. We'll call him Mr. X. He is guilty of conspiring to have a man killed so that the man's wife, who is the mistress of Mr. X, gains his fortune, which they'll enjoy together."

"Go on."

"The mistress is culpable, too, of course, but she may be the weak link. If you get her to admit what happened, you have him. Perhaps once you have him, you can get her. Turnabout is fair play, after all."

"In this fictional account, did Mr. X hire a thug to kill a wealthy older man with a much younger wife during a stroll through a park?"

"Let's say that's the case," Tom said casually.

"But the thug was not caught. We have no idea who he is."

Tom nodded. "Correct."

"So, without any evidence, you are convinced that Mr. X hired the thug."

"Yes."

"Why don't you fill me in on the real story? Hypotheticals make my head ache."

"All right, I will. But the question is important."

"What question?"

"Let's say that you could produce some compelling evidence that alarmed the widow into admitting that Mr. X hired the thug to kill her husband. Maybe she knew about it before hand, maybe only afterwards. But she knows and can offer testimony that damns him."

"By 'produce some compelling evidence', do you mean conjure up evidence and claim it's the real thing?"

"Yes."

Cass drew back. "What are you thinking?" he asked crossly. "If evidence isn't real and you don't have the murderer in custody, how can you know the widow's statement has validity? How can you know she's telling the truth? Don't forget that if she knew about the crime, she is complicit."

"*Mm-hmm*," Tom murmured. "For which she'd likely be offered some sort of immunity from prosecution."

Cass winced. "When she's just as guilty?"

"But if her confession gets him caught? The question is whether the method of obtaining her confession is acceptable."

"Meaning use less than honest means to get a killer off the street?"

Tom nodded resolutely. "Yes."

"No! It is too slippery a slope. It's too tempting for someone to damn someone else to win a reprieve for themselves."

"What if it's the only way to get to Mr. X? A coldhearted narcissist who will damn anyone else to get what he wants."

"Here's a question. What if you're wrong? You believe someone is guilty and so you manufacture evidence to get a confession or to get a finger pointed at this person … and maybe you manage it." He paused. "You, my friend, are a good detective, better than good, but you are capable of being wrong."

"I never said I wasn't. But I'm not wrong about him."

Cass shook his head. "Police standards have to be high or why should anyone have any faith in us?"

"It's a corrupt system through and through," Tom said dispassionately. "And most people don't have any faith in it."

"Too much of it is corrupt," Cass agreed. "Something I would like to see changed. I want to see the bribes and the system of ward leaders come to an end. But that has nothing to do with what you're suggesting."

"At least, my deception would see some good come from it."

Cass sighed. "Let's go to lunch. I will hear you out. This case of yours sounds involved."

"It is."

"You know that I trust your judgment, but our methods have to be held to a standard."

That's why I can't come back, Tom thought.

"I'd like to hear more on the missing boy," Cass said. "Perhaps we can help with that."

Tom got the carriage moving again. "I've got a photograph of him."

"Good. I feel like steak, by the way."

"Of course, you do."

"Nefarious," Cass murmured under his breath.

"The word is growing on you, isn't it? I'd bet a dollar you're going to use it in a sentence sometime today."

Cass chuckled. "In which asylum is the unfortunate lady incarcerated?"

"Oh, ah, she's not anymore. She somehow managed to escape the place just last night, as a matter of fact. Or that's the rumor I heard."

"Oh, Lord," Cass groaned. "We need to get you back on the force before you end up in prison."

"I have no idea what you're talking about," Tom replied, not even bothering to sound believable.

Chapter Twenty-Seven

"Gone?" Blakely Heyer said for a second time.

"Yes," the hospital administrator replied sheepishly. He was a robust man with mutton chop sideburns named Wilford Q. Pugely replied. "I am so sorry."

Heyer rose from behind his desk as he leaned onto it. His eyes were wide with disbelief, his jaw clenched. "How is that possible?"

"We don't know, but the police have been called in on it. Rest assured that—"

"She couldn't *speak* last time I saw her! Couldn't hold a pen in hand to sign her own damned name! She could not possibly have gotten up and climbed out a window!"

"We will find out. I promise you. It's possible she could have—"

"Could have what?" Heyer yelled.

Pugely flinched. "G-gotten confused and wandered out somehow," he stammered.

"Wandered out," Heyer scoffed. "I tell you that she could not speak or hold a pen. She could barely sit, and you tell me she may have wandered out?"

"It's never happened before, so there is no precedent."

"When?" Blakely seethed. "When did this happen?"

"Last night. She was discovered missing at the midnight check. But she was there at eight."

Heyer sank back down in his chair, racking his brain for what might have happened. "There was a doctor," he said, looking up sharply. "A *female* doctor," he said wrinkling his nose as he

153

uttered the word. "From the Women's Hospital. She caused trouble before, trying to see my wife after she'd been dismissed."

The man licked his lips nervously. "We turned over the visitor's log to the police."

Heyer's eyes narrowed. "Had she been there?"

"There were two female doctors who stopped by that night," Pugely replied haltingly. "One of them an attending who checked on a patient."

"Ripley," Heyer exclaimed as it occurred to him. "That's her name. Dr. Ripley. Viola Ripley. Was she one of the doctors?"

Pugely averted his gaze. "Um—"

Heyer slapped the desk. "She was behind it!"

"The police are talking to her, sir."

"My wife must be found," Heyer bit out furiously. "She was put there for her safety. She is a danger to herself and others. You, sir, are responsible! You and your hospital."

Pugely stepped backwards. "I'm sorry. This is not the sort of thing that happens at our facility."

"Except that it did," Heyer retorted. "You had best find her or you will find yourselves sued for every dime in your coffers. If you think for one minute that I cannot or will not do it, you are very much mistaken."

Pugely bowed his head, turned and left.

Only when the administrator had gone, did Blakely Heyer give in to the panic he felt. When the worst of it had passed, he rose and left on shaky legs to go to Lillian. They'd had a plan in place, an excellent plan, but something had gone terribly awry. He felt it in his bones. They would have to adjust accordingly. If Doctor Viola Ripley, that nosy, meddling bitch, had custody of Louisa, she would stop the medication and Louisa might be restored. If that happened, if her mind was made clear, it was possible that all would be lost. Years of planning and careful execution would amount to nothing. Without question or delay, he and Lillian needed an alternative plan.

"What are you doing here this time of day?" Lillian asked a half hour later when she walked into the parlor where he waited.

He heard the annoyance in her tone, so he turned with a drink in hand allowing her to see the expression on his face.

"What's happened?" she asked in a low voice.

"Louisa is missing. She was taken from the hospital."

Lillian's jaw dropped. "Taken? By whom?"

"By an interfering female doctor who tried to intervene before. I don't know how, but she found a way."

Lillian stared in disbelief. "A doctor? You're saying a doctor took her?"

"Yes. That is precisely what I'm telling you. That and we need to come up with a different plan. If Louisa recovers her health and cannot be controlled—"

Lillian walked to a chair and sat, her posture very erect. She was not looking at him. "What is it you propose?" she asked coolly.

He resented her tone, but all that really mattered was coming up with a new plan. "She may insist on a divorce."

She huffed a laugh. "Do you really think so? I cannot imagine why she would."

"Sarcasm is not appealing, Lillian. We need to focus. Louisa may demand a divorce, but I should be able to get a decent settlement. I would settle for the right amount to spare us both the ordeal of a divorce. That's what I'll tell her." He paused and then shrugged. "If that happens, you and I will simply marry and live here." She turned to him looking almost horrified. Her expression sent a sharp chill through him. "Why do you look like that?"

She shook her head. "We … cannot."

He cocked his head. "Cannot what?"

She hesitated. "Marry."

He blinked and waited for her to continue, but she did not. "What are you talking about? We always planned to marry."

"We also planned for you to acquire her fortune. Had that been the case, then *this,*" she said, gesturing around the room, "—would not matter so much."

He came closer. "What are you talking about?"

She looked away from him with a heavy sigh.

"Lillian!"

"The house isn't mine," she admitted.

"What?"

She looked at him again. "The house is not mine. I thought it was, but it's not. I can live here. That's all. For as long as I live, I can reside here. Unless I marry. It's called a life tenancy with restrictions."

He felt himself begin to seethe. Heat suffused him; he felt it eking out his pores. He turned and breathed in and out, in and out, not trusting himself to speak. "Why didn't you tell me this before?" he finally asked turning back to her

She raised her chin. "Do not take that attitude with me," she warned. "Not when you haven't lived up to your end of the bargain."

"What about the money? How much did he leave you?"

"Not enough! I receive a yearly stipend that was deemed sufficient for my needs. He left virtually everything to his daughters who don't even need it."

Blakely looked around the room feeling itchy and provoked. "We could sell it all. Everything. Wall to wall. The paintings and the ceramics are worth a small fortune."

She rose to her feet, clearly disturbed by the notion. "And do what?"

"Go to Italy. We could go live in Italy."

"Oh, Blake! You're talking foolishness. How long do you think the money would last?" She paused and when he didn't reply, she went on. "Not long enough! I can promise you that. And then we'd be back to …what? Scheming? Gambling? Or maybe I can go back on the stage? Is that what you think? Who would hire an American lawyer in Italy? We don't even speak the language!"

He studied her. He'd gotten a bad feeling from the moment she'd walked into the room and that feeling, a feeling of foreboding, had only worsened. "What do you think we should do?" he asked with all the calmness he could muster.

She held his gaze for several seconds and then walked to the sideboard to pour a drink. "Stay calm, for one thing." She poured a glass of sherry and drank it. "The thing may not be as bad as you fear," she said, her tone more temperate.

"What if it is?"

She turned around to look at him and the irritation was back on her face. "We're not selling these things and running off. We'd be stopped before we could manage it."

He knew that expression on her face. For however elegant and refined she could seem, she'd been born to poverty. She'd learned how to survive in life's school of hard knocks. He didn't need her digging in her heels and refusing to budge or to listen. For the moment, he had to retreat. He went to the sofa and sat. "Maybe I am overreacting."

"You are, darling. You are."

"It was so shocking to learn she was gone."

"I'm sure it was," she said sympathetically.

He nodded. "A good night's sleep and it will look better tomorrow."

"Yes," she agreed enthusiastically. She walked over and sat next to him. She reached over and covered his hand with hers. "Yes."

He gave her a shamefaced smile. "Still love me?"

She gave him an adoring look. "You know I do. I hate for us to be in disagreement."

He nodded. "So do I. Maybe tonight we can have a quiet dinner, a few games of cards and then retire early."

She leaned in and gave him a chaste kiss on the lips. "Of course. Things will seem better tomorrow. We just have to remain coolheaded."

He nodded.

"What would you think about lamb for dinner? With mint jelly?"

"It sounds excellent. And a good red."

"Of course." She smiled affectionately and then rose and left to confer with the cook.

How perfectly she was playing the role of the concerned, clearheaded consort. Well, she wasn't the only one who could successfully carry off a part. He'd carried off plenty and his days of plotting and scheming were not quite over yet, as much as he wished they were. His pleasant expression vanished the moment Lillian vacated the room. He glanced around trying to determine where something might be hidden. He got to his feet and went to the door to make sure she was nowhere in sight before he began a search.

Chapter Twenty-Eight

Tuesday, July 24

Cass watched the photograph of William Yardley being circulated around the room during the morning meeting. The sergeant had asked the men to be on the lookout for the runaway as a favor to their former comrade Tom Kassel. He'd explained the boy had done nothing wrong, but that he might feel threatened if approached too aggressively since someone in a position of authority had made a false accusation against him that had frightened him into running away in the first place.

"You'll know him by a scar," Cass spoke up, pointing to the lower side of his face. The scar was noticeable in the photograph, but only when one was paying close attention. Besides, Cass wanted the men to know that finding the boy was something he supported.

"That covers it for me," the sergeant said to Cass. "Unless you have anything else, sir?"

"There is one thing," Cass replied. "I've learned that a new unit will be forming sometime next year, a mounted patrol unit. So if you're a horseman, you may want to consider it."

"What about being full of horseshit?" a brash cop named Crofton asked tongue in cheek. "I'm thinking Fuller might want to consider it."

There was laughter, including from equally brash Fuller, followed by an under the breath response that drew more laughter from those around them. Cass was relatively sure it was, 'don't you mean hung like a horse?'

"That's it, men," the sergeant said with a cockeyed grin. "Go to it."

Cass returned to his office, removed his jacket and tried to begin the day's work, but he was distracted. At the meeting, he'd done a quick mental calculation of the level of talent in the room. It wasn't poor, but what was missing and what Tom's return to the force could remedy was a truly discerning detective with a passion for justice. Was Tom's passion too zealous? Were his methods too reckless?

Only days ago, an eighty-two-year-old man had been found dead, hanged by the neck from the rafters in his attic. Because of crippling arthritis, the man used a wheelchair, although he could still walk short distances. There had been no forced entry on the night of the man's death. All the doors were locked and no one else lived there. The man had grown children, two sons and a daughter, who took turns checking on him and caring for him. It was the daughter who'd discovered the body.

The siblings concurred that their father had become despondent owing to his increasing debilitation. Because of that and despite the mystery of how the man got himself up a steep flight of stairs while hauling a ladder, the death was ruled a suicide at the inquest. Cass didn't buy it, and he was confident that Tom would have gotten to the bottom of it, but Tom was not on the job, and his own position required eight to ten hour days. He could not and would not step back into working a case. He had his wife and daughters to consider. If he couldn't work the job around his family life, the job would have to change. His priorities were clear and they'd been made clearer after Tom's loss of Jacqueline. It was a loss that nearly finished Tom in more ways than one.

Cass swiveled to face the window and thought back on the day he and Tom had been called into the lieutenant's office to learn the sickening news that Jaqueline had been murdered along with her sister and brother-in-law whom she'd been visiting in New York. Hearing the news, Tom had gone stark white, swayed and nearly passed out.

Jacqueline hadn't been the intended victim. It was her brother-in-law, Darren Buxton, the acting Attorney General of

New York who had been the target along with his wife, Deidre. The inclusion of Deidre was for sheer ruthlessness. To send a message. Poor Jacqueline was simply in the wrong place at the wrong time.

It was immediately suspected and later proved that the mastermind behind the murders had been Raymond 'Scissors' Felden, a petty crook turned crime boss of a street gang known as the Whyos. Felden, who owned saloons and casinos, had been charged with racketeering and counterfeiting at the time of the murders. It was his well-funded plan to see that the evidence against him got lost and any uncooperative prosecutors removed. In his experience, enough money solved every dilemma. The first step had been easy. A month after charges were made against Felden, the Attorney General, an older man, conveniently dropped dead while alone in his house. The cause of death was labeled a heart attack.

The assistant Attorney General, Darren Buxton, then became the acting Attorney General. Buxton began getting messages and threats to drop the case against Felden, and some of the messages appeared on his desk, which meant a traitor in the office. Undeterred, he continued building the case against Felden, who had earned the nickname Scissors by attacking his own brother and two other men with a pair of scissors, nearly killing one of them. That conviction had earned him a year stretch for aggravated assault.

In talking to reporters, Darren Buxton used the phrase 'bullying thug' in regard to Scissors. Someone commented it sounded like wooly bug. Or slug, another suggested. The jibes took on a life of their own in the papers with Scissors being touted as a human bug, complete with a grotesque accompanying caricature. The mocking infuriated Felden who determined that both Buxton and his wife would die in such brutal fashion that no one would dare cross him again.

Jacqueline wasn't known to the brutes that broke into the Buxton's brownstone on the stormy predawn morning of April ninth, a Friday, but she couldn't be left behind as a witness even though she was large in pregnancy. They'd been *compassionate* about it, they'd later said. They'd merely cut her throat. They'd done far worse to the Buxtons.

Cass traveled to New York with Tom and stayed by his side before Jacqueline's body was released for burial. He'd stayed by Tom's side for the return trip, the funeral and burial. Afterwards, Tom, locked in a hell of grief and agony, took a leave of absence and left again for New York. He checked into a seedy boardinghouse and subsequently seemed to disappear. Cass wrote and got no response. He sent telegrams and got no response. He went looking for him and was unable to find him. For weeks, he feared the worst.

What he would later learn was that Tom had gone undercover to find the culprits and see them punished. It took Tom seven months to hunt down every participant in the crime and every person that had helped cover it up and made sure each of them paid appropriately. His own life and wellbeing had ceased to matter. Only justice mattered. Revenge and justice. Once it was done, there had been no coming back to the police force for Tom. Too many lines had been crossed.

The Tom who returned to Philadelphia was a ghost of his former self. He had achieved his goal of revenge, but it hadn't resulted in any peace of mind. Slowly, he built a career of privately investigating and found success at it. On a few occasions, he'd even allowed his friends to act as matchmakers, but nothing came of it. Had he fully rebounded now? Cass sometimes felt he had his old friend back and he hoped so. Eight years of mourning was long enough.

Cass wondered if he could forge a path for Tom's return to the force by trusting him regarding Heyer and the widow. He turned back to his desk and picked up his pen to send a note and find out exactly what would be involved.

<u>Chapter Twenty-Nine</u>

Thursday, July 26

Louisa sat facing the window as Betty combed her just-washed hair. Her head was repeatedly tugged backwards, although Betty was trying not to cause discomfort. She truly was the kindest, most ideal helpmate ever, assisting with every task as if it were no bother. Louisa had soaked in a hot bath and her skin was flushed from it. She was clad in one of Aunt Dorothy's surprisingly sensuous silk dressing robes with a flower design in teal and fuchsia.

The backyard was pretty, the air sweetened by a recent rain shower. There were wind chimes in the trees and she enjoyed their discordant tunes on the breezy, late afternoon. Crickets chirped a constant baseline for the strange melody and a train whistle blew in the distance. She appreciated all of it. Everything. The foliage was the deep green of late summer, which was strange since she'd been oblivious for so many weeks, but green was good. Green meant life. The leaves on the trees fluttered, each vying for attention, but the sun was particular with which leaves it lit. One star shaped leaf stood out because the sun filtered through it causing it to glow several shades lighter. It was glorious.

"Almost done," Betty said.

"How can I ever thank you?" Louisa asked and the words had come out almost clearly.

Betty squeezed her shoulder gently. "Having you here is a pleasure for me and Aunt Dorothy." She went back to combing.

"She's in there making supper from a new recipe she found in The Lady's Home Journal. Or was it in The Cosmopolitan?"

Aunt Dorothy had a self-proclaimed weakness for four things, Whitman's chocolate confections, hard cider, good jokes, especially 'dirty' jokes, and lady's magazines. She had five subscriptions including Good Housekeeping. "When I don't care one iota about good housekeeping," she admitted.

"The dish has a fancy French name for trout baked in wine," Betty continued. "I'm going to make strawberry spoonbread, too. The strawberries are so good this year."

"Sounds delicious," Louisa replied, slurring a bit.

"Done," Betty announced. She walked over to put the comb on the table and turned back to assess Louisa. "You're much better today," she said with a smile.

"Maybe I could help with dinner."

"You can keep us company."

Louisa leaned forward and then stood on her own. When she felt steady enough, she smiled. "Another accomplishment." Her words were a little garbled, but at least she was making herself understood. She glanced down at the robe. It didn't feel quite decent to wear it to dinner. "Should I change?"

"Oh, gracious, no. We're not expecting company," Betty added as she started from the room.

Louisa smiled because the words implied that she was family and it was what they made her feel. As she followed Betty, she heard the distant rumbling and the whistle of a train. She'd never realized how much she enjoyed the sounds. Betty stopped and glanced back at her. "I'm fine," Louisa assured her. "I know my way."

Chapter Thirty

The closer they got to her parents' home, the more pressure Vi felt. It was as if the atmosphere around them had thickened and pressed in on her from every direction. Her anxiety was making it hard to breathe, despite that they rode in an open air carriage, a two-seater Studebaker.

"Are you all right?" Cecil asked.

She nodded stiffly, but didn't look at him. She didn't trust herself to because tears were suddenly and infuriatingly threatening. She'd grown up here so she recognized each house on the street. She knew the trees and the lawn implements and the occasional barking dog. She'd thought she could do this, but she hadn't expected this terrible pressure she felt. Was she really ready to forgive them?

"Your nephew is Alan and he's six," Cecil said.

She knew he was trying to distract her. To decompress the atmosphere for her. She loved him for that. She held a finger to her lips to stop their trembling because she could not start crying now.

"And your niece is almost four, and her name is Daphne."

Vi nodded. "Named for Julia's mother," she replied. She looked at him and smiled bravely, having bested the battle for control of her emotions for the moment.

"Julia is your sister-in-law and your brother is Michael. Got it."

"It's possible my grandmother, my mother's mother, may be there. I don't know. Her name is Holiday. Josephine Holiday."

"You haven't mentioned her. Are you not close?"

"No. She adored Michael, but she always favored boys. She favored my uncles over my mother, too. Favors, I should say. Still." She shook her head slightly, remembering. "But she is always invited to family dinners. I resented how she treated my mother. Even more than how she treated me. Nona, my father's mother, she was the one I was close to. Whenever Grandmother Holiday would slight me, Nona would find a way to make up for it, at least in terms of making me feel loved and special."

"I wish I could have met her," he said wistfully.

"So do I." They'd almost reached the house. "This is it," she said, pointing it out.

"It's a beautiful home," he commented.

She took a breath and exhaled. She could do this. It was only one evening and Michael, Julia and the children would be there. She could get through it with grace and aplomb.

"Are you ready?" Cecil asked tenderly when he'd parked.

She nodded but kept her gaze ahead of her. He came around to help her down and she accepted the assistance gratefully. She'd already begun relying on him. Was that right? Was it reasonable? Not that he couldn't have relied on her, as well. She would happily be there for him wherever and whenever needed. "You look very nice, by the way," she said.

His suit, this evening, was blue-gray with faint pinstripes and he'd paired it with a light blue tie. He'd minded the details. She'd noticed the tie pin and the cufflinks and the scented talc he wore. He'd had a haircut and his shoes shone.

"Thank you," he replied. "I tried since you always look so lovely."

She certainly did not look lovely most days of her life. What would he think if he saw her leaving the hospital after a ten-hour shift on a hectic day? But she already knew the answer. He would think she looked wonderful, especially having worked a hectic ten-hour day.

As he retrieved the packages he'd brought and offered his arm, she decided that if the evening got difficult, she would focus on him, how much he cared and how much she cared. Of course, they couldn't admit to the feelings yet. They could hint and allude and tease and flirt, which was enough for now. The rest would come later.

He rang the front bell and Lowery, the butler, promptly let them in. The surge of family happened all at once. Alan ran up and threw his arms around her legs. Michael came hurrying to them next, smiling broadly as he kissed her cheek. "I'm so glad to see you," he said.

"It's good to see you," she returned. "Michael, this is Cecil Lawrence."

"We heard you were coming," Michael said with twinkling eyes as he offered his hand. "Pleased to meet you, Mr. Lawrence."

"Cecil, please."

The rest of the family had converged and Vi felt her breath thicken again. She noticed Julia's worried smile. As they embraced, Julia whispered, "Are you all right?"

Vi nodded, although it wasn't completely true. Her parents were there and they looked as apprehensive as she felt. Her mother was holding Daphne.

"We're so pleased you could join us, Cecil," Julia said.

"Yes, we are," Octavia Ripley echoed as she stepped close. "Hello, dear," she said to Vi. She leaned in to kiss her daughter's cheek.

"Hello, Mother."

"Say hello to your Aunt Viola," her mother coaxed Daphne who was acting shy.

"Hello, pretty girl," Vi said to the child who was watching her warily.

"Glad you could make it," her father said to her.

She couldn't reply. She felt frozen. And resentful. Why had she thought she'd feel differently?

"Both of you," her father said, quickly directing his attention to Cecil who smiled.

"Thank you for having me," Cecil returned. "And happy birthday. These are for you," he said, handing off two beautifully wrapped boxes. Vi knew that one contained a fine cognac and the other Belgian chocolates.

"How kind. Thank you."

"He's sixty," Alan announced.

"Yes," Harrison Ripley laughed. "Old. Isn't that right, Alan?"

The boy looked reluctant to agree.

"Not so old," Julia said playfully.

"There are days it feels it," Harrison said. "But not so much today. Let's go have a drink, shall we?"

"Absolutely," Cecil agreed.

Harrison led the way and most of the others followed, although Octavia Ripley held back. "Would you like to hold your niece?" she asked Vi.

Daphne frowned hearing this and buried her head in her grandmother's neck.

"Don't worry, Daphne," Vi said gently. "I won't snatch you up. I know exactly how you feel."

"Oh, please try, Viola," her mother admonished quietly. "Please. Try."

"I'm here, aren't I?"

"That's only a small part of it, darling."

"It doesn't feel small to me."

"No. I suppose not." She bent to put Daphne down, but the girl lifted her legs to avoid it. "Go," she scolded mildly. "Go to your mother." The child relinquished and then left. Octavia faced her daughter. "Just try to make it a pleasant evening. It's your father's birthday. He may not say so, but it means everything to him that you're here. And to me."

Vi felt tears tormenting the backs of her eyes. There were new lines around her mother's eyes that hadn't been there before. Because they'd lost years. *Years.* She nodded and then stiffly followed her into the parlour.

As they drove back home, it occurred to Vi that, for the most part, she'd been an observer that evening. She had only been a participant when someone asked something that required an answer. Cecil, on the other hand, had been warm and responsive and amusing. He had managed to be supportive of her while acting as if nothing was amiss. He'd impressed everyone. He'd impressed her, and she'd thought she couldn't be more impressed with him.

What did he think of her? That she was petulant? She was a grown woman and an intelligent professional, but had she acted like a wounded child? *Was* she still a wounded child deep down inside? The evening had been more painful than she'd thought it would be. Thinking back, she could only compartmentalize it. Drinks in the parlour. She'd had two glasses of sherry and she had been glad her niece and nephew were the centers of attention. Her father had caught her eye and smiled, and she'd looked away without a response. Her heart had beaten faster and tears had pricked the backs of her eyes, but he could not have known that.

For dinner her mother had carefully placed them. She had been positioned between Michael and Julia and across from Cecil. The food had been delicious, but difficult to appreciate with the knot in her stomach. She was still angry. She needed to admit it. She was still hurt and angry. A big part of her wanted to lash out and demand to know how they thought she could just forget.

"It was a step," Cecil said encouragingly.

"Was it?"

He took hold of her hand and squeezed. "It was. And tomorrow is another day."

"You, Cecil Lawrence, were perfect. Thank you for that. I know I didn't make it easy."

"Vi," he scolded gently. "You're being too hard on yourself. It was a very nice evening. I'm glad I went."

A sigh escaped her.

"May I ask," he began. "Did your father ever apologize or at least express regret?"

"I have never known my father to apologize. My mother once said they regretted the path they'd chosen."

"Ah. I ask because he said something."

169

Vi looked at him. "What?"

"At the end of the evening when you were saying goodbye to Julia, he asked if I knew what it would take. I said, 'Sir?' As if I didn't know what he was talking about. He said, 'We disagreed on her pursuit of medicine and she's still holding a grudge because of it.'"

"A grudge," she repeated scornfully. "Is that what it is?"

"That's how he phrased it, but if you look beyond the phrasing to what he was asking—"

She took his point.

"I guess I'm wondering if you ever told your parents how much their decision not to support you in pursuing your dream hurt you," he said carefully.

"Well, there were hysterics at the time. I was desperately angry and hurt. So, yes, they know. I told them I would never forgive them."

"You didn't ask for my advice," he said.

She shifted to him. "Your opinion matters to me. I want to know what you think."

"Then my advice is to tell them again. Tell them what you need from them. He asked, so tell him. Even if you think it's obvious and well understood, have your say and allow them to have theirs." He paused. "If I'm not mistaken, you want them to understand how much their decision, their refusal, hurt and how much harder everything was without them in your life."

The words laid her bare. Tears surfaced and she couldn't hold them back.

"Oh, Vi. I'm sorry!"

She shook her head. "It's not you."

He pulled the carriage over to the side of the street.

"No, I'm f-fine. You don't have to stop. It's not you."

He put the brake on and then pulled her close. As she cried, he shushed her apologies and kissed her head. She clutched at the front of his suit and drew strength from his calmness and compassion. When she'd regained her composure, he produced a handkerchief before she could, and then drove on. Perfect. The man was perfect.

<u>Chapter Thirty-One</u>

Friday, July 27

The knock on the door was light, as she'd instructed it to be. Lillian, painting on her easel, finished the brush strokes on the petal of the flower before responding. "Yes?"

Sophie, her maid, opened the door. "There are policeman here," she said with apprehension in her tone.

Lillian looked at her with alarm. "Why?"

"I don't know. They asked to speak with you."

Lillian put her brush in the jar and reached around to untie her smock. "I'll be there presently."

"Yes, ma'am. I ... I didn't show them into the parlor yet."

"Well, do it," Lillian snapped. "Offer them something to drink. Treat them as guests, for goodness' sake."

Sophie nodded and started off, but then turned back. "One of them has a bag with him," she said worriedly.

"A bag?"

"Yes, ma'am. With something in it. It seemed strange."

"Go," Lillian said, waving a hand impatiently. She watched the maid scurry off and then she walked over to the wall mirror to check her appearance. Policemen made her nervous, but she needed to appear perfectly composed. And why shouldn't she be? Their business was probably nothing more than a robbery at a neighboring home. Stepping back, she took a deep breath to steady her nerves. She looked back at the painting she was working on. She didn't have a particular talent for it, but she enjoyed it. It was one of her daily diversions and she'd earned it.

172

She had earned her life of ease, and no policeman would make her feel otherwise.

She reached the front parlor where the men, two of them, were still standing. One was tall and remarkably handsome and held a satchel in hand. The other was more ordinary looking with a neat mustache. She would not have pegged either of them for policemen. "I'm Mrs. Holmes. You asked to see me?"

"Yes. I'm Lieutenant Ketler," the man with the mustache said. "And this is Detective Kassel."

"Gentlemen," she said with a tip of her head. "Why have the police come calling at my home?"

"We need to have a conversation, Mrs. Holmes," the handsome one spoke up. Kassel.

Her stomach tightened. "About?"

"About the death of your husband," Kassel replied with what seemed like empathy.

She clutched her hands together below her breasts. "Why? Why now?"

"Some things have come to light," Kassel said. "May we sit?"

"Of course. I instructed for you to be made comfortable."

"Your maid offered," Ketler said quickly.

Lillian moved to a chair and sat, and the men sat facing her.

"We're sorry to distress you," Ketler continued. "But the matter is of great importance."

"What matter? My husband's death was a tragedy, but there is no changing it. He's resting in peace."

Kassel reached into the bag at his feet and pulled out an ornate, oval-shaped silver tray. "Do you recognize this?"

Her eyes widened. "Where did you get that?"

"I'll take that as a yes," he said. He set it beside him on the davenport and reached into the bag again. This time he pulled out a delicate Fabergé egg. "And this?"

She blinked in astonishment. They were her things that had gone missing. She'd searched every conceivable place in the house for them. "Yes. Those are mine," she stated.

"We thought so. The tray is engraved. That's how we traced it here."

"Traced it?" she asked tensely. "From where?"

"These items and more may have been sold to a man who is what we call a fence," Kassel said. "Do you know what that is?"

She hesitated, wondering whether to proclaim ignorance. Of course, she knew what a fence was, but would a properly raised lady know the term?

Kassel didn't wait for her to decide. "It's someone who willingly buys stolen merchandise to resell."

"So someone stole them," she said.

Kassel didn't reply.

She looked from one to the other as a curious dread took hold. "It has to be that, because they were here and now you have them. What else could it be? The thief must have been one of the staff I let go. I don't know precisely when my things went missing, but it seems to me it was about that same time."

"It wasn't a former member of the staff," Kassel stated with a shake of his head.

"Then you know who it was?"

"We know who had them. Yes. Does the name Gullen mean anything to you? Wild Bill Gullen. Does that sound familiar?"

"Of course not. Why would it? What would I know about such a man?"

"What would be your reaction to the man claiming these items and more, along with cash were paid to him to do a job?"

She felt her skin flush. Did she look guilty? "That is absurd! What job? Who would have hired him? For what purpose?"

"I'm very sorry to say it, but … to kill your husband."

Her jaw dropped. She shut it and looked away feeling nauseated. "Obviously, that is a lie," she uttered breathily. She looked at him again. "A deplorable lie."

Kassel cocked his head. "Why is that obvious, Mrs. Holmes?"

He'd asked it so earnestly, she was taken aback. "My husband and I were attacked in the park." She was so tense, her

174

jaw was stiff. "It was a mugging. The man wanted our valuables and my husband resisted."

"That was what we initially believed," Ketler said.

"However," Kassel interjected, "—this man's account is quite different. He claims he was hired to kill your husband and wound you, but only slightly."

She felt tingly and ill. Tears sprang to her eyes and they weren't feigned. "This is outrageous!"

Kassel looked burdened. "Of course, it is upsetting. Do you need a glass of water?"

She glared at him. "No."

"We do not have all the answers yet," the man continued, "but we will in time. What we do have is a sketch of the man who, I believe, hired the thug who attacked you and your husband."

She felt dizzy and strange.

"Ma'am," Ketler spoke up. "None of this has been or can be made public at this point as it is an active investigation. In fact, think of all that we say here today as mere speculation. We simply need to know your thoughts and to get your help, if possible."

She couldn't move, not even to nod her understanding. She watched as Detective Kassel reached into his inside jacket pocket and offered her a folded piece of paper. She took it with trembling fingers.

"Open it when you're ready," Kassel said.

There was no choice. They were waiting for her, so she opened the paper to see a crudely drawn but undeniable sketch of Blake. She couldn't breathe.

"Do you know him?" Ketler asked.

She had no idea what to say. "I—"

"Before you answer," Kassel spoke up, "you should know two things. The first is that we already know the answer to most questions we are asking. Secondly, whether it's true or not, the man in that sketch believes he is in cahoots with you."

She huffed, dumbfounded by the allegation. Had Blake really and truly been so damnably foolish and reckless as to use items from her home to pay the brute that had attacked them? And he had bandied her name about? Claimed they were in cahoots? She felt an unpleasant trickling of perspiration from an armpit and swallowed convulsively.

"That man is Blakely Heyer," Kassel continued. "He's a crooked attorney who was disbarred in New York before moving here."

Oh, my God. They knew. She felt shamed by the words and her association with Blake.

"Approximately the same time you did," Kassel added meaningfully.

God help her! They were watching her. Judging her. "I don't know what you think you've discovered—"

"Speaking only for myself," Kassel said. "I believe Blakely Heyer hired the man who killed your husband. My question is, were you part of it?"

"How dare you!" She rose and walked around her chair, gripping the back of it for support. She felt feverish and chilled at the same time. She felt sick to her stomach. *Murder.* They were calmly discussing Gerald's murder and asking if she'd helped plot it.

"It's not so difficult a leap, Mrs. Holmes," Kassel continued. "You know Blakely Heyer. Intimately, by the looks of his comings and goings from this house. If we are able to prove he hired the killer and if you knew what he was planning or if you planned it together—"

"I didn't have anything to do with it!"

"Do you have any explanation for these items?" Kassel asked, gesturing to the tray and egg.

"No! I knew they were missing. That is all."

Kassel studied her. "It is troubling that you and Mr. Heyer knew each other in New York. You had a relationship there."

He was saying it so casually as if he knew it to be fact. Did he? Could she deny it? But they knew about the forgery and the disbarment. If she denied it and they knew otherwise, she'd lose whatever credibility she had. And they were talking about murder. Gerald's murder.

"And came to this city near the same time. Your affair with Mr. Heyer continued even after your marriage. You will admit to that much," Kassel said more as statement than question.

"Yes, I knew Blakely Heyer." Speaking had suddenly become ridiculously difficult. "And cared about him."

"In New York, you mean?"

"Yes. And I did see him a time or two when my husband was still alive, but not to have an affair. I told him our relationship was at an end. That is why I saw him. It was the only reason."

"You saw him in this house when your husband was out," Ketler said. "Is that correct?"

She hesitated. "Yes."

"It's not that we wish to belabor the matter," Ketler said. "Or to have you give voice to sordid details, but we need the facts to decipher the truth."

She nodded, or tried to, but the muscles in her neck were so tight that her head had begun pounding from the tension.

"You had a stage career in New York," Kassel interjected.

So they were truly found out. Both of them. Him disbarred, her a second-rate actress.

"How long and how well did you know Blakely Heyer in New York?" Ketler asked.

She pressed a hand to her stomach. "Five years, but there was nothing sordid about it. Neither of us was married. I thought I knew him better than I've known anyone," she said tiredly.

"Was it your plan to move here and make a life together?"

She started to answer, but hesitated. She walked back around and sat again. "It was something we thought about," she finally said. "But we both felt it was better to leave our pasts behind and start afresh. It was the best day of my life when I met Gerald. I loved him."

"But you still saw Blakely Heyer again," Ketler said.

"To discourage him," she exclaimed. "He had hopes of a continued alliance despite what we'd decided. I told him it was not possible. That I loved my husband."

"You'd swear to that?" Ketler asked.

There was a pause before she replied. "Yes." It was unhappily spoken.

Ketler nodded. "Was Mr. Heyer ever left alone in an area of your home where he might have picked up these items and carried them out?"

"Yes, I suppose. When I was being fetched. I would never have guessed he would do such a thing."

"I imagine not. He must have felt great passion for continuing your relationship."

She looked down at her hands and nodded. "He did."

"But you told him it was over?"

She looked at him, her eyes wide and beseeching. "Yes. On my life! I did."

"After the death of your husband, how did the relationship begin again?"

She sighed. "Blake was persistent. He cared about me, and I was lonely and frightened. I was injured in the attack, as well, you know."

"Did you know he was married?"

"No. Not at first."

"Mrs. Holmes," Kassel spoke up. "I want you to take a few moments and think, really think, about what I'm about to ask you before answering." He paused. "After considering everything we've just shared, do you think it's possible that Blakely Heyer hired the man who murdered your husband?"

She crossed her arms, grabbing hold of her shoulders and looked away. "The suggestion is so shocking," she said breathily.

"I know it is. And yet it needs an answer."

She nodded but didn't meet his gaze.

"Is that a yes, Mrs. Holmes?"

A tear slowly streaked down her face. "Yes."

"At what point did he admit what he'd done?" Kassel asked.

She looked at him again and noticed his gaze had sharpened. He believed she was guilty. The thought shook her and she swallowed convulsively again. "He didn't!" She released a shaky breath. "N-not per se."

"Not per se," he repeated. "Are you saying he alluded to it rather than state it? Is that what you're saying?"

"I didn't realize it then," she replied weakly. "It's only hearing all this that it becomes clear."

"What did he say that may have been alluding to it?"

"That he had arranged for us to be together," she replied tonelessly.

Several seconds of silence elapsed. "Arranged it," Kassel said. "I see. Anything else?"

She shook her head.

"What did you think he meant by that?"

"That he was leaving his wife."

"When did he say it?"

"I … don't recall exactly."

"Before or after the attack at the park?"

She huffed at the implied insult. The trick. "After!"

"What we will need from you," Ketler spoke up. "Is a written statement. Keep everything you write to the facts you know. Start by briefly describing your relationship in New York and then tell what occurred after moving here."

She wiped her face and looked at him. "Will that provide protection for me?"

"Providing you are truthful, I believe we can assure you that you won't be arrested for complicity in the murder of your husband."

The words were chilling. "I was not complicit!"

"Then we won't find proof that you were. Mrs. Holmes, we believe Blakely Heyer to be a highly dangerous man. The more you can tell us about what he's shared of his actions, the safer you will be. Not only did he hire the thug who killed your husband, he had his wife locked away in an asylum to get control of her fortune."

She tried to look impassive.

"But you already knew that," Ketler observed.

"I had no part of it," she declared.

"That should be in your statement," Ketler said. "Try and remember exactly what he said and when he said it. Dates are important."

She felt cornered and claustrophobic. She glanced at the door, wondering if the servants had been listening. "Do you need this statement today?"

"We do," Ketler replied. "We can allow you a short while of privacy to write it or we can take you to the station and provide a secluded area if you prefer."

The police station? Were they threatening her? It felt as though everything had slipped from her control. "How do I know you won't bring charges against me?"

"As you write your statement, I'll write one for you to keep," Ketler replied. "The same one I just conveyed. If you will provide some paper and a pen?"

"I am innocent," she cried.

"And you will establish that in your statement, will you not?"

She rose with all the dignity she could muster and left the room.

Forty-five minutes later, as Kassel drove away from the home, Ketler reread her statement. "You were right," he said. "It still doesn't make the way we went about it right."

Tom understood Cass's position. He just didn't care. He wanted justice. Of course, at this point, it was all still a chess game. They didn't actually have the killer in custody, so they couldn't really check, much less check mate. All they had done was make a move, which Lillian had considered before making her move. If she had been a full partner in the planning of events, as he suspected, she would be skating away without much punishment. That thought left him cold, but they needed to take things one step at a time. One move at a time.

The good news was that, armed with Lillian's statement, they could strong arm Heyer into accepting a divorce. Louisa would be able to reclaim her life, her home and possessions. It wasn't justice for Gerald Holmes or a fitting punishment for Heyer's betrayal of his wife, but it was something.

"So what's next?" Cass asked.

It was a good question. "Maybe we give Heyer a peek at our hand. But only enough that he only catches a glimpse of an ace or two."

Cass grunted. "He won't be the type to crumble."

"No," Tom agreed. "He won't. We could bring Cecil into it. Have him send a message to Heyer asking to meet in regards to his wife. Cecil could have documents all drawn up for the divorce." He glanced at Cass. "I'm not naïve. I realize I have to think in terms of what can actually be achieved. Can the man be hanged for murder based on what we've got? No."

Cass shook his head. "We can't even explain how we got Mrs. Holmes to give this information."

"But do we need to? When you look at everything, you can tell he's got blood on his hands."

"But can it be proved beyond reasonable doubt?" Cass challenged.

"I don't have reasonable doubt," Tom replied.

"You're a cop," Cass rejoined. "At least, you have the mind of a cop. Speaking of which, have I mentioned I think you should come back to it?"

"Really?" Tom asked with wide-eyed innocence. "I don't think you had mentioned it."

Cass gave him a look. "Trust me when I advise you against pursuing the stage."

Tom's face fell. "Damn. It's always been a dream of mine, you know."

Chapter Thirty-Two

Monday, July 30

William was on a platform eight feet in the air, hunched over while welding a nozzle on a pressure vessel. He was dripping sweat and beginning to shake. He was fixated on finishing his task to the point of having pushed beyond his physical limits.

When he pulled back because of dizziness, he saw stars. He cursed his stubbornness and set down his tools before sitting heavily. That wasn't enough. He felt sick. He was close to passing out and so he collapsed onto his back, breathing shallowly. When the worst of the spell passed, he turned his head. That was when he noticed the parade.

No, not *parade*. Parades were about celebration. This was something else. Another P word. Procession? No, not that. He couldn't think of the right word. He couldn't think clearly. Even his hearing was skewed. The faces of the men that passed were darkened with concern. Many of them were talking, but there was a roar in his ears that prevented him hearing what they said. Some sort of mishap had occurred; that much was apparent. He didn't have the strength to sit up and so he just lay there and watched. A word filtered through here and there and began to form a picture of what had transpired. Words like boy and vat. Fell into a vat.

"Boiled alive?"

"Couldn't get to him."

It didn't take long to understand the sickening tragedy that had occurred. Huge vats of water were used to cool just-formed metal, and they quickly grew boiling hot with use. Hot enough to cook a human being who had the grave misfortune to fall in.

William sighed heavily and covered his face in the crook of his arm.

The plant closed down operations for the day. By the time workers soberly filed out, many with hats in hand, William knew it had been an eleven-year-old boy by the name of Travis Eaton who'd perished. Another man's hands were scalded from trying to save him. All anyone could do was hope that young Eaton's death had come quickly.

Policemen were talking to workers and taking notes for an official report. William avoided looking at any of them, but he accidentally caught the eye of one and he thought the man gave him a strange look. William dropped his gaze and kept walking, but his heart thudded. Had Heyer, that lying devil, made a report on him after all? It was a relief when the cop didn't follow him or call out for him to stop.

<u>Chapter Thirty-Three</u>

Tuesday, July 31

Two days, Blake thought bitterly. He'd wasted two days trying to get Viola Ripley alone. He'd seen her go into the hospital, but she hadn't exited the same way. He needed to confront her privately, but she was always with others. There was no point in making a scene when she would only deny knowledge about what had happened to Louisa as she'd obviously done with the police. No, he had to get her alone to get the truth. He had a small pistol called a Philadelphia Deringer in his pocket for persuasion. He had located and taken it from Lillian's without her knowledge.

As a doctor, Viola Ripley would well know the damage a pistol could do and she would give him the information he sought. *Or I will shoot you,* he would threaten. Later, if she made a report with the police, he would deny it, just as she had denied snatching Louisa. He would get away with it, too, because he didn't own a gun and no one could prove he had one.

He had certainly not wanted to waste his time like this. He'd even gone so far as to hire a private investigator he'd seen advertised in the Public Ledger. The man, whose name was Wolfe, had seemed confident he could locate Louisa's whereabouts after hearing the situation. Blakely's intention had been to leave it for Wolfe, but Louisa had to be found or everything he'd worked for would be ruined. How could he sit around and do nothing when the key was Viola Ripley? Damn her and her meddling.

Today, he'd kept watch on her from within the hospital, keeping a newspaper in hand and hiding behind it when necessary. She'd been on duty before he arrived in the morning. She'd taken a break for luncheon in a small cafeteria on the main floor and then she'd gone back to work, spending a good deal of time on the second-floor maternity ward, especially in Room 219.

There were waiting areas on either end of the second floor, so he was in a position to keep an eye on her without anyone catching on. Finally, at half past four, she left for the day. He followed, keeping enough distance that she wouldn't notice. She had been busy and engrossed in her work all day, but she might be more apt to notice him now.

After a few blocks, it was clear that her intention was to walk rather than take a cab. That was a relief since his biggest concern had been that she would get away and he wouldn't be able to follow quickly enough. He trailed her another block and then another. The late afternoon was muggy and still. The sun had not relinquished any of its punishing power. The brim of his hat kept his face shaded, but heat penetrated his jacket and sweat trickled down his back.

She turned in at a sidewalk, so he picked up speed. She was going toward a house. She started up the steps. He broke into a run to reach her, pulling out the gun from his pocket, but she'd already put her key in the lock. She was opening the door. He reached out, grabbed her, whirled her around to face him and stuck the gun to her side. "Don't make a sound," he whispered harshly.

She'd frozen in fear so he forced her back in motion. He led her back down the two steps and around to the side of the house, keeping an eye out for nosy neighbors. He pushed her between tall hedges and pressed her against the house. "Where is my wife?"

She shook her head. "I—"

She was trying to think of a lie; he could tell. "You had her taken. You were there that night. Where is she?"

185

"I saw her, it's true," she replied shakily. "She was distraught. I told her I would try to think of something. That I would speak with you again."

"You're lying!" He lifted the gun toward her head. "If you think I won't use—"

The gunfire startled him. The noise. The shock on her face. She grabbed her throat and dark blood seeped between her fingers. He stepped back gawking, his heart pounding painfully. He hadn't meant to pull the trigger! He looked around and then back at her as she slid to the ground. *Oh, God.* He stuck the gun in his pocket with a badly shaking hand and hurried away. A few people had appeared and were looking around after hearing the shot. He tried to look calm. He couldn't bolt despite a desperate urge to do just that. He tugged his hat down and kept walking.

Gretchen, one of Mrs. Wolsey's boarders, was coming down the stairs for supper when she heard the shot. She stopped abruptly because it sounded so close. She heard footsteps and both Mrs. Wolsey and Tally hurried into the foyer and looked up at her.

"What was that?" Mrs. Wolsey asked.

Gretchen shook her head. "I don't know."

Tally pulled the front door open and blinked in surprise at the set of keys that dangled in the lock. "They're Vi's," she exclaimed. She quickly stepped out and looked around before coming back. "Did you see her come in?" she asked Gretchen.

"No," Gretchen replied. She turned to look upstairs. "Vi?" she called urgently.

Colleen Wolsey went to check the lavatory while Tally went back outside, baffled. She hurried down the porch steps to the sidewalk looking out at the street in both directions. There were others looking around, as well. Mrs. Burrow was coming from across the street. "Where did it come from?" Tally called.

"I don't know," Mrs. Burrow called back.

Turning toward home again, Tally saw Vi at the edge of the house, leaning heavily against it. Vi's face was stark white and she was clutching at a bleeding wound in her neck. Tally cried out and ran for her, calling to Gretchen that she needed her bag.

Gretchen, standing on the porch, spotted Vi and rushed back inside.

"What is it?" Mrs. Wolsey called as she came toward the door again.

"It's Vi," Gretchen exclaimed as she bounded up the stairs. "I think she was shot!"

The stunned older woman pressed a hand to her chest and rushed out. At the corner of the house, Tally had knelt and was holding Vi. Colleen cried out to see that Vi was dead. The left side of her blouse was covered in blood. Her face was white and still. Tally's hand was pressed against the left side of Vi's throat and she looked frantic.

"The bullet didn't hit a main artery or she'd be dead by now," Tally said.

Colleen Wolsey's eyes filled. Surely, Tally realized Vi was gone.

"I need to cauterize it," Tally continued. "And we need to get her to the hospital."

Colleen was about to speak when Vi moaned. It startled her enough that she jumped. "Oh! Thank God!"

Gretchen came running with the bag and put it at Tally's side, her gaze riveted on Vi. "What can I do?"

Tally lifted her hand and saw the blood flow was slight. "I need clean rags and the bottle of carbolic," she said, putting her hand back to keep pressure on the wound.

Gretchen handed her a clean rag. "Is this the—" she began, holding up a small, dark bottle.

Tally nodded. "Pour some on the rag. We need to get her to the hospital."

"Yes," Colleen said. "I'll get Mr. Mitchell." She started for the house next door.

Tally pressed the carbolic doused rag to Vi's neck.

187

"Who would have done this?" Gretchen cried.

Tally shook her head. "Can you go for the police?"

"Of course. Even if I can't get a cab, I can make it there on foot."

"Tell them I'm taking her to the hospital and ask if they'll let Cecil Lawrence know."

"On Willow Street, isn't it?"

"Yes."

Gretchen squatted to lay a hand on Vi's arm. "We love you, Vi."

As Gretchen hurried away, Tally lifted the rag again. The wound was barely bleeding so she wouldn't need to cauterize it after all. The bullet had seared the left side of Vi's throat, missing a major artery. An inch over and she would be dead. She put the rag back, sat and cradled Vi in her arms. "You're going to be fine. You're going to be just fine. We're bookends, aren't we?" She felt tears threaten, but she would not allow herself to fall apart with Vi this vulnerable. "One short and one tall," she continued in a thick voice. "One sweet while the other won't take guff at all."

"Tally," Colleen called as she hurried back. She was panting, nearly done in by the short trek. "Mr. Mitchell and his son are coming."

Thank God!

Vi moaned. She was trying to surface from unconsciousness.

"Lay still," Tally insisted. "You were hurt, but we're taking you to the hospital. You're going to be fine."

Chapter Thirty-Four

The cab arrived at his office and Blakely paid the driver. He fervently hoped he would not see his landlord. He'd accidentally shot and killed the doctor, so it was time to run. Christ above! Would they suspect him? Had he been seen well enough that he could be identified? He had been in the hospital watching her, so it was possible.

There was a spattering of blood on his jacket. It wasn't obvious to look at, but he knew it. He smelled it. He kept trying to convince himself it was his imagination, but he *smelled* it. It accompanied a sour odor of perspiration and fueled a deep panic he was barely able to manage.

The front door of the office was unlocked. *Damn.* He opened the front door and heard voices, but they were not close. He started toward his office, not noticing the man sitting and waiting for him. Not until the man called his name. Blakely stopped and looked back at him. It took several seconds to recognize the private detective that he'd hired. "Yes, what is it?"

The man stood. "I found where your wife is staying," the man said quietly. He handed over a folded piece of paper. "This is the address. I followed the doctor as you suggested and she led me there last evening."

Blakely blinked in surprise and unfolded the paper. He was anxious to end the meeting before the detective noticed the blood on him. "Good," he said curtly. He couldn't add the man's name because it had escaped him for the moment. "Good day to you."

"And to you." The man started for the door.

"Wait," Blakely said. "Where is this?' he asked, holding up the paper. "Who is she with?"

189

"It's the residence of an old lady on a quiet street. I observed them on a back porch playing a board game. Your wife seems well enough from what I could see. The doctor must have determined the same thing because she didn't stay long."

"Last evening?"

"Yes. I came to tell you this morning, but you weren't here."

Because he'd been stalking the doctor for the very information he now held in his hand. The irony was bitter, but he tried to look impassive. He gestured the interview was over and went into his office. He shut the door behind him and leaned against it, clutching the paper. It was incredible, but everything might have just changed dramatically. If no one had seen him after the shooting, and if he could get control of Louisa again, he might be all right. He had to push on and get Louisa back.

Wolfe. That was the detective's name. How could he have forgotten? He walked over to sit for a few moments. His legs were weak and he was visibly trembling. "Collect your wits, man," he said under his breath.

He pulled the gun from his pocket and stared at it, amazed such a small thing could do such damage. If only he'd known Wolfe had been successful, he wouldn't have bothered with Viola Ripley, but it was a done thing now. Besides, she'd brought it upon herself meddling in his affairs. He allowed himself a single sigh of regret and then he pulled his desk drawer open, retrieved another bullet and reloaded the gun. He had no intention of shooting Louisa or the lady she was staying with, but he had to have a means of persuasion if he needed it.

Louisa, Dorothy and Betty were on the back porch playing a board game called Halma. They'd had a light, early supper and they were enjoying the game and chilled peach cider. The block of ice in the ice box had been replenished earlier that day.

"There and there and there," Dorothy gloated as she advanced by jumping Louisa's pieces.

190

"I told you she was good at this," Betty said.

"Years of practice," Dorothy replied gleefully. "And a killer instinct."

The three of them had spent many pleasant hours on the shaded back porch, playing games and talking. An easy camaraderie had bloomed into a bonding of friendship, especially between Louisa and Betty who were close to the same age.

Betty shook and then rolled the dice, Dorothy finished her cider and poured more, and Louisa looked up at the leaves fluttering in a breeze. Her strength was not yet fully restored, but she'd gotten herself from place to place for the last several days with no assistance and her diction was finally as clear as her mind.

"Oh now," Dorothy said scoldingly. "See, what you should have done—"

Betty laughed. "Let me play my game."

"Honey, I'm trying to pass on some of my killer instinct so you can win every once in a while."

"I know, but—"

"Either you have it or you don't? Is that it?"

"I don't know about that," Louisa rejoined playfully as she shook the dice and rolled. "I plan on developing some. Feel free to teach me all you know, Dorothy."

"That's my girl," Dorothy delighted, lifting her glass to her. "Try and rub off on this one, will you?"

<u>Chapter Thirty-Five</u>

Blakely left the office and began walking while keeping an eye out for a cab. He thought he saw one coming and stuck a hand up but lowered it when he saw it was Lillian in her two-seater carriage. They had not planned to meet, nor could he be bothered at the moment. Not when he had to get Louisa back. "Why are you here?" he asked when she'd pulled over.

"I have to talk to you," she said urgently.

She didn't look well, which wasn't like her. She looked tired and disheveled by more than the wind. He climbed in. "What's wrong?"

"We'll talk as we drive. Are you going home?"

"No. I have something to take care of. Tell me what's wrong."

Tears welled in her eyes and she emitted a shaky breath. "Oh, Blake. I thought I'd know how to say this, but—"

"What is it, for God's sake? You don't look well."

"I didn't sleep again. I haven't slept."

"Why?"

She shook her head slowly. "It's over. They know."

Was she trying to drive him mad? "Who knows what?" She looked away and he sensed something from her that made his arm hair stand on end. Some sort of guilt and remorse. He started to ask what it was about but, on second thought, he didn't want to know. He just wanted everything to be right again. "Listen to me. I have learned where Louisa is," he said, struggling to remain calm. "I'm going to go get her. I'm going to make everything right."

She looked back at him with an expression of defeat. "It's too late."

"It is not too late."

"They know you hired the man who killed Gerald. They caught him."

His jaw dropped. He quickly shut it, but was too aghast to speak for the moment. She was talking nonsense and yet she seemed convinced of it. "What in blazes are you talking about? Who are you talking about? Talk plainly!"

"The police came to me."

"Wha— when?"

She hesitated. "A few days ago."

Then why didn't you come to me then? The question raged in his mind, but he shook his head, trying to clear his thoughts. He needed to focus. "What did they say? What exactly did they say?" he demanded angrily.

"I told you! They caught the man who killed Gerald. He confessed and said that you hired him. Well, he didn't know your name, but he knew your face. He described you and an artist sketched your picture from the description. And the resemblance is undeniable."

He frowned in confusion. She was talking gobbledygook and declaring it truth.

"They were able to track him down from items stolen from my home," she added with a different note in her voice. A note of bitterness. "How could you be so careless and stupid? And not even tell me?"

"Tell you what? You're not making any sense!"

"How am I not making sense? I am telling you what they told me. And they had the items! Taken from my home. A Fabergé egg and a silver tray and more, hocked by the man who admitted to attacking us and killing Gerald. He told the police they were a partial payment for the deed."

Blake swallowed back the bile that rose in his throat. He felt dizzy and strange, as though he was trapped in a nightmare of absurdity guised as reality. "I don't know what you're talking about," he bit out. "I never saw any of those items and I certainly never took them. It's pure rubbish! The man who …did the deed," he added in a hushed voice, leaning toward her, "is dead."

She stared. It didn't look like she was breathing.

"He didn't say anything to anyone because he couldn't. I took care of him right afterwards when he came to collect the rest of his pay. Pay that I came up with!"

"But—"

"But nothing! It is all lies, Lillian. Did you really think I would be so careless in my dealings? After all our planning?"

She looked away, pale and visibly shaken. "You were careless before," she said. "In New York."

He experienced a pain in the pit of his stomach. It was fear with sharp teeth and tentacles. "What did you say when the police spun this fabricated tale?"

She shook her head and refused to look at him.

"Lillian!"

"I said I knew nothing of my things being taken," she replied. She was still not looking at him.

"Nor did I," he insisted, enunciating precisely. "Forget them. It was all hogwash to ferret what they think is the truth from you." She chanced a look at him and she looked full of remorse.

"They said they know you did it," she said shakily. "They said they have proof."

"Which. Was. A. Lie."

"But—"

He waited, but she seemed unable to say more.

"Did you tell them anything?" he whispered harshly, getting to the heart of his fear.

She cringed and looked away.

He felt sick. Sick enough that he might well heave whatever he had in his stomach. "What?"

"They knew about us. Our past. Our affair."

"Affair." The word stung. "Is that what you call it?"

She looked at him with a flare of anger. "It's what they called it."

He faced forward. He wasn't thinking quite clearly, but damage had been done that needed to be undone. Damn it, they needed to move. He needed air in his face in order to think. "Drive."

She didn't move.

"I said drive! I need the air."

She glanced behind her, flicked the reins and got them moving.

"I need to hear it," he said. "Every sodding word that was said. Start to finish."

"You can't be angry with me," she wheedled.

"Oh, really?"

"Blake, they knew everything!"

"They knew nothing. It was a fishing expedition. Can't you see that? I don't care what *they* said or thought. They could not, cannot, prove anything, unless you handed it to them. Are you hearing me? Unless you bloody, fucking handed it to them!" It was time for her to speak, but now she said nothing. "Tell me!"

"I wrote a statement. They made me. I'm sorry, but it was the only way to protect myself."

It felt as if his eyes were bulging from their sockets. "What exactly did you say in this statement?"

"I only confirmed what they already knew. And I said I hadn't helped plan the attack on Gerald."

Oh God! "You told them that …I did?"

"No! Not … exactly. I said I didn't know." She paused before adding. "But that you …might have. That it was possible."

His mind raced. If that truly was all she said, it was damnable and he was furious with her, but it was not proof. "Is that all?"

She hesitated, but then nodded.

She was lying. He could see it. Feel it. She was lying. He had to have the whole truth in order to deal with it. They were coming up on Creedmore Park. "Pull in," he said, gesturing to the entrance. "Find some shade and let us determine a way forward out of this jam you've caused."

"I didn't cause it," she retorted.

"Lil, please!"

She huffed, but pulled in the entrance and drove through the parkway until she found a secluded spot to park. Once there, she turned to him. "We've always found a way around everything, haven't we?"

It was true. They'd met and fallen in love and schemed their way here. They'd known that they could have the good life if they were cunning and daring. They had nearly accomplished it, too. "That's been true until now."

"The tables have turned on us," she acknowledged. "But it doesn't mean they'll stay that way. For now, you need to go. Get clear of here and lay low for a time."

"Why would I do that? Because some cop somewhere has too much time on his hands and got it into his head that I had your husband killed?"

"You did," she said just above a whisper.

"*We* did," he corrected. "But they don't know that. Not really."

"Blake," she pleaded. "They do."

"No. They think they know. They are playing games to find out, but I play better. I play to win. I would have thought you'd know that." He paused to let her wallow in her well-deserved guilt a moment. "They have no proof, Lillian. None. I took care of it. And now that I know where Louisa is, I can go collect her and get her under control again. I can learn from my mistakes. This time I will gain control of the estate. We won't have everything we should have since we won't have your husband's fortune. Which you should have told me," he added nastily.

"Blake, I always know when something important is about to happen. Good or bad. This time, it's bad. It's very bad. We have to get in front of it or everything we've worked for will be destroyed. And I mean everything. Please. Please! Forget Louisa for now. Just go. Leave tonight. Protect me. For now." Her gaze roamed his face as if she were trying to memorize it. "In time, we'll find a way around this mess."

He took hold of her hand and looked searchingly into her eyes. "What else did you tell them?" he asked quietly. "I have to know the worst of it."

She dropped her gaze and tears rolled down her face.

"Darling, I have to know. If I have to run, I will, but—"

"That you admitted it," she said in a whisper.

The words were a shock. So much so that he didn't believe his own ears for several seconds. But she hadn't stuttered. He exhaled long and hard, deflating with it. She'd ruined him. She'd ruined everything. "You told them that I admitted having your husband killed?" The words had come out haltingly.

She looked desperately sorry. "I thought," she sobbed, "that you took those things. I thought they'd caught you because of it."

"No," he replied with a sad, calm resolve. "I didn't. I've only ever taken one thing from you."

"Yes. My heart. And you still have it!"

He laughed derisively and let go of her hand. "Item, I mean. I only ever removed one item from your home without your knowledge."

She wiped her tears away, confused. "What?" she asked as if she hadn't heard him.

"It was only to borrow," he continued, reaching into his pocket. "Not to use, just to have." He pulled out the pistol and enjoyed her reaction of shock and alarm. Had he shocked her as badly as she had shocked him? "For a show of force," he said. "Unfortunately, as it turns out, I had to use it." Her tears had stopped. Had they only been an act?

"What do you mean?" she asked breathlessly.

"That lady doctor who caused me such trouble? I shot her. Her body is not even cold yet."

A noisy breath escaped her.

"I didn't mean to, but I did it. And now I learn of your betrayal." It was queer how calm he felt. He was trapped in a nightmare that had become real. The world was standing on its ear.

She shook her head. "It wasn't a betrayal. They just …they took me by surprise, but we can get out of this. I'll tell them I made it up. Because they frightened me."

He studied her flushed face. She was lying again. She was afraid of him.

"I will," she squeaked. "I didn't understand before. I didn't know it was a fishing expedition. They behaved as if they knew everything. They pretended to care about my protection."

"Ah. Your protection. From the murdering Blakely Heyer."

"We can get past this," she pleaded. "We can even make them at fault. Or we can j-just go. Run. The two of us. Go to Italy like you wanted."

"So now you want to go abroad," he said, his voice dripping with sarcasm.

She began crying again and it wasn't pretty. Or believable. "Why are you being like this?"

"Being like what?"

"Mean!"

"I'm being mean?" He was enjoying the supremely bad playacting. It was playacting on both their parts. He just hadn't seen it before. He'd had a bad feeling lately, but he hadn't admitted how false she was. They'd loved each other once, but not for a while now. In this strange, dead calmness, he saw it clearly.

"Please give me the gun," she said, holding out her hand.

Her hand was trembling and he sobered to see her distress. He sighed as he put the pistol into her hand. She went to pull it to her, but he hadn't released it. When he pulled the trigger, the bullet entered her left breast. She made a choking sound and stared at him in surprise. It was bizarre and surreal because everything had slowed. He felt so odd. "We could have had it all," he said in a strained voice.

"*Guh—*"

Blood was flowering on her chest. It was a growing red flower on her pale pink bodice. He set the gun in her lap at what seemed the correct angle if she'd shot herself. "But guilt got to you," he continued. "Perhaps over our affair. Or perhaps it was missing your husband. That's what they'll speculate." Lillian looked upward toward heaven, although he doubted a place waited for her there. Or for him either for that matter.

He climbed from the carriage and looked around, grateful for the coverage of trees and that there was no one in sight. As he began walking, reality descended. He'd killed Lillian. She had been a partner in his life for so many years, but she had abandoned him to save her own hide, and then she'd had the gall to suggest that he flee in order to protect her. She had betrayed him first. "You led this dance, my love," he muttered. "You."

As he walked, bits of memories besieged him. Unexpected flashes of Lillian in younger years. In his darkest misery, she'd been his rock. When he learned that old man Hammond had recovered and learned of the forged signature on his will, he'd been physically ill. He'd rushed to her and she had calmly stroked his head on her lap and talked soothingly of them getting beyond the patch of mess. That's what she'd called it, a patch of mess. At the time, he'd imagined a rambling garden with a patch of mess that they would carefully skirt to get to the other side.

This city of brotherly love was supposed to have been the other side. The start to a life of ease. They had decided that they would use their good looks, brains and charm to marry into wealth before ridding themselves of the spouses by whatever means were necessary. Afterwards, they would enjoy the spoils of victory. He had imagined them going to a quaint villa in Tuscany. As a boy, he'd read a novel in which a man and woman had fallen in love, escaped terrible misadventure and ultimately begun a new life there. He didn't remember the story except for that, but it was enough to have become his own imagined happily ever after. It didn't matter now. The fantasy was destroyed. Was he also destroyed? He glanced down at his jacket, wondering if he had blood from both women on him. There may have been a spot here and there, but it wasn't noticeable. Not really. Although he could smell it.

Stop it! Breathe deeply, think clearly.

Chances were good, that no one had seen him with Viola Ripley, and Lillian had been killed with her own gun in her own carriage by her own hand. That's what it would look like. No one had seen him with her, no one that could identify him. Two women were dead by his hand and it was likely he was in the clear. It was nearly miraculous, as if he was supposed to get away with it. Perhaps it was because he was supposed to have a new start with Louisa.

The thought surprised him, but it made sense. If he could get her to forgive him, they could continue on and work toward a good and happy marriage. This time, he would try. He simply needed to convince her that putting her in the asylum had been for her protection when he feared her state of mind had gotten the better of her. He would admit that he'd been misguided by a too-zealous physician. It was Backman who convinced him she needed a good, long rest.

He felt better now that he had a plan. He would go to Louisa and offer his deepest regrets. He would plead for her forgiveness, swear devotion and even mean it this time. He could and would reform. He would be the best husband any lady ever had. However, if she could not forgive his mistake and wanted to be rid of him, he would allow it and even arrange for a divorce, as long as there was a fair settlement for him. He wouldn't be greedy. Ten thousand dollars would allow him to move away to another city and begin again with a whole new slate. Maybe San Francisco or Chicago. He saw a cab coming and hailed it.

Chapter Thirty-Six

Tom jotted a note in his pocket-sized notebook as he waited to see Cecil who was with a client. Cecil's clerk was an older man who seemed to distrust him, given the way he kept a disdainful eye on his every move. Occasionally, Tom would give the man a smile or a wink just to let him know he was aware of it, although it only served to make the old gent's gaze narrow with dislike. "Tell me, did I arrest you once, or something?" Tom finally asked.

The man huffed with offense.

"Flirt with your sister?"

The bell mounted on the door tinkled as it opened and a large boned lady of thirty or so stepped in breathing hard. It was apparent she was in emotional distress. "May I help you, Miss?" the clerk asked as he rose.

"Please, yes. Viola Ripley was shot," she stammered.

Tom jumped up and went to her alongside Cavanaugh. He'd just recalled the man's name. "Is she alive?" Tom asked breathlessly.

"Yes. Sh-she was. Tally's with her. Getting her to the hospital."

"When was this?" Tom asked. "Who did it?"

She shook her head. "We don't know who did it, but it happened outside the house. We heard it and then found her."

"She's at The Women's Hospital?"

"Yes."

Tom looked at Cavanaugh. "Let Cecil know right away. I'm going for the police."

"I did," the woman said. "I went there first."

"Good. That's good. Then I'll go to the hospital," Tom said to Cavanaugh, who nodded eagerly, his earlier animosity having evaporated in the angst of the moment.

"May I go with you?" the woman asked. "I took a cab here and I didn't have quite enough money, although the man was very understanding."

"Of course, you can."

"I'll let Mr. Lawrence know," Cavanaugh said. "My prayers are with Dr. Ripley."

Tom opened the door for the lady. "My gig's over here," he said as they walked. Neither of them spoke again until they were on their way. "I'm Tom Kassel."

"Gretchen Lloyd. I live at Mrs. Wolsey's, too."

"I gathered as much."

"How do you know Vi? Do you work with Mr. Lawrence?"

"We have been working on something, yes. That's how I met Vi. Where exactly was she shot?" he asked, gesturing to his body.

"The neck. The side of her neck," she replied in a choked voice, touching the side of her throat as she said it. "It looked very bad."

Tom frowned as he thought about it. Heyer knew about her, but did he know where she lived? Had he learned the address and gone there to learn the whereabouts of his wife? He had to know that Vi had been at the asylum the night Louisa vanished. He would have reasoned she was involved and knew where Louisa was staying.

"I was coming down for supper when I heard the shot," Gretchen said. She rubbed her arms. "Tally came running and we discovered Vi's keys hanging in the lock. We went outside, but didn't see anything at first because Vi was around the side of the house."

"The side of the house," Tom repeated as he pictured it.

Gretchen nodded. "Tally saw her. Vi was on her feet at that point, but she collapsed."

Keys in the door. Shot around the side of the house. Obviously, Vi had been about to walk inside when someone accosted her and forced her around to the side of the house. To get information? To exact revenge? Or both? It sounded like Heyer to him. He flicked the reins for more speed. "Get up!"

"She'd been so happy lately," Gretchen said brokenly. She pressed a hand to her mouth and began crying.

He wished Gretchen wouldn't speak in the past tense, but he just needed to get to the hospital and get the facts.

"I'm sorry," she said, fumbling for a handkerchief. She wiped her face. "I think it just hit me. I was so focused on telling the police and then getting to Mr. Lawrence."

"It's all right," he said gently. "Strong people don't fall apart in a crisis. It's only afterwards that it hits."

At the hospital, they were directed to Tally. She stood in a corridor, still and very pale. As Gretchen broke into a run to embrace her, Tom felt acute dread.

"She's all right," Tally said. She looked over and locked gazes with Tom. "She's all right."

"Thank God," Gretchen cried.

"It was a surface wound. I didn't think so at first, but when the bleeding stopped, I saw."

"You should sit down," Tom urged.

"Yes," Gretchen agreed. "You're frightfully pale."

Tally didn't resist being helped to a chair. Tom sat on one side of her, Gretchen on another. "Your hand is freezing," Gretchen said as she took hold of it. "Are you sure you're all right?"

"Yes," Tally said breathily.

"Is Vi awake?"

Tally nodded. "She was. Yes. They're cleaning her up. They made me leave the room when I ... apparently I swayed. They were afraid I would faint. I *never* faint," she added, directing it to Tom.

"No one would ever accuse you of being a damsel in distress," he said.

"But it was a terrible shock," Gretchen insisted. "And you were so strong taking care of her."

Tom wished Gretchen would show less anguish for Tally's sake. He put an arm on the back of Tally's chair and the tips of his fingers touched her shoulder. "Did she say what happened?"

Tally looked at him and nodded. "It was him. Heyer."

He leaned back feeling foolish and guilt-ridden that he had not considered the possibility and provided some sort of protection for her.

"I'm going to get you some tea," Gretchen said to Tally. She rose. "Mr. Kassel? Would you care for something?"

"No, but thank you, Miss Lloyd." She turned and left and Tom looked at Tally again. She was still trembling. It's true she wasn't a damsel in distress, but she wasn't quite as formidable as she thought either. "I should have anticipated it."

"Don't be ridiculous," she snapped. "Who could have anticipated such a hateful act?"

"Someone who's seen the worst of human nature. Far too much of it."

She grimaced. "I'm sorry. I know I've been rude to you and it's still my inclination, isn't it?"

"It hasn't caused any permanent wounds. Don't worry."

"That's good. Causing permanent wounds goes against my ethics."

"*Hmm.* I'll have to remember that and use it to my advantage."

"I imagine you use your every asset to your advantage," she said wryly.

"I try. There's my obvious charm, although it didn't work on you. There are the skills I learned on the police force—"

Confusion flickered on her face. "You were a policeman?"

204

He nodded. "Appointed by Mayor Stokley as a mere pup of twenty-two."

She considered a moment. "Why did you leave it?"

"Personal reasons."

"Unorthodox methods perhaps?"

"No. Believe it or not, I was orthodox as a cop."

She gave him a look. "Oh, really."

"It's true. And I didn't plan on leaving the force. But something happened and the investigation I got caught up in turned out to be bigger and uglier than I'd supposed. I couldn't let it go and it changed me." He watched a nurse hurry from one room to another. He looked back at Tally and saw she was watching him intently. She had green eyes with golden centers. He hadn't noticed that before. "When it was over, I couldn't go back to my old existence."

"I see," she said. "It fits somehow."

"Why *did* you take such an instant dislike to me?" he asked, purposely changing and lightening the subject. "I'm curious."

"You reminded me of someone."

"Someone you profoundly disliked," he surmised.

"No. Oh, no. I thought I would marry him."

"Ah."

"When I was young," she added. "Not even seventeen." She paused, thinking about it. "I suppose I did dislike him in the end when he decided he wanted an easy life with an obedient wife. But, to be fair, he did give me the opportunity to give up the preposterous notion of becoming a doctor and become the wife I was intended to be. I could doctor our children, he said." She paused. "If it counts for anything, I regretted being rude to you the night we met."

"Don't give it another thought. And if it counts for anything, I think your young man was a fool."

"No, he was right to choose as he did. He's contentedly married with five or six children. It's what he wanted and what she wanted, too. My father still refers to him as 'that man who should have been your husband.' Now *that* is irritating."

He grinned and noticed Gretchen coming back with a cup in hand. "Were the police here yet?" he asked Tally.

"Yes."

"Did Vi say anything other than it was Heyer?"

"Only that he wanted to know where Louisa was. She told him she didn't know. Then he shot her."

"She'll definitely recover?"

"Yes. It was a shock to her body and she's lost some blood, so she's weak, but she'll be fine."

Behind Gretchen was Cecil with a middle aged couple who looked stricken.

Tally drew in a sharp breath when she saw them. "That's Vi's parents."

Tom stood along with her, and Tally started forward to meet them. "She's going to be fine," she told them.

Mrs. Ripley reached for Tally's hands, but her gaze went to Tally's bloodstained blouse. "Is that true?" she asked worriedly, peering back into Tally's eyes.

"Yes. It was a flesh wound." She glanced at Mr. Ripley. "The side of her neck. They're bandaging her, but let me see if you can go in."

"Thank you, Tally," Mr. Ripley replied shakily.

Tally nodded. She glanced back at Tom with what looked like regret, and he nodded although he wasn't sure what he was communicating other than a newfound rapport between them. Cecil walked to him. "Heyer shot her," Tom said quietly.

"My God," Cecil breathed.

"He was looking for Louisa."

"Is she really all right?" Cecil worried.

Tom nodded. "Tally feels certain of it and she would know."

Cecil looked shaky. "Vi. Shot," he said under his breath. "I can't fully grasp it."

"I know. I'm going to go see what I can do to help apprehend Heyer. There is no way he is getting out of this."

"Let me know what you find out."

"I will." Tom braced his friend's arm and walked on.

Charity Cases

Chapter Thirty-Seven

Blakely took the cab to the address he'd been given, but instructed the driver to go another block. He climbed out, looking around. "I should be a quarter of an hour at most," he said as he paid the man.

"Can't wait more than that."

"I won't need you to. Just drive around the block a time or two."

The man drove off, and Blakely started to the house. It was dusk and shadows loomed like ghosts; or did he have ghosts on the brain after killing two women in one evening? He shivered with revulsion at the thought. What had transpired earlier was not something he wanted to think about ever again.

He made his way to the porch and tried the doorknob of the front door. Locked. He went around the house peering in windows for signs of activity. Light shone from a curtained front room to the far left and there was muted light from deeper within the house. Before he reached the back yard, he heard voices and stopped. His breath caught to hear Louisa's voice. She laughingly complained that she'd done it again. How bizarre to hear her! She sounded so normal.

"It's easy to get frustrated," another woman said.

His pulse accelerated as he edged closer, craning his neck to see the ladies through a row of hawthorn trees. He finally caught a glimpse of Louisa sitting and sewing. No, knitting. He couldn't see the other woman from his vantage point.

"I do look forward to giving it to them," Louisa said. "I've never been to an orphanage."

"We went with Aunt Dorothy every year. At least twice a year. She goes more often than that."

"Did she have children?" Louisa asked.

"Yes. A son. Allister. He died in the war in sixty-one. His very first battle."

"I'm sorry."

"I was only six, but I remember him well. He had such a wonderful personality. Like his mother. We adored him."

Blakely moved on, treading quietly. He found the back gate and opened it silently. There were only the two women, but he wanted the advantage of surprise. Fortunately, there were trees and large bushes in the yard. He simply had to segue between them discreetly.

"What was Dorothy's husband like?" Louisa asked.

"Oh, he was a good man. Quiet. You know what they say about opposites attracting. It was true in their case. I remember once—" The lady, he could see her now, gasped and froze when she saw him. Wolfe had said it was the house of an old woman, but she wasn't old. She wasn't even forty.

Louisa glanced at her and then looked at him.

"Please don't be frightened," he said to Louisa. "I would never hurt you. Not willingly." Neither woman said a word. They simply stared in dismay as he closed the distance between them. "I was misguided before," he continued. "I was wrong to allow you to be hospitalized. I'm so sorry for it, but you were so—" He looked at the other woman. "I was afraid she would harm herself." He looked at Louisa again. "The doctor convinced me that a thorough rest was best for you. But you won't go back there. I swear."

"What do you want?" Louisa asked in a steady voice. Anger was beginning to surface in her. It was another surprise since she had no temper that he had ever seen.

"I want to be the husband you deserve. I wasn't before, but I will be. Give me another chance and I will be. I swear it on my life."

"No. I do not care what you say. I do not believe you and I will not go anywhere with you," she said, drawing herself up. The knitting fell from her lap. "Now or ever."

"Please leave," the other lady said.

She also started to stand, but he put himself in motion and merely pointing his finger at her was enough to scare her back into her seat. Louisa was still standing and glaring at him. Somehow, her strength and resolve had grown. "I've told you the truth, Louisa. Only time will prove it, and that's fair, but I am still your husband and you are honor bound to obey me."

She huffed in disbelief. "Honor bound? *Honor*, you say!"

"Sir," the other woman began in a timorous voice. "If you do not leave—"

He looked at her. "What? You'll scream? Stab me with your knitting needle? I have a carriage and men waiting to help me if she resists. Scream if you wish, but it's pointless. They'll rush to my aid as I've instructed. We will get Louisa away from here before anything else can be done." He looked back at Louisa. "I would prefer for this not to get heated, but we are going. I am your husband and you must do as I say. Do you have any possessions here that you wish to take home?"

There were seconds of silence before, "Yes," she said tonelessly.

Good. It was good she realized she couldn't win against him. "Then let us go get them." He glanced at the other woman. "You first, madam. If you please."

She stood, looked at Louisa regretfully, and then led the way inside. The screen door screeched as it opened and it grated on his nerves. He'd feel better once they were clear of the place. Louisa followed the lady and he went third. "No one need get hurt this evening," he said as they made their way single file through a tidy kitchen. "I have no desire to pull the gun from my pocket," he said as they filed into a hall. "Just do what I say, collect your—"

"The problem is," a voice said from his left.

He turned to see an old woman with an antique pistol in both hands and leveled at his head. She was in the front parlor.

"Louisa is my guest and she leaves when she wants."

He hadn't expected anyone else to be there, which had been foolish of him. Wolfe had said an old woman lived there. "You should put that down before you hurt yourself," he said evenly.

"Hurt myself? With my little ole' Pepperbox pistol? Nah. It won't hurt me. It's been a good friend of mine for many a year. It's been much maligned, even by Mark Twain who is otherwise a favorite of mine, but personally speaking, I've never had a bit of problem hitting what I was aiming for." She smiled, but her eyes remained calculating. "You'll want to be getting those feet of yours in motion right about now. Front door is straight ahead."

She was a composed old bird, but her physical reactions would be far slower than his. "You're in the way of the door," he reasoned.

"Mister, I'm like the wind. I will blow back before you get here. Keeping my eyes on you, so you'd best not pull any funny business."

"I only came for my wife. I've been concerned about her."

She grunted. "You'll have to excuse me if I don't believe a word out of your mouth. Now, you were not invited here and I want you out, so move!"

He took a few steps toward her and she stepped back at a matching rate. Could he rush her? Get the gun from her? Her strength wouldn't match his. Speed was the key.

"Put your hands up," she ordered.

Damn it! He put his hands up. "Louisa, I was trying to do the right thing in following the doctor's orders," he said, not taking his eyes off the old lady. "You know I care for you."

"That's a lie," Louisa uttered.

"Move," the old woman ordered again. Her smile had vanished.

He looked at the gun and then at the old woman. He wasn't certain he could get it from her before she pulled the trigger. "This is not over."

"Out!"

He went to the door and unlocked it. He could feel the tension in the room and within himself. He opened the door and then looked at the old woman. She had him dead in her sights. "I can force her back. It's my right."

"Make me tell you again and I will shoot you in your man parts."

Damn the old biddy. He opened the door and stepped onto the front porch. The cab was not back yet. "My cab is not here."

"Keep walking and find one," the old woman said from only a few feet behind, having followed him. "And get your hands back up like the loathsome criminal you are."

The words were infuriating, but he felt the nudge of the muzzle at the back of his skull, and so his hands went up and his feet started back in motion. He would get Louisa another day. Maybe even tomorrow. He went down the steps to the short sidewalk and lowered his hands. It would prove to be his last conscious physical move since the old woman pulled the trigger and proved once more to be an accurate shot.

"Dorothy," Betty cried.

Dorothy watched the man's blood pool on her sidewalk. It looked black. She lowered her hands and turned to the pair behind her. "He wasn't going to stop."

"But," Betty said. "Oh, Aunt Dorothy. You shot him!"

"Think they'll arrest me?" She came closer and chucked Betty's chin. "I doubt it. But don't you worry about your old aunt." She started for the door. "I need a drink. A stiff one. You coming?"

Louisa and Betty clutched hands and stared at the lifeless body on the sidewalk. A cab stopped at the curb and the clearly aghast driver leaned over in his seat to be sure of what he was seeing before snapping the reins smartly and driving on.

Charity Cases

<u>Chapter Thirty-Eight</u>

Charity stood at the open French doors leading to the garden
with her hands supporting her protruding middle panting as
quietly as she could. The contraction finally let up, but it left her
shaken. Without question, labor was beginning. She'd been
having mild contractions since Sunday morning, which was the
reason they hadn't left for home yet. She had hoped they would
stop, but this was it. Behind her, her sister-in-law and nieces
were seated at a table chatting and writing thank you notes for
wedding gifts, oblivious to the discomfort she'd been in.
Thankfully, it had passed.

"Charity," Jack said as he came into the room with a brisk
step. Gregory was right behind him.

"What is it?" she asked, alarmed by their expressions.

"A messenger just came," Jack said. "Vi was—" He cleared
his throat and glanced at his wife and daughters, who had turned
their attention to him. "Apparently," he began again, "we're not
sure why or how exactly—"

"Someone shot Vi," Gregory said as he stepped past his
brother-in-law.

Alma gasped.

Charity cried out and bent forward as another contraction hit
with the force of a speeding train. Gregory braced her, and she
squeezed his arm as warm water gushed from her. It felt so
strange. She'd been lying in bed the first time she'd given birth
and her water had been broken to expedite the birth of the twins.
This felt entirely different.

"Oh, my God," Alexandra cried, jumping up. "Her water
broke!"

214

"Oh, not now," Alma complained. "There's still another reception!"

Eugenia gave her mother a look of dismay. "Mother!"

Gregory and Jack surrounded Charity. She could not fully stand up straight yet. When she could, they got her to her room and into bed. Vi and Tally were supposed to have been with her in the event of her going into labor while here, but Vi had been shot? What in the world? "Is she alive?" she bit out.

"Yes," Jack replied. He'd started from the room to see that a doctor was fetched but turned back at the door. "The injury was not life threatening. Don't worry. You just concentrate on having my new niece or nephew."

A pain seized hold and she grabbed a breath and squeezed her husband's hand. He watched worriedly, his jaw clenched. He hated not being in control. "Keep breathing," he said.

She nearly snapped, *You keep breathing!* but she took tight in and out breaths until the pain passed. "I didn't want to do this here," she said when it let up.

"I don't think he cares," he teased.

"I don't think *she* cares. Her name is Madeline."

"Madeline," he repeated thoughtfully. "I thought we could name him Garrett."

"It is a girl," she insisted. She grabbed a breath and then panted. "But if it is a boy," she said when the cramp eased, "Garrett is fine. We are going to run out of G names though, if that's your intention."

"Not for a while, yet. There's still George. Geoff. Geronimo."

She started to laugh and then made a face of pain. "Don't make me laugh!"

"Madeline," he said again, as if testing it out.

"Madeline Elizabeth. We'll call her Maddie."

"A girl," he mused. "A daughter."

"It's not that strange an idea, is it?"

He considered. "Ask me when she's handed to me."

"What happened to Vi?"

215

He stroked her hand. "We'll learn the whole story soon enough."

"But … shot."

"It's not life threatening. In the meantime, having a baby—"

"I'll be fine," she said tiredly. She'd endured days and nights of on-again off-again contractions. The real work was before her, but she would be fine and very glad when it was over.

There was a light knock on the door before it opened and Alexandra stuck her head in. "The doctor has been sent for and Papa's on standby. Do you need anything?"

"Towels," Charity said.

"Already getting them." Alexandra smiled excitedly and shut the door again.

"The girls have turned out better than I'd feared," she confided. "When I left, they were self-consumed and continually bickering over the pettiest things imaginable." She made a face as a pain came on and then ducked her head and squeezed his hand. When it let up, he leaned in and kissed her.

"I love you," he said.

"I love you, too. So please ignore the truly terrible things I'm going to call you in the next few hours."

"It's all right. I probably deserve it." He put a hand on her abdomen and leaned closer to talk to his unborn child. "You in there. Take it as easy as you can on your mother. You're going to love her, too."

She smiled, but her smile quickly waned. "I wish Vi and Tally were here."

"So do they, I'm sure." He paused. "What G names are there for girls?"

"Her name is Madeline Elizabeth Howerton."

He grunted. "We'll see."

Chapter Thirty-Nine

Tom went to the ninth precinct to let Cass know what had occurred, but Cass already knew about Viola Ripley and a good deal more. What he hadn't known until Tom told him was that Heyer had been the one to shoot Viola.

"There have been five shootings in the city today alone," Cass said in the privacy of his office. "And now we know that three of them are related. I can't say I don't feel some responsibility."

Tom cocked his head sharply. "What do you mean three of them are related? You're not saying related to Heyer?"

"Yes, I am."

"Who are the other victims?"

"Lillian Holmes was found shot dead. Possibly by her own hand."

"That's rubbish! She isn't the type."

"Oh, Tom. It's not like we knew her well. If she's as culpable as we thought, perhaps the guilt of what she'd done finally got to her."

"Rubbish."

"Consider for a moment that she was found alone in the driver's seat of her own carriage and in a park of all places. She'd been shot here," he said, pointing to his chest. "And the gun was on her lap. It looked self-inflicted."

Tom shook his head. He hadn't detected the tiniest bit of guilt from her. She was all about self-preservation. She would not have killed herself. "And the third victim?"

"Blakely Heyer himself is dead."

Tom drew back, utterly stunned. "Are you serious?"

217

Cass nodded resolutely. "I'm very sorry to tell you it was done by a lady you know."

The faces of Jane Behr and Gina Yardley sprang to mind. Heyer had wronged a lot of people. "What lady?"

"She's ninety and I believe you described her as spritely."

Tom's breath vacated his lungs.

"She'll be all right," Cass said consolingly.

"Heyer found them then!"

"Yes."

"But Vi didn't tell him," Tom exclaimed. "She said she didn't tell him."

Cass nodded. "One of your fellow detectives found them, a man by the name of Wolfe. Dorothy's address was written on Wolfe's stationary and found in Heyer's pocket. It'll be easy enough to confirm."

"My God. What happened?"

"Heyer forced his way inside. He claimed he had a gun, although he didn't—"

"Well, he damn well did earlier today!"

"And if we discover the bullet fired at Viola Ripley matches the one in Lillian, you may be right about that, too. But the point is that Heyer's shooting will probably be ruled as justifiable."

"Why probably?"

"Because he was on the sidewalk when he was shot, having been forced out of the house at gunpoint, and he was shot in the back."

Tom tossed his head back and sighed. "Talk about culpability. I have it all over the place."

"Tom, listen. Heyer shot Viola Ripley and probably thought he killed her. So he was a dead man anyway, once we caught him. No one will want to see an old woman charged. It won't happen. Not after what he did."

Tom started to the door. "I'm going to Dorothy's."

"Tom."

Tom turned back.

218

"I won't claim this is a happy ending," Cass said. "But it's not the worst either, all things considered."

Tom nodded and left. The station was busy, so no one noticed him. One woman was seated on a bench, crying inconsolably, although a cop seated next to her was trying. Two cops were leading in a glowering, handcuffed man who had blood on his shirt.

Not the worst ending, Cass had just declared. The words reverberated around Tom's brain demanding an accounting. The fact was, Vi might have been killed. Not only that, but he was the one who had brought Louisa into the home and lives of Dorothy and Betty – and Dorothy had killed Heyer. Did he have blood on his hands because of Lillian's death, too? He didn't believe for a moment that she had taken her own life.

He was nearly to his carriage when a man called out to him. He turned to see two uniformed officers hurrying toward him. "Yes?"

The man in the lead touched his own chest. "Grumley, sir. Del Grumley. That, uh, that boy. The one you were looking for?"

"William Yardley?"

"Yes, sir. I think I saw him. I'm pretty sure."

Tom felt a jolt to his system. He'd forgotten about William for the moment. "Where?"

"Midvale. The steel works."

"In Nicetown?"

"Yes, sir. There was an accident there a few days ago. A bad one. Fatal. A boy fell, probably fainted due to the heat, and fell right into a vat of boiling water."

Tom grimaced. "How awful."

"Yes, sir. It was. We got there right after. The mill had shut down for the rest of the day—"

"Big of them," Tom muttered.

"Most the workers were leaving when we got there and I saw this lad." He glanced over at his partner who shrugged.

"I didn't see him," the other man said apologetically. "But Grum's got a sharp eye."

"It was like … something struck me," Grumley said. "You know? It registered in my mind, but I was distracted. The heat in there, for one thing. It's the heat of hell, it is. Plus the accident. Poor lad was naught but a boy, and there's a smell to a body that's been—"

Tom nodded rapidly to urge the man on. He didn't need the horrific details.

"Anyway, there was something about this lad that trudged by me. It was the scar. I only realized it later, but he had that scar."

"That is the only good news I've had today," Tom exclaimed. "Thank you."

"I feel bad for not recognizing him then."

"No, don't. It's probably better this way. You might have spooked him and if he'd run—"

"That's true. Didn't think of that."

"Thank you again," Tom said, also taking in the other man with a glance. The job of a cop was not often appreciated. He remembered all too well.

"You're welcome, sir. Hope you can find him now."

"So do I."

Blakely Heyer's body was still on the sidewalk when Tom arrived. It suddenly occurred to him that he'd never spoken to the man. He'd never looked him in the eye or heard his voice.

Curious neighbors and onlookers had gathered, although three cops kept them back as a department artist finished sketching the corpse. A horse and wagon waited to take the body to the morgue, and a stretcher was in the yard for transport. The moon was full, and the nearby houses, including Dorothy's, all had outdoor gas lamps glowing, so the scene was eerily lit.

Tom went around back and found Betty and Louisa on the back porch. They were relieved to see him. Betty stood as he approached and he took hold of her hands, which were cold despite the heat of the late July night. "Are you all right?" he asked. He looked at Louisa who had also stood.

"We're fine," Betty replied, although the tension in her body said otherwise. "Aunt Dorothy went to bed an hour ago."

"Is she terribly upset?"

"She is remarkably *unconcerned*," Betty replied ruefully. "After it happened, she came in, set her gun on the table and got out the whiskey. She had two glasses and said she was going to bed. But the police arrived just then so we told them what happened. After that, she went to bed. I checked on her a few minutes later and she was snoring. I thought she might have been putting on a calm front for us, but she was fast asleep. She still is."

He was glad to hear it. "Let's sit."

"Can I get you anything?" Betty asked.

"Aunt Dorothy's hard cider sounds wonderful."

Betty smiled and went inside as he and Louisa sat. "And you?" he asked Louisa. "How are you?"

For a moment, she was at a loss for words. "Shaky. I never imagined it would end like this."

"Nor did I. I didn't consider a lot of possibilities I should have."

She gave him a sad look. "You cannot possibly foresee everything. You can't know what's in another person's mind, especially someone who only cares about themselves and is willing to—"

He nodded when her sentence trailed off.

"How terrible is it to be relieved?" she asked quietly.

"Not," he assured her with a shake of his head. "It's not terrible at all. It's perfectly understandable."

"He would have found a way to finish me. I know it."

Betty stepped back out with a filled glass and the bottle. She handed him the glass and sat back down.

"Heyer shot Dr. Ripley this evening," he said soberly.

Both women gasped.

"She'll be all right," he added quickly. "The bullet grazed her neck. It bled, of course, but it looked worse than it was."

"He shot her for helping me," Louisa said miserably.

"He wanted to find out where you were. She didn't tell him, but he learned it after he shot her. He'd hired a detective."

"Is Dorothy in terrible trouble?" Betty asked worriedly.

"I don't think so but tell me what happened."

Louisa began. "He came around the house, the same as you did."

"I saw him first," Betty interjected. "I knew who he was right away."

"He said he was taking me back," Louisa said. "He said he was sorry for putting me in the asylum, but that I was legally and honor bound to go with him."

Betty nodded. "He also said he had men waiting to help take her away. He said we could scream, but it would do no good. It would just hasten the help of the men."

"It was just the two of you out here?" Tom asked.

"Yes, but Dorothy heard him," Louisa said. "She got out her gun to protect us."

Tom nodded.

"Louisa told him she wanted to take some of her things with her," Betty said.

"It was to buy some time," Louisa said.

"So," Tom spoke up. "He thinks you are going with him at this point. Leaving with him."

Louisa nodded. "What choice did I have if he had a gun, which he said he did, and men waiting to help take me by force?"

"None," Tom replied.

"We'd gone into the hall," Betty said. "That's when Aunt Dorothy spoke up. She was in the parlor waiting for him to pass by. She had her gun pointed at him."

"She made him leave," Louisa said. "I was worried he was going to charge at her and get the gun, but she had it pointed right at him." She paused. "He said he'd be back. He would take me back."

"Then," Betty said after a moment of silence. "He went outside, and Aunt Dorothy followed. We all did. The … gun went off and he fell. He was dead."

"So that's what you told the police?"

The ladies hesitated. "No," Betty admitted. "I said he took me hostage."

Tom smiled and nodded. "That was good thinking."

"I thought it was the only way. If he forced Louisa out with him, well, that's his right, isn't it?"

Tom considered everything. "It will be ruled justifiable homicide. As far as I'm concerned, it *was* justifiable homicide."

"If I'd had the gun," Louisa said. "I would have shot him."

He could see she meant it. "It's good it wasn't you. It would have been harder to justify in the eyes of the law."

"You know what I think?" Dorothy said from the doorway. They all looked at her. "Sometimes the world we've made doesn't make a damn bit of sense."

Betty got up and went to her aunt. "Are you all right?"

"I'm fine as wine. I just needed some water and then I heard the voice of a man I actually like. Not like earlier tonight. Hello, Robin."

"Hello, Maid Marion. Or should I say Annie Oakley?"

She chuckled before turning away. "Goodnight, children," she called. "Sweet dreams to us all."

The occupants of the back porch were left looking at one another in amused bewilderment.

"You see?" Betty whispered. "And she'll be asleep again in five minutes."

"Tom," Louisa said.

"Yes, ma'am?"

"Will you explain everything you know from the beginning?"

"Of course."

"I owe such a debt to so many." Emotion overcame her and she brought the backs of her fingers to her trembling lips and chin. "I want to understand," she continued in a thick voice. "I know there are things you can't repay. How do you repay someone who got shot because they cared enough to help you? Or people who put themselves at risk because of the risk to me?"

"Every person involved made deliberate choices," Tom replied. "And every one of us would stand by them and do the same again. I'll tell you everything I know from start to finish and I'd like to know how your husband got you to the asylum. Did you know what was happening?"

"No! He insisted I see a doctor to make sure I was recovering from the appendectomy."

"Dr. Backman," he said.

"Yes. We went to his office and he started to examine me, but it was his questions." She shook her head. "They were things he shouldn't have been asking. Things that made no sense."

"Such as what?"

"Did I want to hurt myself. Had I ever threatened to kill myself or my husband. Was I aware of how much I was frightening the servants. 'Servants' was his word. I have a housekeeper and a cook whom I love dearly. I don't call them servants. I've never called them that and I have certainly never frightened them. Then he asked… about my last monthly cycle," she said, struggling to get the embarrassing words out. "The entire interview was insulting and wrong. I tried to leave, but they stopped me."

"Who did?"

"The doctor and my husband. The doctor said I was clearly upset and that he couldn't have me leaving in that state and upsetting his other patients. He had his nurse to fetch a draught of laudanum to soothe my nerves. He said when I was calm, my husband could take me home." She looked pained and shook her head. "I was so foolish. I drank it."

"Anyone would have," Betty commiserated.

Louisa gave her a tender look before looking back at Tom. "Blakely escorted me from the doctor's inner office. I was so anxious to leave. I'd found Dr. Backman repellant. But the room began to spin. I couldn't remain on my feet. I don't know what I

224

was given, but it was not laudanum. I don't remember much after that, but I know that I was taken to the asylum."

He nodded. Dr. Backman had some explaining to do.

"Now your turn," Louisa said. "Please."

"Of course. Well, let's see. I received a note from Cecil Lawrence," he began. "He's an attorney Dr. Ripley had contacted."

Chapter Forty

At six o'clock the next morning, Tom walked into the Midvale Steel Works compound amongst the stream of workers. He had dressed to blend in. The vast size of the place was astonishing, and this was only a mid-sized mill. He kept his eyes peeled for William but did not spot him amongst the throng of bleary-eyed men, all of whom knew where they were going.

He knew he could go into the office and elicit their assistance, but he was only going to do that if he could not find William on his own. It seemed unlikely the boy was using his own name. If he wasn't, would they remember his face, even with its identifying mark? Besides, he didn't want to scare William off if word got out that he was being sought. It was better all-around if he found William on his own. He knew how to talk a man down from a more dangerous situation than this. There was one other reason for keeping the mill's administration out of the equation. What if they balked at paying the young man if he had misrepresented himself?

Tom walked by a long building housing a blacksmith shop, a mixing room and other shops. At the end of the building was a narrow road. Across from that was a tire mill. Walking on, he reached a large building, a steel foundry, and went inside. He was recognized as an outsider, and occasionally asked if he needed help. Each time, he shook his head, waved a hand in thanks and kept going. His skin prickled uncomfortably from the heat. The day was new, but it was already close to a hundred degrees inside the building.

Tom left the foundry and went toward an enormous welding shop. He hadn't yet seen a quarter of the buildings. There were other steel foundries and a rolling mill and a gas producing house and a dozen other buildings. This was a large business manufacturing steel, axels, locomotive tires and more.

He got odd glances as he did an unsuccessful circuit of the welding shop, but no one stopped him or asked him his business. He was making his way back out when a young man caught his eye. He was the right age. The right hair color. The right look. He was standing at a table full of tools cleaning one off.

Tom started toward him, and the young man looked over at him and tensed. The scar! He had the scar. The boy was wary, ready to bolt, so Tom stopped. "Your mother would like you to come home, William," he said speaking loud enough to be heard over the din. His ears would ring from it after he left.

William set down the tool and rag without taking his eyes off Tom. He was still poised to run.

"I'm a friend," Tom said. "I met your mother when I was trying to help Louisa Heyer who was put into an asylum by her husband."

William's jaw went lax. "What?"

Tom wasn't sure if William hadn't heard him correctly or he was remarking on how outrageous it was. He chanced a few steps closer while replying. "Mrs. Heyer was put into an asylum by her husband who was trying to get control of her finances."

"An asylum? For lunatics?"

Tom nodded.

"She's not crazy," William exclaimed with a fervent shake of his head.

"I know. She is out now. She's fine and well. I cannot say the same for Blakely Heyer. He's dead."

William took a step backwards, panicked. "I didn't do it!"

"I know that, William. We know who did it. You're not in trouble."

The young man blinked, hardly daring to believe it. "He said—"

"I know what he said. That you stole his cufflinks. It was a lie to get rid of you. I've been looking for you to take you home."

He paused as he watched the words sink in. "Your mother is worried sick about you."

William lowered his head, close to tears.

Tom walked over and touched William's shoulder. "Come on," he said. He turned and led the way toward the door and William followed. Men looked at them curiously, but no one tried to stop them. They stepped out of the building where the air was cooler. Tom reached for his handkerchief and mopped the perspiration from his face and neck. "I guess you get used to the heat."

"You never get used to it," William replied. He slogged along like a sleepwalker, numb and expressionless.

"Do you want to go collect your pay? Tell them you're leaving?"

William shook his head. "Can we just go?"

"Of course, we can. You can collect your pay another time. Or I'll get it for you, if you want."

William didn't respond. In fact, he didn't speak again until they were in the carriage and in motion. The moving air felt heavenly. "I'm really going home?"

There was so much vulnerability in the young man that Tom felt a lump in his throat. He nodded while waiting for it to subside. "Unless you want to go to wherever you've been staying and collect your belongings."

"No. I don't have anything worth taking and I'd rather never see that place again."

They rode in silence for a few blocks. "I found you because of the boy who died," Tom ventured.

William looked at him curiously. "Travis?"

Tom nodded. "I'd asked the police to keep an eye out for you"

"One of them looked at me funny. I was afraid Mr. Heyer had made a report on me, after all."

"He looked at you funny because your photograph had been passed around and he recognized you."

"My photograph?"

"I got it from your mother." He glanced at the younger man with a smile. "I'll need to return it now."

"You're saying he was looking to help me?"

"That's right."

William thought about it a moment. "I never think of the police as helping."

"It's the main job. Or it's supposed to be. I used to be one."

"You were a cop?" William said disbelievingly.

"I was. Yes. I was a regular beat cop and later I became a detective."

"Is that what you do now?"

"You could say that, only I work for myself." William was finally beginning to relax. He'd initially been distrustful enough that Tom had wondered if he might jump from the vehicle and make a run for it. Of course, even if he had, surely he would have gone home on the sly to verify the truth of the matter for himself.

"The cops must still like you. To pass my photograph around because you asked them to."

Tom nodded. "They like me and I like them. Most of them anyway. My closest friend is still there, a lieutenant now, and he's one of the best. As a policeman and as a person."

They reached an intersection and stopped behind a wagon.

"I don't think I'll believe it until we get there," William said.

Tom looked at the boy. "I'm sorry for what you've been through."

"Mr. Heyer wasn't a good man, at all," William said bitterly.

"That, my young friend, is an understatement." Tom flicked the reins and started them moving again.

"This one time, I thought he might be up to something with Miss Louisa."

"Oh?"

"I saw him put something on her food. It was a kind of powder. When he saw me, he said it was something to help her headache, but not to tell her since she didn't like taking medicine."

Tom felt a chill. "Is that so?"

William nodded. "I'd have believed him more if he hadn't acted so squirrely about it. But I never thought he'd do what he did." He paused. "He's really dead?"

"He is. It happened last night. He found out where his wife was staying, hiding from him, and he tried to force her to leave with him. She was at the home of two ladies, one of them near ninety, and it was her, Aunt Dorothy, that shot him. One shot. Back of his head. Done."

William huffed in astonishment.

They stopped at an intersection again, one close to the precinct. "Do you want to go to the station house and meet the man who spotted you? They're in a morning meeting now."

The question seemed to throw William. "Swear to God it's not a trick?"

"Of course, I do. But we don't have to. It was just an idea since we're not far from there." He flicked the reins and got them moving again.

"I guess we could go."

"Consider yourself in the driver's seat, William. Straight home or to the station. You call it and we will go."

Tom led the way toward the precinct's meeting room. William seemed reluctant, but he'd chosen to come. The plan was to hang back at the door and then speak to Grumley in private when the meeting ended. They reached the open door where the morning meeting was in session. The men in the room were particularly attentive as they listened to the lieutenant speaking.

"You all know that with heatwaves, come waves of violence," Cass was saying. "Although yesterday was an exception. At least we can hope so," he added wryly. A hand shot up and Cass pointed at the individual. "Yes?"

"Can you say what happened at The Rabbit Den? Was it really a massacre?"

"It was gory, but not a massacre. Thankfully, that mess belongs to another precinct."

"Tell us, Lieutenant," someone said.

"All right. The brothel owner found one of his girls pocketing some of her take and decided to teach her a lesson by marking her face. She fought back and her jugular got punctured. In the screaming and gushing of blood, the other girls went berserk and all hell broke loose. Eight people ended up with stab wounds and one was shot, although not fatally. The only fatality was the girl he tried to mark. She was dead before police arrived."

Tom noticed William looking around the room curiously.

"So now the brothel owner awaits trial for murder," Cass concluded. "Over two dollars, I believe it was. But back to our own backyard, be especially vigilant—" He broke off abruptly having seen Tom and then William. "Is that William?"

The men in the room turned to look at them. "It's all right," Tom said under his breath as William stiffened.

"Yes, sir," William replied nervously to Cass. "I'm William."

Cass smiled. "Gentlemen, this is the young man we were looking for," he announced. "And it is ironic, but the man who'd made the false accusation against him was none other than the recently deceased Blakely Heyer."

A feeling of shock and astonishment rippled through the room.

Cass gestured an invitation to William who glanced at Tom before starting forward. Tom followed a few steps behind.

"You found him," Cass said to Tom with a pleased smile.

"Actually, Del Grumley was the one to spot him working in a steel mill." Tom looked around until he saw Grumley. He pointed at him. "I simply went and collected him."

Grumley beamed and nodded. "Welcome back, William," he called. He started clapping and then the entire roomful of men got to their feet clapping and cheering.

William was no longer skittish on the way back home. He was buoyant. When they stopped in front of the Heyer home, he sat staring at it in awe. "It's never looked so good," he marveled. "It looks like heaven." He looked at Tom. "Thank you, Mr. Kassel. A thousand times over."

Tom grinned and nodded. "I wish I had this kind of conclusion for every case I work." He paused. "I have an idea. Let's go to the front door like company."

"All right," William agreed, his eyes twinkling.

When they reached it, Tom knocked. William had stepped aside so he wouldn't be seen right away. He agreed that it was better to prepare his mother.

Georgina promptly answered the door. "Oh, Mr. Kassel! Thank you for sending word about what happened. We couldn't believe it. But there it was in the paper this morning."

"I wasn't sure they'd get the story to print so quickly, but in case they did—"

"It's shocking. Will Louisa be home today do you think?"

"I would think so. I'll go when I leave here and see if I can give her a ride home."

"That would be wonderful. Will you come in for some breakfast?"

"Yes, but actually, I came by for a different reason. Something that will make you very happy."

"William?" she asked breathlessly. "Have you learned something?"

He smiled. "More than that."

A hand flew to her chest. "Have you found him?"

He nodded and stepped backwards. She followed as if she was on an invisible rope. She saw her son and cried out. In a moment, they were embracing and rocking, laughing and crying at the same time. Tom enjoyed it, discretely swiping at his eye which suddenly had an itch.

<u>Chapter Forty-One</u>

Friday, August 3

Charity followed a maid through the Ripley home carrying her sleeping infant in a Moses basket. Vi was in the music room playing the piano, Bach if she wasn't mistaken. They stopped in the door and Vi noticed them. She cried out, rose and hurried toward them. The maid deftly moved aside, and Charity met Vi a few steps into the room.

"Oh," Vi breathed as she stared into the basket.

Charity's gaze went to the angry looking abrasion on Vi's neck. It looked like a deep burn.

"She is so beautiful," Vi said. She looked up and kissed Charity's cheek. "Congratulations."

"Thank you."

"Come and sit. I want to hear everything."

"So do I. How are you?"

"I'm … well." Vi looked as if she might say more, but was at a loss for the right words.

They went further in the room and Charity set the basket on a table before sitting on a curved settee beside it.

"Tell me about her," Vi said, peering back into the basket. "Little Maddie."

"It's hard to tell too much yet since she sleeps ninety percent of the time, but I can tell you her favorite waking hours are between one and four a.m."

Vi laughed as she sat beside Charity. "How was your labor?"

Charity made a face. "Not as bad as last time."

"Tally said she came at midnight?"

"A few minutes after," Charity replied with a nod. "I'm so glad it's over."

"When do you leave for home?"

"This afternoon. I needed to see you first."

Vi reached over and squeezed her hand. "I'm so glad. You must miss the boys terribly."

"I do. We both do. I'm trying not to dwell on it because I get so anxious." She paused and glanced at the door. How has it been here?" she asked quietly.

"I won't say it feels perfectly natural, but we're all trying. They'd like me to stay."

Charity already knew this from Tally. The Ripley's had also offered Tally a room of her own, but she'd declined. "Will you?"

Vi nodded. "For now, it feels right."

"That's good. You need time to get beyond what happened."

Tears sprang to Viola's eyes and she shook her head. "I wasn't badly hurt. Not really. My life was never in danger. I should be able to bounce back from it more easily. But I feel this close," she said holding her thumb and forefinger apart by a few inches, "to falling to pieces all the time. It's so frustrating."

"Oh, Vi. Any of us would be shaken to our core given what happened. Give yourself the time you need and don't feel frustrated by it. There are people who love you and want to take care of you, so let them."

Vi reached for the handkerchief in her pocket and dabbed beneath her nose. "It's harder than you may think."

"No, I completely understand. Not only have you been independent for years, you've been the caregiver of others. To have that reversed is not easy."

"No, it's not."

"I hear that Cecil is a daily visitor."

Vi smiled. "Yes."

"Do your parents like him?" She already knew the answer, but she wanted to lighten the conversation for Vi's sake.

"Do they like him," Vi repeated musingly. "I would say so. They think he walks on water."

Charity chuckled.

"I saw Louisa yesterday," Vi said. "She and Betty Lee came for tea."

"How is she?"

"Happy. I would say she's back to being her old self, but I never knew that person. I met her when she was ill and fearful." The baby made a squeak and both women leaned forward to see her. Maddie was stretching and stirring, trying to wake. "Come on Maddie, you can do it," Vi said. "Auntie Vi wants to hold you."

"You can hold her," Charity laughed.

It was all the invitation Vi needed. She rose, picked up the baby and breathed in the soft scent of her with great appreciation. "This is the best medicine yet. And they said I only needed salve three times a day. What do doctors know?" She began to gently sway.

"You'll be yourself again in no time," Charity said reassuringly.

Vi did not look away from the infant's face. "Will I? I don't know. I feel … changed. Not better and not worse, just different." She looked at Charity. "I'm going to take some time away from work."

"Of course."

"I mean more than a few days."

Charity waited for her to continue.

"I don't know when I'll go back."

"You'll know when you're ready again."

"What if I'm never ready again?"

"If not—" Charity broke off, wondering how to phrase her thought. "Are you worried you're going to disappoint someone if you choose not to return to work?"

"Not someone. Everyone. No," she relented. "Not everyone, but my closest friends and the hospital administrators." She shrugged. "Nona."

"Your grandmother would want you to be happy and so do your friends. In your heart, you have to know that's true."

Vi looked back at the baby. "She's so beautiful. Is her papa completely smitten?"

"Oh, yes. I'd forgotten how touching and sensuous it is to see him with a baby."

Maddie began to root at Vi's breast and so Vi returned her to her mother. "You will stay for lunch, won't you? There's so much I want to hear."

"I'd love to."

"Good. I'll be right back," Vi said cheerfully and she left the room with a lighter step.

Charity looked down at her baby girl. "That is your Auntie Vi," she said softly. "You will love her as I do."

<u>Chapter Forty-Two</u>

Thursday, August 16th

Louisa and William strolled side by side through the University of Philadelphia campus after William's admission's interview. William stopped and watched some young men playing football on an athletic field.

"I can't believe I might get to come here," he said with an amazed expression. He looked at her. "Thank you for this."

"You have thanked me. A dozen times or more. All I ask is that you embrace your studies and learn all you can."

"I will. I swear it." They resumed their walk and passed College Hall on the way back to Market and 9th where their cab was waiting. "All this brick and stone and turrets and towers. I can't believe I might get to go here."

The last part of it was said more to himself than her, so she didn't comment. She understood his feelings. The nearly hundred- and fifty-year-old university was grand. It had begun when Benjamin Franklin was a prevailing influence of the day. "I feel like celebrating with an ice cream sundae," she suggested. "What do you think?"

"That sounds good."

"Home?" the cab driver asked as he opened the door for them.

"One stop first, please. We are in need of ice-cream."

"Breyer's is close by."

"That is perfect."

As the cab started in motion, Louisa looked over at William who was staring out at the campus. "What do you think you might like to study?"

"I don't know. I had no idea they offered so much. I'm glad the first semester is almost all required courses."

"It's so hard to know what you want to do with your life when you're young."

He nodded. "Although I've been thinking—"

"What?"

"That I might consider being a police officer," he said haltingly.

"Oh?"

"Would that disappoint you?"

"Of course not. I'm surprised, but ... no."

"Do you think it would disappoint my mother?"

"No, William. I do not. She'll want you to be happy and contented with your life's work."

"I told Tom last week."

"What did he say?"

"He asked me why."

"It's a good question."

He shifted toward her. "When he picked me up at the mill, I didn't know if I could trust him or not. I thought it might be a trick to get me to jail."

She felt a crush of sorrow for what had befallen him but tried not to react too strongly.

"Then, on the way home, he suggested taking me to the police station to meet the man who'd spotted me. They'd all been looking for me because Tom asked them to. I guess I always feared cops. I mean, if one of them comes around, you're generally in trouble."

"I suppose that's true," Louisa said.

"But we went. Well, first he suggested it and then ... I guess he saw my reaction, so he said never mind, that we didn't have to go. That's when I thought it would be all right, but I was still nervous."

238

"I can understand that."

"When we got there, they were in a meeting. It was a room full of big men in blue uniforms. Then the lieutenant saw me. He's a good friend of Tom's. He got this smile on his face and said, 'Is that William?' And he called me up in front of the room. As I was going, he complimented Tom on finding me, but Tom said that he'd just collected me. It was another cop in the room that had spotted me. Tom pointed him out and the man, his name was Del Grumley, he looked so glad I was there and that he'd helped. He yelled, 'Welcome back, William,' and he started clapping. Then all the other men started cheering." Tears sprang to William's eyes, and he looked out the window until he'd bested the surge of emotion. "It was something," he concluded.

She nodded. "A powerful moment."

"They're just men who have a job to do. They're not bigger than life. Not all that scary. Their job is to help and protect. Figure out crimes. Anyway, I said all that to Tom, and he said it's still a dangerous job. He said if I decide it's my calling, I'd be good at it and I'd probably like it, but he doesn't think I should set my mind on any one thing yet."

"That's sound advice," Louisa replied. "Especially when you're just starting university."

He looked back out the window, captivated by all they passed. "You know, there were good things that came from the bad," he said thoughtfully.

"Yes, there were," she agreed.

He looked at her.

"It was a dreadful time," she said, "but now I feel such an appreciation for everything. People, food, freedom."

"Plus, new friends and new beginnings," he said.

She couldn't speak for a moment because of the lump in her throat, but what she thought and what she said when she could speak was, "And we won't waste it, will we?"

"No, ma'am!"

Note to Reader:

I first introduced Gregory Howerton and Dr. Charity Werthing in *Down in the Valley.* (Zebra/Kensington Books) It is still a favorite story, and has my all-time favorite male protagonist, Tommy Medlin in it. I hope you will check it out.

Please take a moment to rate this book. The importance of book ratings and reviews cannot be overstated, especially for indie authors. Thank you.

Jane Shoup enjoys writing different genres, but her mainstay is historical adventure with suspense and romance.

Jane lives in Greensboro, North Carolina with her husband, Scott, rescue-dog Gabby, and near her three grown daughters and their families, including five grandchildren four grand-dogs and a grand-cat who showed up one day, declared he lived there and has since accepted the name Bob Sahara Tigercat.

Visit her website at www.janeshoup.com,